# CHOSEN
# FOR
# THERMOPYLAE

Belinda Harrison

ISBN-13: 978-0-6483721-4-1 (US/EUR Paperback)

# DEDICATION

This one is for all the people I forgot the first time ... and for all the new fans – your support has been amazing, and very much appreciated.

# ACKNOWLEDGMENTS

Thank you to you – the reader, I'm glad you enjoyed the first book, and decided to come back for the second, This one is a little different to the first, but I hope you think it is 'good different' and will dive into book 3 when it arrives. I'm also loving your reviews and comments on Goodreads and Amazon – both positive and negative – that you're leaving, it helps me to grow as a writer! It's awesome that my long-held dream to be a published author is coming true. THANKS TO YOU GUYS!

To my editor Kristie – who has once again 'tightened the ship' for this manuscript and pulled me up when I go overboard! We're getting better at this whole writer/editor thing I reckon!

There are also two rather important people I should thank – my partner and daughter – for putting up with me *accidently* making every conversation about 'my book or sales or reviews or fans or Instagram account or fantastic book swag ideas I've thought of' the past few months. You two are troopers and I promise the shine will wear off (okay no it won't, but I'll get better at not making it all about me!)

To my friends and work mates in my new job and my old one, thanks so much for your kind words and support, and you too can tell me to shut up when I talk too much about myself or my books as well!

Once again I have made my own version of a prayer to the gods – hope they don't mind too much!

Don't forget you can connect with me online on Instagram at: belindagharrison, on Twitter at: beharrison78 on Facebook at: Belinda Harrison Author or through my website at www.belindaharrison.com or via email at: belinda@belindaharrison.com

Book Three of the Thermopylae Bound Series *The Ker at Thermopylae* will be out late 2018.

# 1

## Palace of Trachis, region of Thermopylae
## 8th waning, Moon of Skirophorion, 509bc

I stood at the window of Alexis' room – which I now shared – and watched as the pale dawn illuminated the stables to the left and mountains to the right. Three moons had passed since Alexis and I spoke of our love for one another and announced our intention to be together. I had had to kill Melanthios and his brothers for the privilege of it, and though my final actions towards Melanthios were not as honorable as I always prided myself on, I knew if I had the time again I would not behave any differently. Not only had I been determined to keep Alexis as my lover and protect her from his cruel nature, I had wanted to punish him for what he had done to her before I found them at the hot springs.

My father had left Trachis almost a moon ago, his wandering nature getting the better of him, though I knew he would have remained to make his home in Trachis as I was if he could. His destination was north, not to Thrace as I had believed he intended when he first spoke of leaving again, but to Konitsa, to visit friends, and a woman who had once been his lover. I offered to join him, but he said it was a journey he must make on his own. In a way I was glad, for I would not have wanted to ask Alexis to leave her own family when she had so recently been reunited with them. She and Queen Melina had started to repair their damaged past and though at first it was difficult for them both, I knew it made each (and King Agrias) glad to finally have the chance.

I turned as the brown-haired mass in the bed beside me moved, a smile lighting my face automatically. "The dawn greets us once again," Alexis murmured, the bright green of her eyes finding my blue ones in the dimness of Eos' light.

"It does," I agreed, returning to our bed when she held her hand out.

She trailed her finger down my naked thigh. "Does this mean you are leaving me to join Moeris and Thaddeus at the barracks?"

"I do not have to leave just yet," I replied, feeling the caress deep inside. I slipped beneath the coverings, stretching out on my side to face her and placing my hand at her hip. I pulled her body against mine as our lips met, my tongue darting out to taste her soft, warm lips. She sighed into my mouth and the deep hunger of desire began in my stomach, quickly travelling down between my legs when she pushed against me. Alexis slid her thigh between mine, her heated skin slipping across my wetness. "Gods," I moaned.

"Love me," Alexis insisted, pressing harder against me.

I captured her lips again as I rolled her onto her back, placing my own leg between hers. I moved atop her, my thigh dragging across her sensitive flesh, pushing her towards her end with each measured stroke. She tightened her hands at the small of my back, eyes fluttering shut and I dipped my head to graze my teeth along her collarbone.

After I had killed Melanthios at the hot springs, Alexis had wanted me to make love to her, to help her forget he had ever laid his hands on her. I had been unable to then – too afraid I would hurt her; that Melanthios had scarred her in ways I could not heal with my love alone. But now I held no such fears and there had barely been a night since that we did not spend proving the depth of our love for one another with abandon.

I slowed my movements, silencing her protests when I covered her mouth again.

"Skylar," she panted when we parted.

"Yes, Princess?" I smirked.

"Must I beg?"

"Mmm … tempting."

"Gods, please. I need you to touch me. Now."

Pleasurable heat ran the length of my spine. I pushed down as Alexis' hips rose to meet mine. I knew she could feel my arousal against her skin when she captured her bottom lip in her teeth and her hand moved to the outside of my thigh. "No touching," I warned.

"Skylar," she pleaded. I smiled again, enjoying the desire and frustration war across her face. "I want to."

"Not yet," I insisted, taking both her hands and trapping them above her head beneath one of mine. My other traced her jaw and the length of her breastbone.

She writhed beneath my touch, her hips lifting again in response. Slowly I lowered my mouth to her breast, taking the taut nipple between my teeth and flicking my tongue over its end. Alexis jolted beneath me and I repeated the motion before doing the same to the other. I knew if I attended her in such a manner she would soon find release, but I did not want it to be so today. Today I wanted her to feel me deep inside, to want my touch with every fiber of her being, my mouth on every inch of her body.

I kissed my way lower. She opened her legs, the dark curls tickling my stomach when she lifted her hips. "Down," I commanded. She exhaled loudly but complied. I rewarded her obedience with my hand; bestowing the lightest of touches between her thighs. "You are so ready for me."

"Always."

"Hmm ... should I taste you?"

"Gods, yes," she groaned, her hips rising again.

"If I release your hands you shall keep them above your head, yes?"

"Yes. I give you my word. Just ... please touch me."

I smiled and lifted my hand. Hers remained where they were as I kissed the soft skin just below her hip. I felt the sharp intake of breath above me as well as the increase of her heartbeat and shifted lower still.

"Skylar," she whispered, her hands clenching at the pillow beneath her head.

I leaned forward. Her hips rocked upwards again as I ran my tongue the length of her. Tasting. Reveling. I slipped inside the waiting warmth and Alexis' will broke. She gripped my head hard, pulling me against her heated flesh. My hunger for her exploded and I did not order her to release me. Instead, I possessed her – body and soul.

"Skylar, oh gods. I love you," she cried, her flesh tightening around me as she surrendered.

When she quieted, she put her hand beneath my chin. "Come here." I moved up until we lay face to face again, Alexis' hand immediately straying to my chest.

"I believe it is time I made you beg," she smiled.

I returned her grin but shook my head. "I would not last long enough." I took her hand and placed it between my legs. "I am so close already."

Alexis massaged my sensitive flesh as the first ripples gripped me. "Then be quick," she demanded, slipping one finger inside.

"Gods! Alexis please!" I cried, losing myself to the wave as she worked my body relentlessly. When she felt my muscles relax again, she drew out, resting her hand on my hip. "Gods," I muttered.

"Indeed," Alexis agreed with a grin.

"Have I told you how much I love you?" I whispered, resting my forehead against hers.

"Not since I woke," she replied, tracing one finger over my ribs and across the straining muscles of my stomach.

My heart continued to race beneath my chest, the familiar stirring of desire beginning again as though we had not just reveled in one another, nor spent most of the night doing the same. "How remiss of me," I grinned, leaning forward to kiss her. "I love you."

"I love you," she replied, adding in an urgent whisper, "I want to have a child with you."

"What?" I asked, my body instantly tensing, the flutters of desire replaced with a different type of adrenaline.

She tightened her grip at my waist. "I want to have a child with you," she repeated.

I shook my head and pushed back the light blanket as I threw my legs over the side of the bed. The cold marble floor was a shock after the heat of our passion, but I paced naked across it between the bed and the high window.

The initial shock of Alexis' words began to wear off, replaced instead by too many questions and an underlying fear I could not quite name. She allowed me the stiff movements and the time to arrange my thoughts without interruption. I could not look at her. I knew if I did I would not ask her the questions I must. Questions that could not be overlooked or dismissed so easily. Questions I knew would hurt to ask if she gave answers I did not wish to hear.

Finally, keeping my eyes on my feet and the marble below them, I spoke. "It is not as simple as me taking you to bed, of making love to you. I cannot simply lie with you and put a child inside your belly."

"I understand that Skylar, but there are ways for us to have a family together."

"How?" I asked, looking up and watching her carefully.

"Thaddeus," she replied, color rising in her cheeks.

I stopped pacing. "Thaddeus?" I repeated, anger flaring in my chest.

"He has offered to aid u–"

"You spoke with *Thaddeus* before you spoke to me about this? Before we could discuss how I felt about having children? A family?" My hands clenched and unclenched, the fear growing within. "What if it is not what I want? What if I say no?"

"Nothing has been decided. You can say no if it is not what you wish for," she murmured, dropping her eyes.

I stared at her a long moment, willing the racing of my heart to calm before I spoke again. "Why now when we have only just begun our life together? Why must we rush to add children?"

"If we were betrothed, it would be expected of us."

"So, you wish for us to be betrothed?" I asked, raising my eyebrows. "I have travelled to many places and known many ways, but I have never heard of two women being betrothed before. Besides, you are a *Princess*, how would that be viewed by your people here in Trachis?"

"It is not betrothal with you I seek, Skylar. I do not need to be called wife, or call another the same to want children," she replied, raising her eyes to mine again. She crawled across the bed and joined me on the floor, taking a deep breath before she reached out to lay her hand on my arm. "You know that Basileios and I could not have children of our own. I do not know why that was, but perhaps it is as you once said to me; that he was not the one worthy of that gift. Perhaps I have always been waiting for someone who truly loved me; someone who wanted to be with me because they loved me so completely, not because it satisfied someone else's strategic alliance."

I shook my head in frustration. "But *I* cannot give you what you want Alexis ... and I would rather spend eternity in Tartarus than allow Thaddeus to lie with you."

"Skylar, it is the only way."

"No. I forbid it." I shook her hand from my arm and took up my pacing once more.

"You forbid it?" she asked, her eyebrows rising high on her forehead.

"Yes."

"Why? If he can give us what we want, why would you not allow it?"

"I should not have to explain my reasons to you," I shouted. "You should know I would *never* allow anyone else to put their hands on you in such a manner. It is torturous enough knowing Melanthios did."

"Skyl–"

"No. You are *mine*, Alexis. You encouraged me to claim you from Melanthios and I did. I killed him so we could be together. So why do you think I would now allow someone else to take you to bed?"

"I could have just gone ahead and done it; not told you until I was with child," she said, her voice barely above a whisper.

I spun to face her, my feet as heavy as the marble beneath them. Every hair on my body stood on end. Hot anger infused my stomach, clenching against her words.

Was Alexis truly capable of such a betrayal? I had not believed it to be in her nature. This was the woman who had asked me for protection before she asked me for love; whom I gave my unquestioning protection to before I truly loved her. Perhaps some of Melanthios' cruelty had been left inside her. My jaw clenched at the thought.

"You considered the action?" I managed, pulling my tunic roughly over my head and picking up my weapons.

"Of course not ... Skylar, wait, please," she began, reaching out for me.

I kept out of her reach, yanking open the door and slamming it behind me as I left. I headed out of the central chamber and made my way to the barracks. I needed to spar, to sweat and ache from the physical exertion training had always brought. I needed to silence her words and my own thoughts. My anger burned hot and I wished Father was still in Trachis. At least he would understand my unwillingness to have Alexis lie with another, to share in my rage that she could even suggest such a thing. But I did not know when he would return. I was alone with Alexis' request, with her desires. It was true that I had never been able to deny her anything she wanted, but this ... how could I gift her this when I did not have what she needed and could not allow what she asked of me to make it so? It was impossible.

# 2

The dark hair of the God of War sat perfectly in place even as he moved above his lover. She held his gaze, accepting him inside her body and writhing below him, her own satisfaction being sated just as much as his was. Their relationship, the lust and love they felt for one another had never wavered in its intensity though they had been together uncountable immortal winters.

Aphrodite dug her fingers into his back as they rode waves of exquisite pleasure, finding release together. Ares rolled onto his back, Aphrodite now above him. She kissed his chest, the dusting of hair tickling her nose and cheek. She rested her chin on his sternum and ran one finger over his moustache and goatee and along his lips.

"Now you have satisfied me, you may speak of the mortal," she said with a grin.

Ares smiled, showing off his perfectly white teeth and nipped at her fingertip, curling a lock of her long, blond hair around his hand.

"As I told you, Skylar is not just any mortal. She is my Chosen One and it is time she knew of her past, and of her destiny."

"Are you certain that is who she is, and not just wishful thoughts?"

"Yes. She is powerful. I feel my blood run within her, though it is true that I have not always felt it. I believe that she is the one the Valkyrie spoke of long ago. Her half-mortal blood distinguishes her as different from the others. It was always said that the Chosen One would be different to any who had come before."

"So, what is it you believe I can aid her in? You do not need me to convince her to love, or to find love, she has already done so, though it was not what she expected when she arrived in Trachis."

"No, that was a surprise to both of us, but it appears an advantageous turn of events. I want them to have a child."

Aphrodite's brows rose until they were hidden beneath her hair. "A child for your Chosen One and her female lover?"

"Yes."

"From what you have told me, it does not appear that Skylar wishes for children."

"She never spoke those *exact* words. She believes there is no other way than to have Alexis lie with another, and I understand her refusal to grant such a request; I myself would kill the man or god who ever dared share your bed."

"As I would any goddess or mortal who shared yours," Aphrodite nodded.

"Skylar loves Alexis with a fierceness well recognized among my Keres; focused, intent, unwavering in the intensity. She also displays loyalty and loves with a passion that shall see her agree to a child to keep Alexis by her side if another solution is provided to them. Just as she claimed Alexis from Melanthios, so I claimed you from Hephaestus, and tell me, would you really wish to still be known as his?"

"You know I do not."

"Neither does Alexis wish to be with anyone else. She wants for all she could not have with the man who was good to her, kind even when she could not bear him an heir. She dreams of sharing that special bond with Skylar, and only Skylar, but she too knows of no other option. You speak of the strength of love, and that was never more evident than when Zita turned her back on her family to be with the Bessoi boy, when she hid this child from me so I could not train her and test her as I should have. Love can begin wars and love can bring about glorious endings. Need I remind you of your hand in the affairs of young Paris and his Helen?"

Aphrodite smiled, not only at the mention of Paris and Helen, but at the length of Ares' speech; her lover was not known for long dialogues. "Their coupling certainly brought *us* closer together – love and war working side by side, glorying in the lust at Troy; both pleasure and bloodshed."

Ares raised his head and kissed her. "As it should always be," he murmured when they parted.

"So, what can I do for your Chosen One?"

"Test her. Skylar must face her past and make peace with all that has gone before. She must allow Alexis' love to heal her, to strengthen her. The fear she still carries for what happened to Kuria in Corinth must be dampened."

"Kuria was one of my best at the temple, before Stamatis bought her,"

Aphrodite interrupted gently.

"Indeed. Many men gladly parted with their coin for the chance to share her bed for the briefest of times," Ares nodded. "Skylar must revisit those fears, that truth with Alexis. She must allow Alexis to know even more of her ways and who she was before she arrived in Trachis. She cannot be afraid that Alexis shall leave her, she must trust that they shall stay together, no matter what they face in their future.

"Only once she allows every part of herself to be truly accepted by Alexis shall she be strong enough to stand at my side with the amulet. Only then can she aid me in my desire to sit on my father's throne, with you by my side."

"You ask a great deal of their love."

"I do."

"What if she is unable to put the past behind her?"

"You doubt the power of their love?"

"Not at all. As you say — love is a powerful force. But mortals do not always follow their love; fear can be just as dominant if it takes hold deep enough within."

"That is true, and if they cannot, all is not lost. This test shall be for both of them. If their love is strong they shall receive a child who shall enter the world not only as an heir — as it shall certainly be named as heir to the throne of Trachis — but as a symbol of their love which shall bring them closer until it is time for them to be parted.

"If not, then their parting shall provide me with easy opportunity to convince Skylar to join me for she shall not have anyone to stay for. When Dianthe speaks of past truths kept from her, she shall not wish for her father any more than she wishes for her lover."

"You have given much thought to this matter," Aphrodite noted.

"Yes."

"I can give them a way to overcome their past, but I cannot put a child inside Alexis' belly any easier than Skylar can. Do you intend to make Skylar an Adonis so they can lie together to produce the child?" Aphrodite asked with a smile, though she was not certain her lover would not do so if he had such means.

He returned her grin and shook his head. "No. Do you forget that my mother is the Goddess of Childbirth? If anyone can do it, she can; after all she speaks of producing my brother Hephaestus without aid from my father. I am certain she shall know of a way. Besides, Hera has always favored me as a son. She shall agree to aid me in anything I ask of her."

"But you cannot speak of your true plans with her; your defeat of your father means your defeat of her and she shall not be pleased when she learns of your betrayal."

"True, but I shall deal with her when the time arrives. There is much to be done before she has a role in this. You are willing to play your part?"

"Of course. For just as Skylar is unable to deny her Alexis of anything, so too am I helpless to deny you of what you seek," she said, kissing Ares thoroughly and pressing her body the length of his to emphasize her point.

## 3

Fear burned as bright as the distaste deep within my gut as I trained with the soldiers. My shield and sword worked in unison, a blur of bronze and iron, as the sweat dripped from my brow. How could Alexis think I would allow her to be with another? With Thaddeus of all people? He was friendly and charming, that was true. And he was certainly loyal to her long before we met, but that only increased the jealousy I felt as my mind threw up picture after picture of them locked together in a lover's embrace. I screamed and doubled my attack against Moeris, his training serving him well as he protected his lightly clad body against me.

The first time I had met Thaddeus was in the bathing area at Trachis not long after I arrived. That night I had questioned Alexis on his feelings for her. She had told me that there had never been anything more than friendship between them, that he was a loyal friend she had known for many winters. But now ... What if she had not spoken true? At the time there had been nothing more than the blooming of a friendship between she and I, though I had already wished for more. There would have been no reason for her to keep the truth from me. But had she?

I reminded myself that I had also believed Thaddeus' wife Hesper to hold Alexis' heart, until Alexis assured me that she thought of Hesper as a sister, as she had since childhood. There had been more between us then, Alexis having requested I meet her though we were supposed to be separated. I had almost kissed her that night. Had wanted to more than anything. I wondered how Hesper felt about Alexis and Thaddeus' plan to create a child together. Had he spoken of it to her? Had Alexis? Was she uncomfortable about her husband lying with another or was the multiple wives custom so ingrained in the ways here in Trachis that she would not blink if Thaddeus suggested it?

I knew Hesper had wanted to see Alexis and me together but now I could not shake the feeling that perhaps Thaddeus had only wanted to see Alexis and I together so he could offer to give her a child.

I growled. I should not believe such thoughts. Thaddeus appeared to adore Hesper, and she him, the times I had seen them together when they believed no one was watching spoke of a deep love and commitment to one another – their love continuing even after so many winters together. Something I could only wish to experience with Alexis.

I should find Hesper, perhaps she would not approve of the plan either and together we could deny our lovers of the same. I only had to hope that Alexis would forgive me if I denied her of this.

"Such fire within you this morning, what causes it to be so?" Moeris asked, drawing me from my thoughts.

I drove my sword towards his stomach. He blocked its path solidly, driving me back with an attack of his own. "No specific cause," I replied, catching his blade with the edge of my shield.

"Your attacks are unfocused and messy. Were you to find yourself in battle you would offer only careless slashes and earn yourself scrapes and wounds – if you were fortunate. If you faced a fierce opponent I am afraid I would not wish to return to the palace at day's end for fear of having to tell the princess of your untimely demise." I said nothing, parrying and defending as the dust rose around our sandals. "I am fond of Alexis, just as I have grown fond of you these past moons. If something troubles you, I would listen just as your father would if he were here."

I continued my attack and defense against his weapons as I considered his offer. I trusted Moeris after what he had done to assist in freeing Alexis from betrothal to Melanthios and wondered what advice he might be able to give me in my father's absence.

"Alexis wishes for a child," I finally said.

"Ah," he acknowledged with a nod. "That appears a problematic wish given your pairing." I only grunted as reply. "Do *you* want a child?" he asked, raising his shield to crash against my sword.

"For many winters I had not considered them to be in my future," I told him, just getting my own shield into place as he swung his blade in my direction.

"You speak as if that were in the past. Your mind has been changed since you joined us here?"

"Perhaps," I acknowledged, my sword finding his arm.

Moeris smiled and looked down at the small cut. "Your focus returns."

I nodded, both of us halting our weapons. "Thaddeus has offered to assist us," I told him.

"He is a good man. But I gather you are not comfortable with the idea of his help."

"No. I told Alexis I forbid her from lying with him to create a child."

"Why? You are fond enough of him."

"I am fond of you too, but that is not reason enough to allow such an action." Moeris waited for me to continue. I drew in a deep breath. "Can I trust you not to repeat what I am about to say?"

"I give you my word," he nodded.

I waited another beat. "It would be their child – Alexis and Thaddeus' – not mine and Alexis'. Every time I looked at it or held it, it is all I would see. Alexis and Thaddeus have been close for many winters and, I can only imagine, shall be for many more to come. The child would begin to see him as a parental figure and I cannot have that."

"If the gods offer you a solution for a family with the one you love, you must take it."

"No. Absolutely not."

"Do not regret the opportunity you are handed, for there are those who would gladly trade places to have what you can have," he said quietly.

I regarded Moeris a long moment. "Your wife is unable to gift you with children?" I ventured.

"We attempted for many winters, but to no avail. I was as you are now – unwilling to allow her to lie with another to see it so. It became something we could not overcome. She died this past winter, from a broken heart perhaps, childless and disappointed in me. In us."

"Apologies Moeris, I did not know. But I cannot allow another to touch Alexis, I just cannot. After Melanthios ..."

"Thaddeus is not Melanthios," Moeris interrupted gently. "He shall not hurt Alexis. He cares greatly for her."

"That is just as difficult to accept. Perhaps it is what he has always wanted, or what she always has. Perhaps this is their way of being able to be together without hurting Hesper."

"It is not," Thaddeus' voice cut into our conversation. "Alexis chose you Skylar. She loves *you*. Do you not understand how much? She wants a family with you because finally, after so many winters of knowing it was expected of her, she has found herself truly wishing for it."

"So you say," I replied stiffly, scratching at the ground with the tip of my sword.

"Perhaps I shall leave you to your words," Moeris said, squeezing my shoulder as he passed. I nodded in reply.

"The child I help to create shall not be mine, not really," Thaddeus said. "It is not for my own hidden pleasure or some deep desire you believe I hold. The act itself would not be as it is when I am with Hesper or as you are with Alexis, you must believe me when I speak these words." I gripped the handle of my sword but said nothing. "I wish only to see Alexis happy. You have made her so already, and yet there is something she still desires, something she wants for you both. Allow me to help. I shall not question the decisions you and Alexis make on your child's behalf. I give you my word. Besides, I have enough responsibility with my own three boys and Gnosidicus has just confirmed that Hesper is again with child, she is due in Gamelion, the first moon of the winter."

"My congratulations to you both," I murmured.

"Thank you," he nodded. "I do not wish to be a father to your child Skylar, but I hope you shall allow me to be in their life. If it is a boy I would teach him as I do my own sons, and if it is a girl I would watch over her, to be a man she could look up to and respect as she shall King Agrias and your own father when he returns. I am certain Moeris too would wish for the same if given the opportunity. I am no threat to the relationship you and Alexis share and if you truly believed it to be so, I fear my own children would be forced to grow without their father. I have borne witness to the lengths you would go to in protecting what you have with her, and I respect that." He held his arm out as he continued. "Allow us both to make Alexis happy. Your child need not grow alone in this world as you and Alexis had to. My own children shall treat yours as kin; my boys have already begun to call you aunt. My heart always has and always shall belong to Hesper just as yours shall always belong to Alexis."

I blew out a deep breath and sheathed my sword, taking Thaddeus proffered arm and gripping it tightly.

"I shall take your words under consideration, but it is not a decision to make lightly."

"I understand," he nodded. "If it was me being asked to allow such an act I am not certain I could consent to it either." He released me and picked up his shield which lay on the ground not far from us. "Consider it at least," he added.

He slid his arm into the holds on the inner side and crossed the courtyard, tapping Brygos on the shoulder and motioning for the young man to follow when he turned.

"Easier said than done," I murmured to their departing forms.

# 4

I hesitated under the veranda on the southern side of the palace, torn at my destination. King Agrias had asked me to see him when I rose this morning and I had intended to go directly after training. Until Alexis had made her request. Now I paused because I knew how close he and Alexis were and I did not know if she had spoken with her father about wanting us to have a child, and if that was what he wanted to speak to *me* about. Agrias and I had got along well since we met, but I had not shared as much with him as Alexis had shared with my own father – she having admitted her feelings for me to him before speaking of them to me.

I decided I was not ready to speak to Agrias just yet, and continued to Hesper and Thaddeus' apartment instead. I knocked and the door opened almost immediately – the elderly palace healer, Gnosidicus, filling the doorway ahead of Hesper.

"Ah, Skylar, I am glad to meet you this day," he said.

"Gnosidicus," I nodded.

"I would have words, if you shall permit them. Were your intentions to see Alexis after you were done here?"

"Er, perhaps. I believe her to be in our room if you wish to go on ahead," I replied.

"I shall wait for you outside and we can go together," he offered. I drew a deep breath but nodded as Gnosidicus exited the apartment and I entered.

Hesper closed the door and crossed the room to a tall table. "I imagine I know why you are here," she said, offering me a skyphos of wine.

I took it, draining half before I spoke. "Thaddeus says you are to welcome another child in the winter."

"Yes," she smiled, her eyes following her hand to her stomach before they met mine again. "But that is not the reason I meant." I drained my cup but said nothing. "Alexis has spoken to you of her wish for a child, Thaddeus as well I imagine if you know of our news."

She held the amphora out again but I shook my head. "How long have you known it is what she wanted?" I asked, my voice slightly harsher than I intended.

She hesitated, sitting the amphora back on the table. "For some time."

"And? What do you have to say on the matter? Do you allow it without question? Without hurt at the thought of what must occur for it to be so?" I growled, beginning to pace across the room.

"Skyl–"

"She is your friend and he your husband, how could you allow such a match?" I cut her off, my hands clenching. "Perhaps they have always cared for one another more than they should. Had Agrias had his way, it would have been the two of them betrothed, not Alexis to Basileios. Perhaps your children would be their children."

"Skylar, stop!" Hesper demanded, halting my steps with a firm hand on my arm. I flinched at the contact, only just holding myself back from reflecting her blow and inflicting pain in return. I saw a flash of fear in her eyes, but she continued as though there had been no interruption. "You torture yourself with visions, I see that, and it is not easy for me to turn thoughts of my husband with another woman from mind either. But I love them both so much and with what Alexis endured with Basileios; the disappointment she felt with herself for being unable to give him what she was supposed to, as well as what would have happened to her had she became Melanthios' wife, I cannot begrudge her this request. She is my dearest friend and you make her exceptionally happy. You saved her, you breathed life into her existence when she did not realize anything was missing.

"From the moment we met at the bathing area, when your father told the story of you interrupting the bathing couple when you were seven winters old, I began to grow fond of you; I could see why Alexis was so drawn to you." She paused and for a moment I wondered if she intended to place hands on me as Queen Melina once had. I was about to take a step back when Hesper continued without nearing, nor her hand on my arm tightening. "I saw how you looked at Alexis, what you believed was hidden from her that night, and her own reaction to your nearness spoke words she could not yet express. I saw what was happening between the two of you before Alexis even realized it, before she lost her heart to you. And I saw what your apparent rejection of her did – how she felt when she found you with the slave girl after you asked her for more."

I opened my mouth to speak, but no words came out, and my face heated with shame and embarrassment at how much Alexis had shared with Hesper of that night.

"You are everything to her, and she wants to give you so much in return. She wants to give you what you have never had – a family, a full family which extends past just you and your father. A family with children and two loving parents. Grandparents to fuss over their grandchildren."

I stood silently, absorbing what Hesper said. At length I found my voice. "Gnosidicus waits for me," I murmured.

"Do not shut her out. Not again," Hesper advised, removing her hand and stepping back. "Speak with her. Share what you keep inside so misunderstandings do not keep you apart and miserable." I passed her the skyphos and turned, my fingers on the handle when she spoke again. "She loves you more than she ever knew was possible. Please do not break her heart, she would not survive, and neither would you."

I only nodded in reply, closing the door quietly behind me, the truth of Hesper's words finding their way to my core. Gnosidicus waited patiently and I indicated we make our way to the room Alexis and I shared as I blew out a deep breath.

"I wanted to speak with you and the princess on a … delicate, yet important, matter," he said.

I slowed as we reached the central corridor. Had Thaddeus or Hesper spoken to him already? Had Alexis? I held my hand out to halt his progress. "Before you do, may I speak with the princess alone for just a moment?" I asked.

"Of course. Take as much time as you need." I nodded and opened the door to our room, closing it and lowering the wooden lock into place before I turned to face Alexis.

"I did not know if you would return," she said, her back to me as she drew a fine-toothed implement through her hair.

I took a deep breath and crossed the room, drawing my fingers through the long brown strands that lay over her shoulders and down her back, the softness tickling my arms. I did not know how to speak of my fears with Alexis. No, that was not true. I did not *want* to speak of them for I feared how they would sound out loud to the one I loved more than any other in the world. "I have never been able to stay away," I murmured.

"I saw you with Moeris. You were angry. Hurt. I made it so."

"I am not always controlled, my defense is attack and I did not want to hurt you. It was best I left for a while."

"I apologize for the words I spoke earlier, I know they hurt you and I would ne–"

"I know," I cut her off, leaning down to expose the side of her neck and placing a gentle kiss there. I felt the shiver slip down Alexis' spine and I smiled, pressing my lips against the soft skin again, my teeth grazing her slightly.

Her breath caught and she reached up to tangle a hand in my hair, drawing me closer as I felt her pulse quicken. "Skylar," she whispered, turning so her lips met mine. "You seek to distract me from the words we need to speak to one another."

"Yes. Do you think it shall work?" I grinned, drawing the pin from her chiton.

Alexis made no attempt to stall the material as it fell around her hips, my hands following its path moments later. "No … ah … yes," she breathed.

"Good." I stroked the defined bone of her cheek and slipped my tongue into her mouth. In a smooth motion which caught me by surprise – and started a burning fire between my legs – Alexis stood. Her tongue tangled with mine as she pressed herself against me. I placed enough space between us again so my palms could trace the contours of her body.

"Gods, please," she groaned, fisting her hand in the material at my hip as my hand slid down her stomach.

I willingly obliged, drawing through the wetness that had accumulated as I touched her, my pulse hammering beneath my chest. I lifted her onto the table and slid my hands down her thighs. She closed her eyes, her head flung back. I entered her quickly, not rough, but not as gentle as I had been earlier that morning; before talk of children and Thaddeus had shattered our intimacy. I needed to feel her in every part of my being.

She wrapped a hand around the nape of my neck and pulled me to her with abandon, her tongue possessing me before mine had the chance to do the same. My desire, the wanton lust I felt for her was a wild thing and I kissed her as she opened her legs wider, inviting me to fill her, to own her and bring her to her climax. I gladly complied, her fingers finding my nipple through the linen tunic I wore and bringing it to life with her ministrations.

I gasped, feeling the building pressure within me and when she pulled out the pin at my shoulder and ripped the material from my body, I groaned deeply into her mouth. She positioned her knee between my thighs; urging me to move against her as I thrust inside her.

I continued my steady movements, her breath shortening and her stomach tightening as I pushed her higher. Her fingers dug into my hip as she neared her end and as she fell over the glorious edge, I did the same, the depth of my pleasure almost sending me to my knees.

"Gods," Alexis whispered again, her body convulsing beneath me as she attempted to catch her breath.

"My princess," I whispered, my heart pounding beneath my chest.

"Please do not leave without words again, we must speak of everything, always. I want to know all your thoughts," she said, her mouth brushing mine again as she spoke.

"That would not always be for the best," I told her. She leaned back slightly, her green eyes capturing mine. I lifted her hand, kissing each of her knuckles. She opened her mouth to speak again, but I put my finger against her lips. "I cannot speak the words you want me to right now. But know that I love you, so deeply it hurts sometimes. I want to give you everything you desire. I do not think of you as Melanthios did – as a prize to be won, a possession, but you are *mine* and I cannot allow anyone else to place hands on you as I do. I cannot bear the thought of it."

"I know. It pains me to think of you with another as well."

"There is more we must speak of, I accept that, and though I would rather spend the remainder of the day showing you just how much I love you, Gnosidicus waits outside and then I am due to meet with your father."

"Gnosidicus is outside and you just came in here and …?"

I smiled wickedly and brought her hand to my lips, kissing her knuckles again. "Yes. Whatever else the day may bring, I needed to know we were still solid. Connected."

"Always," she promised, taking another kiss from my lips. "Now get dressed before the old man grows impatient and enters without warning."

"He would not dare," I grinned.

# 5

When I had re-dressed and Alexis' chiton was settled around her slim body, I opened the door to the healer. He held out his hands to Alexis, his face creasing into a smile as he spoke. "Good morning, Princess."

"And to you Gnosidicus, how does this day find you?"

"Very well. Hesper wished me to pass on the news that the suspicion the two of you had was correct; she is again carrying a child."

"I am pleased for her," Alexis replied, though I noticed her smile held a touch of sadness.

I closed the door and returned to Alexis' side, offering Gnosidicus the chair that now stood in the middle of the room; far from the table whose contents were slightly disturbed due to the recent activity atop it.

I swallowed a smirk and cleared my throat. "You needed to speak with us?"

"Indeed," Gnosidicus confirmed as he sat down. "I very much hope I bring you and the princess pleasing news."

Alexis turned curious eyes in the old man's direction and sat on the end of our bed, facing him. "Please, speak."

I remained standing, shoulders tense and uncertain what the healer would say, though many ideas danced behind my eyes, none of them particularly appealing.

Gnosidicus cleared his throat. "Last evening, as I lay slumbering, I found myself enter Morpheus' realm and I was visited by the great god Asclepius. My ancestor often visits me when I pray to him to aid me with a particularly difficult patient or when the herbs and medicines I have tried do not appear to be working. I had not asked a question of him, but I have learnt the gods work in strange ways and I received an answer just the same."

"The answer to what question?" Alexis asked.

"It was about you, Princess, and your desire to conceive of a child."

Alexis' mouth silently opened and closed several times and I sat down heavily on the bed next to her. It was as I expected – he was there to tell me that Alexis must lay with Thaddeus if she was to have a child, that unless I wished to disappoint her, I would have to allow them to be together. "What did Asclepius speak of?" I asked, finding my voice first and feeling Alexis stiffen slightly beside me.

"He spoke words of encouragement, of hope. He understands that Alexis is almost past her child-bearing age and has produced no offspring, but if you are willing to walk the stony path together, you shall be provided with a child in a manner agreeable to you both," the old man replied, his eyes meeting mine with certainty.

"How is that possible?" I asked, a frown crossing my features.

"He did not say, but you must travel to Epidaurus where a temple to him is newly constructed. You must spend the night there at the healing temple they call the Asclepeion. The answers shall be provided as you slumber in his midst."

"Do you trust his words, Gnosidicus?" Alexis asked quietly.

His gaze shifted back to her. "Always," he assured her with a nod.

"Then we must prepare for travel," she said, reaching for my hand and squeezing it tightly between her own. "Please," she implored, holding my gaze.

I drew a deep breath. I could see how much it meant to her; how much she wanted it. A gnawing fear settled in my stomach and I exhaled slowly as I stood. "I shall consider it."

"Skylar," Alexis began.

"I have to go. Your father is expecting me," I told her, hoping I was not walking into a similar conversation so soon. "Gnosidicus," I added, nodding in his direction. I closed the door to our room and squared my shoulders, attempting to set aside all thoughts of children and Alexis and Thaddeus or the potential journey to Epidaurus, and headed for the Throne Room.

As I neared, the voices of Agrias and Melina floated out through the open doorway. I slowed, not wanting to interrupt what was obviously a heated and long-fought conversation, but when I heard my name, I continued toward the room, leaning against the cool stonework outside to listen.

"She is more than capable, as you well know, and I cannot see that she would refuse the request," the king said.

"But should we not take both of them with us? Amyntas would want to see Alexis after so many winters, and if you are determined to cite Skylar's presence for the further changes you wish to make, would it not make sense to have her along to introduce?"

"Perhaps, but I wish her to forge stronger alliances with the men here. It is fortunate we do not need to face enemies this summer, it gives her more time to learn their strengths and weaknesses … and offer guidance to those whom require it."

"I suppose," Melina conceded.

"When the assembly meets again in the autumn, I want Skylar to be at my side. These next moons are important if that is to happen. She has already proven herself loyal to our people by working tirelessly to ensure those lost in the battle with the Illyrians were properly sent to the afterlife, and by overseeing the induction of the new soldiers two moons ago. But there are a few on the small council who remain doubtful of her intentions to remain, especially now Leandros has left."

"One only has to see the way she looks at our daughter to know she shall remain here, at her side, until their days come to an end," Melina murmured.

"Indeed," Agrias replied, and I thought I detected a grin in his voice. "Sometimes I wonder how Alexis stands to be the focus of such intensity."

"She loves her," Melina replied. "Skylar can make her feel as though no one and nothing else exists outside the two of them when they are alone."

"Alexis spoke of this with you?"

The queen laughed. "A little. Though I had to share some of *our* past with her to hear her say the words."

"Oh?"

"Do not tell me you do not recall just how single-minded you were when you came to Trachis and laid claim to me? It is an intoxicating feeling to be the subject of someone's undisguised wanting and desire."

"And when the feelings are returned, it is a heady mix indeed."

"Oh yes," Melina agreed.

There was a long pause and I decided I had remained outside long enough. I strode into the room, finding Agrias holding his queen tightly, her hands at his chest as their lips met. "Pardon the interruption, King Agrias. You wanted to see me?" I asked, bowing in his direction. "Queen Melina," I added, nodding to her as well as they parted and her eyes found mine.

"Skylar, come, please," Agrias grinned, waving me over with one hand, his other still pressed to the small of Melina's back. "You need not be so formal with us, I consider us family." I only nodded in reply as I made my way to them, seating myself on Alexis' throne when Agrias offered it to me. "There are two matters I wish to discuss with you this day." He and Melina took their own thrones and the green eyes of the king captured mine as he leant forward. "I have had further word from Epirus," he told me.

I tensed slightly. After Melanthios' army had been defeated, Agrias spoke with the leader of the Illyrian soldiers who had joined the Epirotes and told them Melanthios had attacked unprovoked. At first the Illyrians did not believe him, but when they saw the preparations which had begun for the wedding feast, and Antigonos – a former Epirote living in Trachis – confirmed that Agrias had agreed to become a vassal, they spoke apologies at having followed him into battle. *There is no faster way to bring shame to your people than to attack an ally when they have done nothing to warrant such an act,* the warrior had noted. The following day, Agrias sent a messenger to Andreas, along with the bodies of his sons, and ordered him to rescind his family's claim on Alexis. Andreas agreed, sending the messenger away immediately so he could mourn the loss of his boys alone.

"Andreas shall be kept busy over the summer campaigning period; the Illyrian tribes are furious with Melanthios' behavior here and intend to march on the Molossians. If he lives, Andreas shall come here afterwards."

"What for?" I asked.

"Not to fight. He wants to see where his sons lost their lives."

"I have not heard of such a desire before. Should we be concerned?"

The king grinned, his eyes flicking to his queen as he spoke before settling on me again. "No, *we* should not. I agree it is an unusual request … but allow me to deal with Andreas and his visit should it come to fruition. Your concern should be only with the happiness of my daughter, and I have no doubt you have that well in hand," he added, his grin widening.

"Er …" I cleared my throat, dropping my eyes from his.

"All is not well between the two of you?"

"We are …" I paused and blew out a deep breath, uncertain how to share Alexis' request with them. "What is the second matter you wish to discuss with me?" I asked instead, returning my gaze to theirs.

Agrias did not answer immediately, exchanging a look with Melina before he replied. "I have spoken previously with you of how I have incorporated more of the southern Greek ways into our life since I arrived here in Trachis; their gods and their clothing to name but two. Now that you have decided to remain, I want to embrace further Greek festivals and battle formations, I am particularly intrigued with the phalanx you told me of. And I intend to go visit my brother to discuss it with him."

"I have made my concerns in this matter clear," Melina interrupted. "I am afraid Agrias' brother – Amyntas – shall not accept the changes, that he shall take our titles, or our lives, for the dissent or apparent disrespect we show their heritage."

Agrias smiled at his wife with fondness and reached for her hand. "And I have told you not to worry yourself so, my dear." He brought her fingers to his lips. "You know my brother and I have always been able to speak openly and strategically when it comes to matters on how I rule here. I do not believe this time shall be any different." Melina opened her mouth, but the king continued. "Amyntas shall understand why now we should act in the same manner as the Greeks around us. I can assure him that it is not to align ourselves with Athens, for that shall no doubt occur to him because he has aligned himself with the Persians."

"He would wonder if your intent was to march on Aigai with the force of Athens behind you and take the capital to rule for yourself," I noted.

"Exactly," Agrias nodded. "The Greeks are strong and would possibly defeat him if they attempted it, but they continue to squabble between themselves for the time being, so I do not believe there is any danger of that, or *we* would be their first target."

"But you cannot know for certain that Amyntas shall accept your reasons. When you did not follow him in becoming a vassal to Persia, he threatened to take your life and your throne. It was only through wise council that you were allowed to remain ruling," Melina countered.

"I would have denied him of both title and position then, as I would now, if he sought to attempt the same." Agrias frowned. "I do not wish to be at war with my brother, but if he does not allow me to rule as I see fit, then I shall have no hesitation in making it so."

"But Agri–"

"No Melina, my mind shall not be changed in this matter. If I wish for our soldiers to fight as the Greeks do with their hoplites and phalanx formations, then it shall be so. If I wish our people to worship the same gods and celebrate the same festivals, then it shall be done. And any who dare stand against me shall find themselves banished or at the end of my sword; my brother included if he chooses to make it so."

"Agrias, Melina, please do not invite division between yourselves or your family on account of wanting to make *me* feel welcome or comfortable here," I interrupted before Melina could respond to her husband's outburst. "I …" I paused again, drawing in a deep breath as I considered my next words carefully. "I need to speak with you both about something."

# 6

I stood with a suddenness that caused Agrias and Melina to jump. "Alexis wishes to travel to Epidaurus," I told them.

"What is in Epidaurus?" Agrias asked.

"Gnosidicus speaks of a temple dedicated to Asclepius, God of Healing."

"A healing temple?" Melina echoed.

I nodded, blowing out a deep breath. "Perhaps ... perhaps your journey to Aigai could be postponed a short while as Alexis has come to me with a request; one which I am not certain I can agree to. She may need the two of you here to speak with. We might both need that," I added quietly.

"What has she asked?" Agrias asked, rising from his throne and tentatively placing his hand on my shoulder.

I exhaled another long breath and raised my eyes to his. "She wants a child."

"Oh?" the queen asked, pushing herself to her feet and joining us. "She does not wish for the two of you to remain together? She seeks the arms of another?"

"No, no," I frowned, shaking my head. "She ... she wants it for the two of us."

Agrias took his hand from my shoulder. "I wondered when she would speak of it to you," he said, silencing words of question and outrage from both myself and his wife by raising a hand. "What is it that troubles you most about the request?" he asked gently.

"You cannot imagine?" I replied, my voice catching.

"The manner in which it must be gifted," he offered, nodding. "I do not know if either of us can aid in the decision. I fear it may be something only the two of you can find agreement – or disagreement – on," he continued. "But I want you to know I am here if you want to discuss it."

I remained silent, uncertain what I could say in response, not that he appeared to need an answer.

"I imagine there is much about this request that scares you," Melina said. "I have made so many mistakes where my daughter is concerned. The … the morning I laid hands on you and pulled you into my chambers," she paused at my sharp intake of breath. "You have not spoken of it with Alexis?"

"No. I do not want to cause another rift between the two of you."

Melina nodded. "You challenged me that day as though you knew of the history between Alexis and I, you allude to knowing of it now." I nodded in reply. "May I attempt explanation for my behavior?" I swallowed loudly but nodded once more. "We had a son," Melina said, reaching for Agrias' hand and threading her fingers through his when he took it. "He died when he was two winters old and it devastated me. I could not bear the thought of not watching him grow and learn and fall in love. I could not imagine not being a mother to my precious little boy. I longed to have him back and became pregnant again soon after with Alexis, believing another child would bring me the same joy. Unfortunately, when Alexis was born, I could not see past her gender. I did not see that she could bring me that happiness, if only I nurtured her as I had him. Though we remained beneath the same roof, I showed her nothing of what a mother should be, taught her nothing of what it was to be a girl, a woman.

"And then she was betrothed to Basileios and I realized I had failed her. I recalled my own fears at fourteen winters when I was to become Agrias' wife. My mother and the women of my tribe spent much time preparing me for the event. They spoke at length about how Agrias would come to me, what would be expected of me and what I must do to ensure an heir was produced for my husband. But I had passed none of my knowledge onto Alexis and when I finally attempted to share what I knew with her, we could barely stand to be in the same room as one another and she left without proper instruction, or warning."

"She was fortunate Agrias betrothed her to Basileios, who was kind to her, rather than Melanthios," I murmured.

"Yes. You cannot imagine how I regretted my actions and how I feared for her when I met Melanthios and his brothers; I was certain I would never see her again. But then she returned to us and though it was a kind husband who saw her back in our arms, Basileios could not remain at her side.

"I watched her as she cared for you, how she was around you. I saw that you touched something deep within her, something I did not believe she had had with Basileios, or anyone before. I could not find words to ask her – did not feel I had any place to. But I longed for you to wake, to see if she stirred the same in you. Having spoken with your father, I was in no doubt it was a woman's touch you preferred."

"I do not recall much of that early time after I arrived, but I remember conversations between the two of you; of your insistence she ready herself for her betrothal to Melanthios. Why did you push her towards him if you did not want that?"

"I hoped she would rebel against me, against her father, to stand up for herself. I wanted her to refuse to marry a man from such a brutal tribe. When my mother told me I was to be Agrias' wife I was frightened and did not want to. Of course after we were betrothed, I came to know of his gentle nature and fell in love with him, but at the time I could not see any other choice, and it was not as if my heart belonged to another I would rather be with. I went along without question of what was expected of me, just as Alexis did when it was her turn.

"I so desperately wanted for her to choose the life she wished for herself, rather than the one that was to be forced upon her. That is why I attempted to incite your desire for her, to claim her for yourself before it was too late. I know I did not go about it in the correct manner, but I did not know what else to do." Melina reached out, the tips of her fingers resting at my cheek. I stiffened slightly beneath her touch but did not move away. "From the first moment you saw her, you knew she was special, you wanted her, did you not?" she asked, her voice barely above a whisper.

"I did, though I did not want it to be so; I did not believe myself worthy of her attentions," I replied. I also had not believed it safe for Alexis to want me so near, though I was as incapable of keeping away from her as she was me.

"You were everything she needed," Melina said in earnest. "And so, I say to you now with complete truth and certainty; do not allow your fear to drive Alexis from your arms or drive an unbridgeable divide between you. Do not face your future with regrets for what might have been, for it is no way to live." She took her hand from my face and stepped back. "If you can find a way to make a family together, then I shall do nothing but support you. Both of you, in whatever way you need. I am glad you came into our lives when you did."

"We are *both* glad you and Alexis found one another when you did, and that you remain here with us to complete our family again," Agrias added.

"Consider all we have said this day and really think about what *you* want, not just about what others may want," Melina counselled.

"Melina speaks true. What Alexis asks is huge we understand that. It is not a decision to make lightly. But we are here to listen and help anyway we can."

"And what if I cannot agree to what Alexis asks? Where does that leave us as a family?" I asked.

"Our fondness for you shall not diminish. We love you not only because you love our daughter, but because of who you are as a person."

"Thank you," I murmured, though I did not know how a parent would be able to still love someone who had hurt their daughter as I was afraid I would hurt Alexis.

"Ask Alexis for time to decide how you feel about what she has asked of you if time is what you need. She shall understand," Agrias said.

"I hope so," I murmured, and we all knew I was not just referring to his last statement.

# 7

# Epidaurus, north-eastern Peloponnese
## 2nd rising, Moon of Hekatombaion, 508bc

The sun had begun making its descent when Alexis and I arrived in the south a little over a week later. My decision to take her to the Asclepeion in Epidaurus had not been reached easily and I was still not certain I had made the correct choice. But I made it after a great deal of time alone with only my weapons for company, and long conversations with Moeris and Melina.

The large, black ox we had brought with us from Trachis was just as hot, dirty and smelly as we were; dust sticking to the sheen of sweat across its fur and swishing tail as closely as the dirt on our faces and legs.

Alexis had blisters on her feet from her sandals – unaccustomed to walking such distances by foot. I fared better, the winters of journeying with my father serving me well, though I was weary and more than a little apprehensive about our arrival.

We had taken no one else with us, though Thaddeus had implored Alexis to allow him to accompany us for protection. I had already told him he was not needed, that I could take care of us both, but it took a direct order from Agrias to ensure Thaddeus remained in Trachis. I was certain his pride was wounded, but the thought of him travelling with us to Epidaurus was more than I could bear and when thoughts of what possibly lay ahead between Alexis and Thaddeus surfaced, I attempted to divert them; focusing instead on the Asclepeion and wondering if Asclepius truly ever provided answers or healed those who travelled there.

We stayed in only a few towns on our way south; Alexis having convinced me to allow her to experience how Father and I had often slept beneath the night sky, rather than finding lodgings with local traders. Of course, finding a homeowner prepared to house both us and the ox for the night was challenging enough, so it made agreeing to the request easier.

It amused me that the gentle, sparkling lights above, and the isolation of our surroundings, made my lover even more amorous than usual, despite her obvious weariness each evening. She eagerly relieved me of my sword and removed the pin that held my bronze cuirass over my chest, discarding my tunic with the same fervor when she reached it. My concern that someone would come across us in such a vulnerable position dulled when she ran her hands over my skin, and when her lips met mine I found myself abandoning my misgivings at our travel and lost myself in the freeness and hunger with which she offered her body to me. I trusted that my winters of experience ensured I would hear danger long before it got near enough to harm us.

After our pleasurable coupling each night, Alexis quickly succumbed to Hypnos' realm and, though I was also tired from the travelling, I slept little during the dark candlemarks; determined to remain watchful and ensure we reached Epidaurus without incident. I knew the animal accompanying us would be of no use as protection if it came to that and thankfully, the paths were free of travelers and mercenaries alike – those attending the Games in Olympia having long since passed, and the traders preferring to travel only during the daylight to ensure they arrived at *their* destinations with their goods intact.

I had ensured we took the farthest route around Corinth with its haunting memories to reach the southern Peloponnese region. The land that stretched between the Saronic Gulf and the Gulf of Corinth – known as the Isthmus – was the slimmest in the region at forty-three itinerary wide, but fortunately, I could not see the massive acropolis in the distance as the sun set that particular evening.

The town of Epidaurus itself was on the water, picturesque as it looked out onto the Saronic Gulf, though unlike the last time I had been here, we did not venture that way; the new temple to Asclepius being fifty itinerary to the west of the town in a wooded valley, which we had entered half a candlemark ago.

The sweet scent of thyme accompanied us as we passed beneath the tall pine trees, and I knew if we had travelled through the grove in the winter, the aroma of pine needles would also have surrounded us. The trees were a welcome relief after the heat of the day, thick enough to block most of the sun yet set far enough apart to keep a little of the warmth trapped inside.

We followed the overgrown path west through the pines, a mixture of calf-high wavy grass and white colored flowers with yellow centers growing across the track. More than once I had to tug on the thick rope yoked around the bull's neck to encourage him to move, rather than stop to taste every stalk of vegetation, and when the trees thinned out we emerged from the dense wood, finding ourselves facing a large, columned structure.

"The Shrine of Artemis, just as Gnosidicus spoke of," Alexis noted.

I nodded in reply, taking her hand when she reached for mine. Hers was damp and I wondered if it was just the heat or her own trepidation that caused it to be so. I tightened my grip and led her and the ox around the rectangular building.

The open walled structure was less than six-and-a half-feet across at the main entrance with four Doric columns standing proudly almost twenty-four feet high and evenly spaced. Nine columns ran from the front to the rear on both sides and another four stood at the other end. The longer sides were a little over double the length of the front and back and the roof appeared to still be under construction, with wooden beams exposed and no tiles to keep the weather or birds out. The western side was the only one to have a pediment above the columns – carved warriors in a scene I was familiar with: the siege of Troy.

An older man dressed in a simple white chiton and, despite the heat of the day, a short himation, came bustling towards us. His hands were clasped together at his chest and he wore a welcoming smile. We continued past the shrine to meet him.

The ox found the small flowers far more interesting than the man up ahead and I did not pull him too vigorously to follow, allowing him the small treats, for I knew his time in this world would soon be done and I wished his last memories to be happy ones.

"Greetings, friends," the man said when he reached us. "Welcome to the Asclepeion of Epidaurus. I am Head Priest Deacon."

"Thank you," Alexis replied, taking her hand from mine and placing it in the older man's.

His eyes roamed curiously over our small party, his lips lifting as he took in the fine form of our sacrifice. "You seek answers from the great God of Healing?" he asked, his gaze finding Alexis' face again.

"We do. We have travelled from Trachis in the region of Thermopylae on the advice of our healer Gnosidicus, he speaks highly of you and the work you do here," Alexis replied.

"My dear Gnosidicus. He is a good man indeed. I have often attempted to entice him to join me here, but he prefers the weather in the north, and the hot springs. Do the days find my friend well?"

"Very. He sends his regards to you and the other priests and says to tell you that though his body ages, his mind is still sharp and he hopes it shall be many days until you are reunited in Hades' realm."

"That is happy news indeed. Speak words of the same when you return to him, for it has been many winters since we found ourselves together."

"We shall," Alexis promised as I nodded my agreement.

"Good. Now tell me, what answers do you seek from Asclepius? You do not appear to be lame or ill. What has brought you so far from home?"

"We understand that men travel to the healing temple for cures for external ailments or complaints, but we hope he can aid with an *internal* problem," I answered.

"Oh?" Deacon enquired, his eyebrows rising.

"We wish for a child," Alexis added.

"You both wish for children? You have attempted with your husbands without success?"

"No. We ..." Alexis looked across to me briefly before she continued. "For five winters I called Basileios my husband and, though we attempted many times, I was unable to provide him with an heir."

"And you?" Deacon asked, his eyes sliding across to me. "You too have attempted to bring a child into the world without success?"

I hesitated. Deacon was a priest, a religious man who was not permitted to take a lover at all, and whilst he may have seen many injuries and miracles of his god's healing powers, I was not entirely certain he would be as quick to aid us if he knew of our coupling. And despite any misgivings I may have, I would not jeopardize Alexis' opportunity to enter the temple and implore the great god himself to aid us. "No. I am here only to support my friend. I offer protection for her journey from and back to Trachis. To ensure she returns to her family in health and able to bear the child she so dearly wishes for."

Alexis gave me a small nod, understanding my words and the reasons behind them without requiring an explanation.

I met Deacon's eyes again as he spoke. "Very well. You may assist up to a point, but you shall not be privy to all we do here."

"I cannot leave her."

"She shall not be in any danger, I give you my word."

"I—"

"Skylar," Alexis said quietly putting her hand on my arm. "We must do as Deacon suggests." She squeezed, her eyes speaking more than her actual words.

I blew out a breath and nodded. "I shall remain as close as permitted."

"Indeed," Deacon smiled, turning from us as he added, "come, we must offer your sacrifice to Asclepius."

"Thank you," Alexis whispered, sliding her hand down to take mine again.

"You know I would do anything for you, though I do not enjoy the idea of being separated from you in this place."

"I know."

Deacon had his back to us as he made his way to a large, light-colored stone altar, so I lifted Alexis' chin and planted a quick kiss on her lips. "I hope Asclepius visits you quickly." She only smiled in reply, separating our entwined fingers as we arrived at the altar.

It stood at three and a half feet high, nineteen feet wide and just over forty feet long. The top held a circular formation of rocks, with lengths of wood and pine needles for tinder inside; awaiting the official burning of sacrificial offerings. Four black and red clay urns stood empty at each of its edges. The closest to us showed a man – presumably Asclepius – speaking to a lame figure leaning on a wooden stick. The urn on the opposite side pictured men kneeling before an altar and offering libation and a rooster for sacrifice. At the far end on the near side, I could just make out a tall figure laying hands on the head of a soldier; bandages covered the warrior's arms and right leg, his left missing.

Deacon paused at the mid-point of the altar and indicated we do the same. "You are familiar with ritual sacrifice? You have performed it before to your gods or goddesses of choice?" he asked as I brought the beast to a halt beside the slab of stone.

"Yes," I replied.

"I have witnessed it, but never been involved myself – it was not expected or asked of me," Alexis said at the same time.

Deacon nodded. "Sacrifices are normally only performed by the males in your household, I understand. Though here in Epidaurus, the one who seeks aid must personally bring the animal and sacrifice its body to Asclepius."

"Oh," Alexis murmured.

"I shall be right here with you. It is how it must be if you truly want to be with child," I said.

"To raise a child with the one I love more dearly than any other in this world is what I want," Alexis replied, her eyes meeting mine.

I did not respond; I would not lie to her and tell her I wished for the same when I was not certain it was how I felt. I simply nodded in reply.

"If we are ready to proceed, there are several items I must collect," Deacon said, circling the altar.

"I ... I do not know if I can take a life, even one of an animal," Alexis whispered, her hand finding the ox's flank.

"Do not think of it as an act of violence. Deacon will ensure that all of us, including the ox, are willing participants."

"How?" I did not have the chance to respond as the priest returned, setting several bowls on the altar.

"First, we must prepare your sacrifice so he is pure and ready to meet Asclepius. We shall begin by washing the dust from his body," Deacon announced. I nodded and shed the bag I had brought with us. Deacon picked up an amphora of water and passed it to me. I poured it over the ox's rear and back, noting the barley seeds mixed in with the liquid. Alexis smoothed her hand down the animal, removing the dirt embedded in its course hairs.

Deacon threw more barley seeds and I knew it was so he, as a priest of Asclepius, participated in the ritual, encouraging the great god to hear our prayers and look favorably down upon us. When we reached the ox's head, it dipped its nose towards the ground several times and Deacon smiled. "Your ox has given his consent to the sacrifice. We can proceed and offer him to the God of Healing."

Alexis and I finished cleaning the animal and when I handed the amphora back to Deacon, he passed me a length of material. "Place this around his neck," he instructed.

Alexis whispered her thanks to the ox as I tied a knot in the ends, giving him a quick pat on the nose as well. When I finished, I turned to find Deacon giving Alexis a knife from his bowl of barley. The guard and pommel were asymmetric, the cutting edge of the blade curved as opposed to the back, which was flat. It was a typical weapon used in sacrifice, though I knew just as many kings and soldiers who used their xiphos for the same purpose. It was less than half the length of my sword and I wondered how Alexis would handle it against the throat of the large animal.

"You must use this makhaira to slit the throat of your sacrifice. Do it quickly so he does not suffer. I shall collect the blood in this bowl and if all is in order, we shall offer its body to the flames," Deacon told her.

Alexis said nothing but took the weapon from him and stepped closer to the ox. She blew out a deep breath, raising her hand and placing the knife's edge against its throat. She drew another breath and let it out, slower this time. "I cannot," she whispered, lowering the blade.

"But ..." Deacon began. I held my hand up to him and crossed to Alexis.

I stood behind her, placing my fingers at her hip and wrapping my other hand around her trembling one. With my lips at her ear I spoke. "Do not be afraid, think only of what you want to ask Asclepius. The sacrifice and offering of the ox shall please him and he shall consider your request far more favorably if you prove to him you are strong enough to do this, to face what you find frightening or distasteful." I pressed the knife against the ox's throat as I continued. "A makhaira blade is single-edged, rather than double as my sword is, so you must bring it up as well as across the ox's neck when you slice."

"I do not know if I am ab–"

"You must," I interrupted gently.

"But Skylar ..." I loosened my grip around her hand and lowered the knife.

I circled her, capturing her eyes with my own and dropping my voice. "If this truly is what you wish for us, you have to."

She drew another deep breath, letting it all the way out again before nodding. "It is."

"You are not alone. I am here and I love you," I assured her, squeezing her hand and taking my place behind her again.

She nodded again and closed her eyes. "I am ready."

Her hand clenched beneath mine and she brought the blade back to the ox's neck. She drew in two quick breaths as I inhaled a deeper one, tightening my hand around hers and preparing for what lay ahead. Deacon began a prayer, his words obviously not for us to hear; his voice barely audible.

Alexis sucked in another breath, her shoulders pressing against my cuirass with the motion. She lifted her hand and the blade flattened the ox's hair. I felt her body tense as she forced the knife harder against the flesh, the ox lowing as we broke the skin.

I kept my hand firm on hers, ensuring she did not pause as we met the sinewy muscles within and the first drops of blood hit Deacon's bowl.

A rush of air flew from Alexis' lips and her hand slackened, but I kept it trapped beneath mine and pulled the knife up and across, severing the chords and bringing its life to an end. The animal went limp, its front legs lowering it to the ground as though it were kneeling before Deacon, who kept the bowl beneath the dropping liquid.

Blood flowed swiftly from the open skin, coating my fingers and running down my, and Alexis', wrists and forearms, dripping off the end of my elbow to stain the dirt below.

Alexis' hand came off the makhaira and I took it from her, allowing her out of the circle of my arms. She turned her face from the sacrifice, her hand gripping the altar for support as she swallowed loudly. I wanted to take her in my arms and lessen the regret or disgust I believed she felt. Instead I dropped to my knees and held the ox's gaping flesh open above Deacon's bowl. Its eyes were still open, glazed in death, reminding me of many a soldier whose life had been ended by spear or sword in battle.

"I have all I require," Deacon said, setting the bowl aside a moment later. I nodded and Deacon took the ox's back legs as I gripped the front ones, turning it onto its side.

"She does not need to use the makhaira again?" I asked.

"No, that is for us to do," Deacon replied. I assumed he referred to him and me, but he raised a hand and three men, dressed in the same plain chitons and short himatia as he, joined us. I stood, giving the priests room to work.

# 8

Alexis' sandals sent up a puff of dust as she turned to face me and I put a finger beneath her chin, surveying her pale face before meeting her eyes. "You did well," I told her. "It is always difficult the first time."

"You have ..." she swallowed. "You have done this often?"

"Enough to have learnt how," I replied. In truth I did not know how many times Father and I had made our sacrifices to the gods, or assisted someone else in theirs, but I knew how hard it had been that first time. I pressed my lips to Alexis' forehead before releasing her chin.

She looked down to the blood on her hands, scrubbing uselessly at the redness. I covered her fingers with my own, casting a glance to Deacon and the priests. They had cut open the ox's stomach and extracted the liver and entrails and were examining them closely. I returned my eyes to Alexis' hands, sliding my thumb over them. "This part shall soon be over and the blood shall come off easily with water and oils," I assured her.

"I hope so," she whispered. "It ... it reminds me of your hands when you emerged from Melanthios' tent."

I drew a deep breath, closing my eyes momentarily before drawing Alexis into my embrace. I thought I had removed all his blood before I returned to her, but obviously I had missed enough that she noticed. "Do not allow yourself to be reminded of such thoughts today." I felt her nod and released her again.

"This animal is a worthy gift to Asclepius," Deacon announced. "Warrior, would you aid us in lifting the beast onto the altar?"

I did as asked and when the carcass was in place, Deacon handed one of the priests the bowl of blood and addressed Alexis again. "Come, we must prepare you also." She looked to me in alarm.

"Do not fear, Asclepius seeks to heal, not kill. He does not ask for human sacrifices," I grinned, attempting to settle her unease.

"Indeed," Deacon agreed. "It is time you spoke your wishes to our god." He offered his hand to Alexis and she took it, managing a small smile for me as I gathered our bag and fell in behind her, Deacon and the priests.

Deacon led our small group across a narrow stretch of grass to the temple of Asclepius. It was a far more impressive structure than the Shrine of Artemis – and it was complete. The priests entered via a ramp, leaving Deacon, Alexis and I to admire the outside of the building.

Six fluted columns comprising of three parts stood at the short end of the temple as we approached. They tapered upward, drawing my attention to the decorative triangular pediment that formed the terracotta gable above.

I recognized the scene as an Amazonomachy; Amazonomachiai were fierce, ancient battles between the Amazons and any one of a number of Greek heroes who had long since passed from this world and into the next. The pediment on the temple before us featured at its center Heracles and the Amazon queen, Hippolyta. Heracles' wooden club was raised high, his other hand freeing the girdle at her waist. Either side of them were Hippolyta's women warriors and the men who had accompanied Heracles on his journey.

I was well aware of the tale – Heracles having been set twelve labors as atonement for killing his wife and children, the retrieval of the girdle his ninth. I drew a deep breath; it had been several winters since I had thought of the hero and his journey throughout the Peloponnese and beyond, but after Kuria was killed, thoughts of Heracles' atonement was my constant companion.

Alexis' eyes followed mine to the carving. "Do you recognize the battle?" she asked.

I nodded. "It is Heracles' battle with Queen Hippolyta of the Amazons. Do you know of it?"

"Yes. Heracles' feats were told to us as children, though I knew him then as Aretos. His success with the twelve labors of purification made him the greatest of our heroes."

"It is no surprise," I said with a nod. I returned my eyes to the building, noting the terracotta cornices which formed the base of the triangular pediment. They sat out wider than the pediment itself, plant motifs on the facing side softening the rigidity of the building.

"This temple is our most impressive building, though it is not the most important," Deacon smiled, leading us to the longer side. "Here you shall speak of your wishes. The abaton is where those wishes are acted upon by

Asclepius."

"Acted on how?" I frowned.

"Asclepius hears your prayers in the temple and whilst you sleep, he brings about what is asked."

"He shall lie with Alexis to gift her of what she seeks?" I asked, my chest tightening painfully, breath refusing to come.

Deacon smiled but shook his head. "No, that is not his way."

"It would not be the first time a god has laid with a mortal – Heracles' own mother Alcmene was one such woman and her son was forever subjected to the jealousy and torments of his father's wife," I growled. The thought of Alexis carrying a god's child worse than the thought of her carrying Thaddeus'.

Alexis reached out, settling her hand on my arm. "Do not be afraid. It is answers on *how* to have a child that I seek. I do not ask Asclepius to gift one to me."

I clenched my jaw shut, stepping away from Alexis and focusing on the temple itself again so she did not feel the tremble of fear that coursed through me with each beat of my heart. Eleven fluted columns supported the stone cross beams of the slightly concave architrave and the decorative frieze above. The frieze alternated between flat stone panels and black, carved upright bars in groups of three. The bars were weight bearing of the roof above them and placed directly above a column, which provided a pleasing sense of conformity. "You may not have the choice if he comes to you as you slumber," I murmured, even less willing to leave Alexis at the abaton when it came time.

Slanted cornices overhung the architraves in front and the terracotta tiled roof was low pitched. The two corners of the rooftop above me held sculpted figures standing proudly against the clear sky; the one to my left an amazon mounted on horseback, on the right a sea nymph riding a seahorse.

I continued to the opposite end of the temple, willing myself to remain calm. After I had shared the details of Kuria's death with Alexis, she had still wanted to be with me and I had promised myself I would always be strong and brave for her, no matter what. I needed to show her that side of myself now.

I sucked in another long breath. The pediment on the third side of the building told the story of Theseus and Periphetes. Deacon and Alexis joined me, Alexis' warm hand settling at the small of my back beneath my cuirass, her fingers drawing light circles over the material of my tunic.

I exhaled, leaning into her touch as Deacon spoke. "Do you recognize the tale on *this* pediment?"

"Theseus' defeat of Periphetes at Epidaurus," I replied. It was another tale of daring feats I had heard long ago, and Father and I had spoken of the hero at length before visiting Theseus' hometown of Troezen.

"I am not familiar with it," Alexis said.

"Would you allow me to speak of it, or would you prefer to hear of it another time?" Deacon asked.

"Please, speak of it now," Alexis replied. I heard the smile in her voice as she answered, and my own broke out – her insatiable quest for knowledge and a well-told story shining through, even here, at this time. I turned slightly to watch Alexis' face as Deacon began, the tightness in my chest lessening at her look of excitement.

"Theseus was the son of King Aegeus of Athens, though until he reached sixteen winters, he did not know it to be so. His mother had never spoken of his father, and they lived in the south of the Peloponnese in Troezen, far from Athens itself. When Theseus reached the age, his mother told him of his father and told Theseus he should go to him in Athens where, upon his father's death, he would assume the throne. Theseus' mother took him to a large rock, beneath which were a sword and a pair of sandals that Aegeus had hidden many winters before."

"Did they possess some sort of power?" Alexis asked, her eyes bright.

"No," Deacon smiled. "But Aegeus left his own belongings behind so he would recognize his son when he came."

"A clever plan," Alexis noted.

"Indeed. Theseus' mother wanted him to travel to Athens by boat, which she considered the safe route, but the young man was ambitious and was determined to follow the more dangerous inland path around the Saronic Gulf."

"Which would see him have to pass by the six areas believed to be entrances to the Underworld," I added.

Alexis' eyes widened, but she allowed Deacon to continue. "Each of the entrances were said to be guarded by a fierce enemy which Theseus would have to fight before he could continue on and, as you may imagine, his mother wished only for him to arrive safely in Athens to claim his father's throne."

"So, Epidaurus is considered an entrance to the Underworld?" Alexis asked, a shiver gripping her.

"It was once, but no one has referred to it as such for many winters," Deacon replied.

"But Theseus faced Periphetes here?"

"It was actually just outside Epidaurus," I amended.

"And who was Periphetes?"

"He was a giant of a man who carried a solid brass club, frequently killing anyone he came across if they did not give him the coin they travelled with – or anything else he asked for," I replied. "He threatened to smash Theseus with his club, but Theseus outsmarted him, telling Periphetes he did not believe the club to be brass at all, but a thin sheet of bronze over wood as other clubs were. Periphetes insisted that was not the case, and when Theseus asked to be allowed confirm it by holding it himself, Periphetes could not resist proving the boy wrong and he handed it over."

"Whereby Theseus smashed the club onto Periphetes' head and killed him!" Deacon finished with delight. "Do you know the other stories of Theseus' travels to Athens?"

"I do," I acknowledged.

"Please, tell me," Alexis said, smiling in my direction.

"Should we not continue inside?" I asked.

"We have time for other tales, if you are happy to speak of them," Deacon replied.

"Please?" Alexis asked, her hand tightening against my back.

I shook my head, but grinned. "As you wish," I conceded. "There was the thief named Sinis who captured travelers at the Isthmus and tied them between two pine trees which were bent towards the ground. When he allowed the trees to spring back into place, his victim would be torn in two," I began.

Deacon cleared his throat and cast an apologetic look at Alexis. "Perhaps some of the particulars of their punishments need not be shared," he said.

"Do not fear that I am too delicate to hear of them, I have known of many ways," Alexis replied, her chin set defiantly.

"Apologies, I did not mean to offend, I just tho–"

"Though I struggled with the ox at the altar, I shall not faint from mere words you or Skylar speak of deeds long past," she assured him with a quick smile.

"Very well," Deacon nodded.

I swallowed a grin and continued. "Theseus defeated Sinis by exacting his own punishment on him. Also, at the Isthmus, at Krommyon, Theseus killed the wild sow terrorizing the area, then he travelled near Megara where a giant named Skiron forced passers-by to wash his feet. Skiron carried a huge axe, so few denied him the request, but when they knelt to bathe him, he kicked them over the cliff and into the waiting jaws of an animal far below. Theseus jumped aside when Skiron attempted to do the same to him and pushed Skiron to his death instead. Theseus then defeated Kerkyon in a wrestling match at Eleusis before meeting Procrustes, who was also known as the stretcher."

"He does not sound particularly friendly," Alexis said.

"No," I agreed. "When Father spoke of what he did to travelers, I was glad he was long dead when we passed by."

"What did he do?" Alexis asked quietly.

"Procrustes had two beds in the plain of Eleusis. Weary travelers often stopped to speak with him and he offered them relief from their journey. The beds were of differing sizes and for those who were too short for the small bed, he attempted to stretch them by tying their hands and feet to either end and tightening, or if they were too tall, he would tie them down and cut off their feet so they would fit." Alexis shivered and I attempted to lighten the conversation by saying, "Though the bed I first found myself in at Trachis was small, I am glad *your* father did not know of Procrustes' ways and attempt to fit me to it."

"At least now you have no such worries," she grinned.

I nodded, returning the smile, wondering how long it would be before we returned to Trachis and the bed Alexis and I shared.

"I am a little afraid to ask, but how did Theseus defeat Procrustes?" she asked.

"He tied him to the larger bed and used Procrustes' own axe to relieve him of his head," I replied, seeing an entirely different bloodied body behind my eyes.

"Oh," Alexis murmured, reaching for my hand. I took it gratefully, wishing we were far from Epidaurus, the journey long behind us and talk of a child finished with, or alternately already in our midst if that was what was meant for the two of us.

"Your knowledge of Theseus' feats is impressive, you were taught of him as a child?" Deacon asked.

"Yes," I replied, my eyes still locked with Alexis'.

"Where do you call home – Epidaurus? Sparta? Troezen perhaps?"

I exhaled slowly, finding the priest's open gaze as I replied. "None of those. But it is not the first time I have found myself at Epidaurus nor speaking of Theseus and his deeds," I murmured, offering no more explanation.

"I am pleased that his heroic deeds are still spoken of, for it shall be a sad day when our children do not hear of them," he nodded. "Shall we enter the temple now?"

"Perhaps I should wash the blood from my hands first," Alexis said, indicating a spring up ahead. "I cannot imagine Asclepius would want such obvious reminders of death brought into his temple."

"No. You shall bathe before you go to the abaton, that is where Asclepius shall truly receive you and what you ask of him," Deacon replied. "But already he knows of your sacrifice and shall be pleased."

"What is an abaton?" Alexis queried.

"The sleeping chambers," Deacon replied, leading the way back to the east entrance of the temple and stepping between the columns.

Alexis gripped my hand tighter, holding me back and turning to me as she spoke. "Perhaps when we are alone again you can speak with me of your time in Epidaurus and what happened there," she murmured.

I raised an eyebrow, wondering how she knew there was more to my acknowledgement of being in the area than I had shared with Deacon. I drew a deep breath and nodded. "When we are alone again," I promised. "I pray that time is not long in arriving," I added as we followed Deacon inside.

# 9

The temple was fragrant with a familiar scent and I soon found the source; bowls of dark liquid attached to the walls of the building above brightly burning torches. I inhaled the woody aroma I had long ago learnt was frankincense, and which I now wore within the perfume I had come to favor since arriving at Trachis. There was also a sweet, fresh smell given off and I believed it came from the plant known as *Nardus*, named for the Assyrian city of Naarda to the southeast of Greece's shores near Egypt. The two scents together, along with the earthy smell of myrrh were almost always found in temples around the Peloponnese and Attica, the priests believing they increased the holiness of the places.

The ceiling was coffered; large squares made of thick slabs of white marble inset between lengths of dark wood. Deacon waited for us by a large statue of Asclepius and though I searched for them in the dimmer confines, I could not make out the other priests. The statue was almost twice as tall as the priest, the carved relief of the healer standing proudly in a chiton and sandals. In his left hand, Asclepius held the familiar length of wood he had always been said to favor (and which appeared to be a javelin without its bronze tip). A sculpted snake was wrapped around that, its head beside the kind, bearded face. His right hand sat on his hip above a large stone hound which reached his mid-thigh.

Deacon offered his hand to Alexis and she stepped to his side. I followed her, near enough to intervene if I deemed it necessary, but far enough away to allow him to guide her as he must without interference.

"You must repeat a prayer after me, then quietly speak your desire to

Asclepius," Deacon instructed, lifting his fingers from hers and moving back a pace.

Alexis nodded, closing her eyes as Deacon began.

"O mighty Asclepius, blessed healer of mortals

Come, bringing health and happiness to we who seek your aid

Honored son of Apollo, enemy of illness and death

We ask for your aid this night

To bring us the good end we seek."

Alexis repeated each line after the priest, her eyes remaining shut as she rested one hand against her stomach and spoke her words to the statue of the god.

Deacon returned to Alexis' side, placing a hand on her shoulder as I joined them. "Asclepius has heard your wish. Now it is time to bathe and ready yourself for him to come to you."

"I pray he shall grant my request," she murmured. My heart beat faster as I watched Alexis' face light with hope, but I said nothing.

"I am certain you shall be rewarded. Go now to the sacred spring outside and we shall join you shortly. Skylar, if I may have a brief word?" Deacon asked. I hesitated momentarily then nodded, Alexis casting a curious look in our direction before heading out of the temple as directed. I willed myself to remain still, though my heart hammered faster beneath my cuirass. "You care very deeply for the princess," he began.

I stiffened at his words but nodded. "How did you know who she was?"

"I have not visited Trachis for many winters, and Alexis would not recognize me for at the time she was preoccupied with her upcoming betrothal to Basileios. But her simple elegance and distinctive, beautiful face have remained throughout her days in Epirus, for which I thank the gods." I frowned, but Deacon continued before I could question him. "The two of you are lovers?" Again I hesitated, but he waved off the answer when I opened my mouth to give it. "You do not need to hide who you are here, nor feel that I shall be uncomfortable in your presence. You fear for what she asks Asclepius, but you care for her and want to give her what her heart desires. All that is plain to see but do *you* wish for a child for the two of you?"

"I want to make her happy and if this is what pleases her, then I shall do what I can to ensure her wish comes true."

He regarded me silently for a moment. "That is not an answer to my question."

I swallowed, dropping my eyes from his and paced across the marbled floor. "I have asked myself the same question many times since she spoke of it. I have not lived as she has, my father never insisting I marry or begin a family of my own. He never encouraged me to find one to settle with until we arrived at Trachis – until he learned I had feelings for Alexis, and she for me. But children … I cannot imagine having one grow inside me and I fear for what shall happen to Alexis if she does. I cannot lose her as my father lost my mother." The words tumbled from me, giving voice to the fears I had been unable to name until that moment. I swallowed again, effectively preventing anything else from coming out as Deacon spoke.

"Alexis knows of the loss of your mother?" I nodded. "Have you spoken of your fear of what may happen with her?"

"No," I replied, shaking my head.

"Do you believe she would not want to know?"

"I cannot be afraid. She does not deserve someone who acts in such a manner."

"She deserves someone unafraid to be true to how they feel. Someone who can be vulnerable in her presence, even if that is not the face they show the rest of the world. Have you ever allowed yourself to be so with her?"

"Yes," I replied, recalling how vulnerable and exposed I felt the night I spoke of Kuria.

"And she did not flee from you, did she? She was strong when you felt weak." I nodded. "Tell me, when she spoke of wanting a child with you did she ask you to carry it?"

"No."

"Why do you believe that was?" I shrugged, not having considered the question before. Deacon leaned in close. "Perhaps because she knew what it would remind you of and she did not wish for you to carry that burden. Perhaps she suggested *she* carry the child, though she had not been able to previously, to save you from the decision. Do you believe it an easy thing for her to offer, given her history?"

I drew another deep breath and frowned. I had not considered any of it; I had not considered Alexis' feelings or her own sacrifice. How could I not have? I had thought only of myself, of how *I* felt about children. I had not stopped to consider what it would cost her.

"With great love comes fear stronger than you can imagine and courage deeper than you ever thought possible. Speak to her of your thoughts and allow the gods to take care of the rest. Do not deny her of your truths now and hear of her own reasons. Only in true togetherness can you walk this path."

"How so?" I asked.

"If having a child with her is what you truly wish then call on Asclepius to hear your words before Eos lights the sky with her dawn. If you speak the truth, he shall know, and it shall be done."

"May I remain in the abaton with Alexis?"

"No, that journey she must take alone, but speak together before she enters and perhaps you shall find the answer to the question I asked."

Deacon gave a final nod and made his way out of the temple as Alexis had before him. I inhaled sharply, wondering how I could make such a decision before the morning arrived. I knew without doubt that I wanted to be with Alexis, to make her happy and be everything she not only deserved, but everything she wanted. But I also wished I could ensure she would survive the birth of a child. Perhaps *that* was the question I must ask Asclepius to answer. I drew a breath and followed the priest outside and over to the small spring where Alexis waited for us.

"Is all well?" she asked, looking from Deacon to me.

I nodded in reply, setting our bag aside once again and taking the strip of material Deacon held out, crouching down to submerge it in the warm spring. The water was clear but shallow, only as wide as my arm from fingertips to shoulder, the sandy bed almost the same color as the hot springs near Trachis.

"In the temple I … I cannot explain, but I felt as though Asclepius was there with us," Alexis announced. "Do others speak of feeling the same?"

"Some," Deacon replied with a nod. "I shall go prepare your bed in the abaton. Take as much time as you require to rid your body of the dust of your travel. There are no other guests at this time and the area is private enough for you to comfortably disrobe. When you have made your goodbyes, I shall see you settled."

"Thank you," I said, straightening up and squeezing out the linen as Deacon took the stony path and disappeared into another building which I presumed housed the sleeping quarters.

# 10

When the priest had disappeared from sight, I turned my back on the path and exhaled a long breath. "May I?" I asked, indicating the fibula at Alexis' shoulder.

She nodded but caught my hand as I reached for the bone pin. "What is it?" she asked.

I shook my head. "Nothing, all is well."

"I know when you do not speak truth with me," she murmured, threading her fingers through mine and stepping closer. "Tell me. Please."

"Perhaps you see my struggle at allowing you to be naked by a hot spring without being able to touch you as I wish," I replied, allowing a smile to escape in an attempt to keep the mood between us light. To distract Alexis from further questions, I raised the wet length of linen and squeezed it, tiny droplets snaking along her collarbone and beneath the neckline of her chiton. I dropped it, tracing the water's path with one finger and exposing more of her skin to the evening air.

"Skylar," she scolded, but the pulse point in her neck jumped and a flush crept up her neck. I smiled, slowly drawing the pin from her chiton and aiding the clothing to meet the ground below. I pressed my lips to her neck, feeling the beat of her heart mirrored there. "Skylar," she murmured again, her chest rising and falling in quick succession.

Her hand found its way beneath my hair and she gripped the nape of my neck, pressing my lips against her heated flesh. She sighed as I placed my hand at the small of her back, drawing her body against mine, careful not to hold her too hard against the bronze of my cuirass.

I claimed her lips and she pressed herself against my thigh. I drew my tongue along her bottom lip, tasting her, enjoy the shortening of her breath in my mouth. She tightened her grip on my neck but I did not hurry, content to allow the growing heat in my stomach to spread to the rest of my body. I slid my hands lower, resting them on the outside of each of her thighs, my fingers drawing lazy circles over the smooth skin.

Alexis shivered, a guttural sound escaping her. She put her hand on my chest and pushed me away slightly. "Skylar," she whispered, leaning her forehead against my own. "Gods, the things you make me feel when you kiss me in such a way, I do not ever want you to stop."

"I never shall," I promised, raising my hand to cup her cheek.

She turned her head and kissed my palm. "Deacon may have spoken words of privacy, but we cannot lie together, not here," she murmured.

"He already knows of our love. It would not surprise, or offend, him if we did," I countered, though I did not know if it was truly wise to do so – not when he had encouraged me to speak of so much before Alexis left for the abaton.

"That may be true and believe me I want for nothing more than to make love to you right now, but I must go to the abaton. I must know if Asclepius is able to aid us."

I swallowed loudly, briefly closing my eyes as I nodded. "Yes. And your nakedness distracts me, so turn around so I may bathe you in readiness for such a visit," I directed quietly, the corner of my mouth lifting in a grin. Perhaps if she did not look at me I could ask her the questions I must.

"I wish you too could be naked, and that this spring was deeper and wider," she said, doing as I asked.

"It is as warm as the one in Pylae," I said, speaking the old name for the area.

"I recall how much you enjoyed it on your first visit." I could hear the smile in her voice.

"Our second visit was not so sweet," I murmured, remembering how the water had turned red with Xylon's blood when I had landed his spear in his neck.

"I choose to remember that day as the one where you ensured we would be together always," she said, reaching down to pick up the strip of linen and handing it back to me. "I always saw the hot springs as a place of beauty, now I know they are the place of new beginnings. Of fresh starts."

"Mmm." I drew her hair aside, squeezing the warm water onto her shoulder and rubbing at the dust gathered on her neck. Her skin shone in the fading light of the afternoon, darker where the dust clung to it.

"There was more I did not speak of when I told Deacon how I felt Asclepius' presence in the temple."

"Oh?" I asked, raising an eyebrow.

She turned to face me and I did not attempt to stop her. "Yes. Somehow, I know that Asclepius does not intend to lie with me in the manner you fear most. He seeks to find a way to allow my body to carry a child, not gift it to me."

"Perhaps it is a trick, so you do not fear him coming to you."

She gave me a smile and placed her hand on my cuirass above my heart. "I wish you had felt his presence too. You love me so fiercely that thoughts such as those torment you. I wish I could make you see that they are not necessary."

"I love you more than I ever knew was possible. More than I ever wished to when we first met. I do not enjoy feeling that I am inadequate for you."

"Skylar," she said, her voice as soft as a caress. "You are all I have ever wished for. You are never inadequate, please hear me when I speak the words to you."

I held her gaze for a long moment before placing my hands on her shoulders and turning her from me again. It was a long time before either of us spoke again, and I moved my gentle ministrations down her thighs and calves, thinking only of her cleanliness as I drew the material over her body.

Eventually I straightened and drew a deep breath to drown out the rushing blood in my head. It unsettled Alexis' hair when I blew it out again. "Do you believe I could be a good mother?" I asked quietly, focusing on a particularly dirty spot behind Alexis' ear. "I am not certain it could be so, not having had a mother of my own to learn from as I grew," I added in a rush before my courage to speak the words failed me.

"You do not believe you learnt of a parent's love from your father?"

"I learnt how to ensure we remained safe as we travelled, and of the towns and villages themselves. Even when we assisted those who asked it of us, Father used the opportunity to teach me of specific ways or people or of heroes long past. But you and I would not find ourselves in the same situations – at least I would hope we would not."

"Go on," she encouraged, keeping her back to me.

"Our lives would be settled in Trachis. We would have no need to seek shelter beneath tall trees or with families in strange villages. I would not need to teach our child, nor would it be their duty, to fight. I would do that on their behalf, as would Moeris and the other soldiers."

Alexis turned, my eyes unintentionally straying down her body before meeting her deep green ones.

She rested her hands on my waist. "If I did not think you could teach our child all he or she needed to learn, I would never have suggested it for us. Our different backgrounds mean we each have something unique we can teach them. They shall know not only one way, but of many. They would be fortunate to have such an upbringing."

"What if … what if I did not love the child you bore?" I murmured, afraid of hurting Alexis with the words.

"Why would you not love our child?" she asked holding my gaze as she tilted her head to the side, no accusation beneath the question.

I inhaled deeply, letting it all the way out again before I replied. "Because it would have no part of me inside. I am not able to contribute to its creation. Perhaps it would feel the same about me and not love me either. That would put you in a difficult position."

Alexis took my hands, her bathing forgotten as she brushed the linen to the ground. "Skylar. I see how you are with Hesper and Thaddeus' children. You have grown fond of them, you laugh and play with such freedom. You give them so much of yourself, your time and love. I have no doubt you shall love a child that comes from my body even more, even if it contains no part of you. It shall be *our* child. The two of you shall form a firm bond. A special bond."

I swallowed loudly, considering her words. The eldest of Hesper and Thaddeus' children – Nikomachos – was six winters old and he and I often fought mock battles with a wooden sword I crafted for him, the two of us debating the merits of different weapons as we sparred. Pamphilos was four and followed Nikomachos wherever he went. I had made him a sword as well, but for the most part he was content to sit and watch us rather than join in, his bond with me formed when I spoke of heroes and poets. Tritonos was barely three winters with tight brown curls that bounced up and down as he ran to clutch at my legs. He barely spoke due to difficulties Hesper had when birthing him, but his face lit up each time I visited and I found something oddly comforting in the snuffling noises he made against my shoulder as he slept.

The first time Tritonos had fallen asleep at my shoulder was on our second meeting. Hesper and Alexis were discussing a banquet and I had picked Tritonos up when he toppled off one of the couches in Hesper and Thaddeus' apartment. I went to his aid, holding him a little awkwardly as I checked him over. His cries had quieted, and he began twirling his fingers in my hair, laughing as he drew them out again, the soft ends obviously tickling his chubby little hands. I had smiled and, satisfied he had had more of a fright than been injured, tucked him against my chest and sat back on the nearest klinai. I watched him playing with my dark hair, tickling his cheeks and nose with other strands and when he tired of the game, he simply nestled against me and fell asleep.

I offered to put him into his small bed, but Hesper said I should remain where I was as Tritonos was a fussy sleeper and may not settle again once he was put down. She added that he rarely went to strangers, and never allowed them to hold him for long, or whilst he slept. Alexis had smiled at me as she told me I had obviously charmed him as quickly as I had her. I had blushed at her words, but they warmed me at the same time and I remained holding the boy until he woke almost a candlemark later.

It was true – I adored Nikomachos, Pamphilos and Tritonos far more than I had expected to when I finally met them, and they shared no blood with me.

"I am afraid to lose you. When it comes time for you to birth that child, it scares me that you may not remain in our lives to aid me in raising it," I admitted, finally dropping my eyes from hers.

"Do you believe I do not fear the same?" she asked, her hands tightening at my hips. "I fear losing you to sword or an errant spear each time you join our soldiers at the barracks. You cannot know how relieved I was when Father said there was to be no summer campaign, for I knew you would take up arms and join them to ensure me and my family were safe."

"I would have, without question," I agreed.

"Gnosidicus is the most capable healer I have ever met, that I have ever heard of. He speaks of descending from the very god we seek aid from here. He shall not allow any harm to come to me if I am to birth a child. You *must* believe that."

"I could not bear for it to be so," I whispered.

Alexis pushed up onto her toes to place a kiss on my lips. "It shall not," she insisted.

"If you had had children from your betrothal to Basileios, I do not know if I could have loved them."

"But I do not. That honor has been gifted to you. To us," she replied, her voice barely above a whisper.

"You wish very much for a child for us," I said, searching her eyes again.

"Yes."

I nodded, but said nothing further, leaning forward to capture her lips instead. "It is time you went to the abaton," I told her when we parted.

# 11

The sun had almost disappeared as Alexis and I made our way from the spring to the abaton. Deacon awaited our arrival, holding a bright torch.

"You are ready to enter?" he asked. Alexis nodded.

"May I join you, just to see where Alexis shall be?" I asked the priest. He hesitated. "Please, I give you my word; I shall leave when you ask it of me."

He looked to Alexis and then back to me. "Very well." He turned and led us down a set of stone steps, the torch throwing long shadows up the walls, the head getting dim briefly before Deacon stepped out into an underground hall.

The priests reappeared, their voices melodic and soothing as they sung in a language I did not recognize. The scent of incense was again present in the abaton, though this time I did not know the scent which accompanied the frankincense.

There were no beds in the room, but over forty klinai stood in rows, far enough apart to appear singular, but clustered together enough to be part of a larger formation. Short tables stood beneath or beside each, the ones alongside holding instruments or amphorae.

Geese wandered about between the couches, chattering to one another and pecking occasionally at the floor. A number of hounds also padded about, whilst others slept beside klinai or at the feet of the singing priests. Some looked up as we entered, but did not approach, nor pay us much attention; yawning widely before resting their heads back on their paws. As my eyes adjusted to the darker space, I began to make out other, much larger yellow lumps in the corners of the room or stretched out along the walls. Alexis appeared to notice them at the same time and moved closer to me. "Serpents?" I asked, indicating the closest one.

"Oh yes. They are a most favored animal of our great god. The geese and hounds as well. They aid him in healing those who come here," he replied.

The snake I had referred to lifted its head at our voices. The scales of its back were a shining, olive-yellow, almost the same color as the bronze of my shield. It slithered in our direction, revealing white-edged scales akin to drops of water across its long, slender body; which made the dark color appear even more metallic. They were in stark contrast to its brilliant yellow stomach and deep ochre eyes. When it stuck out its tongue I backed up a step.

Deacon chuckled quietly. "Our serpents are not poisonous, you need not fear them," he said.

"That may be so, but it is not only poison these creatures are famous for using as their means to kill. That one in particular appears big enough to swallow us whole," I countered.

"Indeed, though their natures are tame. They do not hunger for human blood," Deacon assured me, running his hand along the creature's wide back as it passed him. "The legendary serpents of past days no longer walk this world, their descendants far more accustomed to we mortals, and we to them."

The snake wended its way between Alexis' legs and mine, the smooth scales surprising me with both temperature and softness as it glided over my foot.

Alexis suddenly crouched down to run her hand over the scales just as Deacon had. "I believed serpents to be cold, but this one is as warm as the air in here," she said, a look of wonder on her face.

"Yes. Their skin remains the temperature of the air around them and though they are not very active, they prefer the warmer days. When the winter comes we increase the number of torches to keep them comfortable," Deacon replied.

The serpent wound itself around Alexis' arm and I rested my hand on the pommel of my sword. "Are you certain it is safe for Alexis to remain here with them so near?"

"Completely," Deacon nodded as one of the priests approached. He handed a steaming skyphos to Deacon, who took it with a nod. The man retreated again and Deacon put his other hand on Alexis' shoulder. "It is time for you to prepare for sleep."

Carefully, Alexis removed her arm from the serpent and stood. The snake allowed her to move away, sliding silently back to its former position.

Deacon led us both to a nearby klinai and indicated Alexis sit down.

When she did, he handed her the skyphos. "What is it?" we both asked at the same time.

"Chamomile tea," he smiled.

"Ah," I muttered.

"Why?" Alexis asked a moment later.

"Chamomile aids to induce sleep – it relaxes the body," I replied before Deacon had the chance.

"Indeed," he replied, grinning wider. "You surprise me with how well versed you are in so many areas. Trachis is fortunate to have you now call it home."

"We are very lucky indeed," Alexis murmured, reaching out to squeeze my arm.

I returned her grin, coloring slightly at both their words. "Thank you. Now drink your tea while I remove your sandals."

Alexis smiled and made herself comfortable, taking a sip as I knelt before her. Most nights since settling in Trachis I had removed Alexis' sandals from her feet. It had begun as a game; a delicious seduction where I removed first her sandals, then her hair from its hairpins, fingers trailing teasingly across her skin until I reached the fibulae on her chiton and freed the soft linen from her body. I would slowly skim my hands across the smooth skin of her shoulders and the small of her back before reaching far more interesting places.

I swallowed as the usual fire began deep in my stomach, firmly reminding myself that I could not have her in such a manner this particular night. I wished again I could stay with her in the abaton but, even if Deacon allowed me to, there were questions I needed to ask myself and answers I must give Asclepius before the sun rose in the morning. And I would not if I remained. I set Alexis' sandals aside and she drew her feet up onto the couch.

"I must fetch a number of items, but when I return I shall walk you out," Deacon said. I nodded and blew out a deep breath, straightening as he turned and made his way behind a large pillar.

Alexis reached out for my hand and I took it, sitting beside her. "Thank you for bringing me here. For coming with me." I only nodded in reply. "It has been more than three moons since we spent a night apart. I wish it did not have to be so, but I ... I have to know if a child is a possibility for us."

"I hope Asclepius provides you with the answers you seek. But I shall miss you lying beside me, your head on my chest as you slumber. Your leg wrapped around mine and the blanket very much on your side of the bed," I grinned, tracing the line of her jaw with my finger.

She returned the smile. "And I shall miss your steady heartbeat beneath my ear and the way it quickens when my fingers draw across your stomach."

I leaned forward and kissed her. Soft, slow, a deep need snaking its way through my body. Though I knew there could be no sating the desire, I did not pull back, wanting to take the feeling of her, of us, with me. To have the reminder of my desire for her during the long candlemarks of the night. Her tongue met mine as I slid my hand beneath her hair to the nape of her neck and she pressed her body to mine.

Catching the sounds of Deacon's return, I reluctantly pulled back. "I love you and I want you to be happy," I whispered when we parted.

"I want us both to be happy," she replied, her breathing shallow.

I nodded, uncertain that would be possible. Deacon sat a number of pyxides on the table beside Alexis' klinai and I pressed my lips chastely against her cheek. "Till the morning," I said. She nodded, echoing my words as I stood.

"Come," Deacon directed, heading once again for the entrance to the abaton. I looked back to Alexis, giving her a nod and a tight smile. She returned both and I inhaled deeply as I turned from her and followed Deacon back up the stone steps.

The priests followed us to the outside of the abaton, carrying torches and moving off towards the altar after silently nodding in my direction. "You should join them," Deacon said. "They shall cook the ox you brought and partake of its flesh, encouraging Asclepius to come down to the mortal realm to visit the one who seeks his healing. If you eat with them you too shall receive answers, if you have not already made your decision and spoken of it with Asclepius."

I watched the pyre on the altar come to life when the men pressed the heads of their torches to the tinder. "You may sleep in the temple of Artemis or beneath the darkened sky, the choice is yours. Anywhere but the abaton," he added, though I did not need reminding of where I could not go.

I nodded again, waiting until Deacon had descended the steps before making my way towards the altar. I set my bag down and unfastened the belt that held my sword around my waist, placing it on top before settling on the ground not far from the priests, who had begun their quiet singing again. The flames rose high into the air around the large ox, its skin sizzling as the heat infused it. Before long my stomach rumbled in appreciation of the sweet aroma of the beast's cooking flesh and I leant back on my elbows, searching the tiny lights far above for the patterns I knew they sometimes wove.

Deacon's questions from the temple echoed through my mind, along with Alexis' insistence that I could be a good mother. A *worthy* mother to our child. I wished I shared her confidence but could not understand how I would know what to do. My concern about how I would love a child which did not come from my flesh played most on my mind. Over the winters, my father had been with a number of women, though none remained with us for very long. Part of it I knew was due to our nomadic lifestyle, others left because my father still mourned the loss of my mother and had no room for them in his heart as well. But sometimes the women had left because of me. Some spoke occasionally to me, others not at all. I had not been borne of their flesh, so no matter how much they may have enjoyed Father's company, or the satisfaction of his body, he came with me and I did not belong to them.

There was only one woman who ever came close to treating me as she did her own daughter – and they too travelled together – but by the time Father and I met Nasrin and Ava, I was too old to wish for a mother figure any longer. Father would see Nasrin in Konitsa, I believed that was why he suggested he travel there alone. After encouraging me to find love in Trachis, perhaps he believed it was time he found his own; that his love for my mother could remain alongside his affection for another woman. Though he had never spoken the words, I knew he had grown fonder of Nasrin during the short time she travelled with us than any other before or after her. While I grew he had never sought love for himself, but now I was older he should be allowed seek it, if that was what he wanted. I missed him being with me of course, especially since Alexis asked something so foreign of me, but I did not begrudge him a chance at happiness again.

I pushed myself to a sitting position, the pyre heating my feet and legs, and though the evening was still warm after the day, it was not unpleasant. Long flames and shooting sparks licked the flesh of the ox in their race to reach the dark air above. The priests poked at the wood, dislodging several larger pieces and sending even more sparks skyward. I watched with interest, briefly wondering if the ox was going to topple off the altar altogether as they continued their prodding. I swallowed a grin and removed the pin of my cuirass, setting the bronze aside as I drew my legs up and wrapped my arms around my knees. The priests, having had their fun, allowed the beast to finish cooking without further interruption and I returned to my thoughts.

The dark of the night outside the range of the pyre began to deepen, settling around me as though my lover embraced me. A sense of calm and certainty washed over me. I realized that with thoughts of Nasrin and Ava, I *did* have comparison for how I would wish to be with my own child should Alexis and I have one. They had laughed and spoken of everything together, just as my father and I had. There were lessons learned, tall tales told and tragedies in their past they spoke little of ... it was enough that the two of them found themselves free and together, safe from what had come before.

I did not have to travel with our child to teach him or her what I knew. The agora at Trachis would provide rich veins of knowledge, stories of far off lands, exotic foods, jewelry and scents. I too could ask for items to be brought to Trachis and teach our child of their uses just as I had once been taught. I knew of herbs and medicines, should our child fall ill on a cold, winter night. I would soothe them in my arms, keeping him or her warm against my chest as I paced in our room or before a roaring fire in the palace kitchen.

One of the priests called my name, drawing me from my ponderings and indicating the ox was cooked. The warm, calming embrace released me as I stood and made my way to the altar. The men pulled the animal apart, handing a large portion to me and I joined them; our backs against the altar.

# 12

As we ate the ox, a number of geese and hounds wandered over from the direction of the abaton and the priests threw small pieces of meat to them. I was pleased to note none of the serpents deemed the feast worthy of their presence – I did not want to think of them with a taste for flesh.

When the food was gone, the priests got to their feet and nodded their goodbyes. I expected them to return to the sleeping quarters, but they headed in the opposite direction – back along the path Alexis and I had arrived on and towards Epidaurus. I questioned the priest who had given me the food on their destination.

"We have done our part here this night. Deacon insists he alone takes care of your friend, and as there are no others for us to tend, we shall return to the town until the dawn."

"She must be important indeed," another of the men noted. "For even on a quiet night we remain here to receive travelers."

"I see," I murmured, my eyes finding the abaton again and wondering if I should be concerned. When I turned back to farewell the priests, they were already well down the path, having passed the Shrine of Artemis, two entering the dense wood as I watched. I felt my sudden isolation with their departure. Deacon and Alexis were only a hundred feet or so away, but for a brief moment, the distance felt insurmountable and my breath caught as I attempted, and failed, to draw a full breath.

My doubts returned, more pronounced than before. Unsettled, I crossed to my bag and took out a sharpening stone. I unsheathed my sword and sat down again, drawing the stone the length of the blade, sharpening each side to a deadly point.

The familiar gesture helped and my heartbeat took up a slower pace, a whisper of the certainty and calm I had felt as I watched the flames before I ate returning, heightening the more I worked on my weapon. I would tell our child stories of the heroes and gods I knew, recreating the terror and triumphs the heroes felt as they faced fierce beasts with a hundred heads or tusks as sharp as swords. I would speak of journeys to Colchis and Troy, of individual heroism, or the braveness of many. I would speak of women warriors and wise men, ensuring that the tales lived on for many generations to come.

There would be certain tasks expected of a child of the royal line, and I would want for him or her to learn of them. Alexis would know of those things, but through the knowledge *I* shared, our child could become a great ruler – fair and just – learning lessons from those who had ruled both well and poorly before.

And love. A child with Alexis' deep green eyes and brilliant smile, kindness and laughter in equal measures I would love without question. Alexis spoke of sharing such a gift only with me. How could I deny her when I wanted to give her everything she had never had, everything she deserved?

As our child grew, candlemarks could be spent at the hot springs making wonderful memories of the three of us splashing and laughing together. Alexis and I would take turns to hide behind the waterfall before appearing again as though we were immortal; able to appear and disappear at will.

I did not need to fear that the child would not love me in return, for how would it know until it was older that other children's families were not as ours was? It would feel my love, Alexis' love, and it would be enough. It would know we were part of one another, even if we shared no blood ties. The three of us would be together as often as we could. I would remain a soldier, protecting our home with the other soldiers – many of whom were also fathers, but I would live at the palace rather than the barracks; I was certain Agrias would approve such a request.

Our child would know I took up sword and shield for them. For its mother and grandparents. They would know that I loved them so much that I would do anything I could to ensure they remained safe. They would not need to wonder where they would go next, whether they had enough food to last such a journey, or when they may next find a warm bath. Their place would be in Trachis; happy, safe and loved with Alexis and me. A new life for me had begun when I arrived at Trachis. Now it was time to add a family of my own to the one I had been welcomed into when I spoke of my love for Alexis and stopped her becoming Melanthios' wife.

I paused, my hand halfway down the blade, as a disconcerting thought occurred to me; what if Alexis remained barren, unable to carry a child for me, just as she had been unable to for Basileios? "What if you cannot heal her?" I whispered, my voice cutting through the quiet of the night as I turned my head to the twinkling lights above.

"I can heal her," came a quiet reply. I jumped, scrambling backwards and dropping the sharpening stone as I wrapped both hands around the handle of my sword. I held it up, the blade level with the seated man's throat. His bearded face broke into a smile and he held his hands up. "Do not fear, my child, I mean you no harm. I am sorry to have startled you."

I kept my weapon where it was, studying the face, before slowly lowering it again. Though the carving inside the temple of Asclepius was fairly accurate, it did not do justice to the handsome features of the god sitting across from me. With brown curled hair and a neat beard, it was his eyes that spoke most to me. Dark brown and warm, they called me to trust, to return to his side and speak words with him, to ask him the questions I most wanted answers to.

I blew out a deep breath and sat back down, setting my weapon aside. "You fear your Alexis shall remain barren for all her days in this world?" he asked gently.

"Perhaps, but ..." I hesitated.

"Speak of your fears, Child. What troubles you most about that thought?"

"She would be devastated," I replied. "For many winters she was expected to provide a child to her husband and she attempted to. But now, when it is what she wants more than anything else, what if she cannot? When I was in Athens I heard stories of a king and queen who had attempted and failed, and then, by some turn of good fortune, they were triumphant. But I do not have what is needed to gift her of this. I have love, yes, I have stubbornness and determination, but I do not have what she requires most ... I wish I could be all she needed."

Asclepius regarded me a long moment before he spoke again. "You have a body, a vessel that, though you have never attempted it, could carry a child for the two of you." He reached out to press a warm hand against my stomach.

I opened my mouth several times, but no sound came out. Finally, I shook my head. "I cannot carry a child for her, for us."

"You mean you do not *want* to," Asclepius corrected, though he did not say so unkindly. "You speak words of great love for her, yet you would not be prepared to do this if I could not heal her?"

I drew another deep breath. "My mother ... she died bringing me into this world."

"That does not mean you would suffer the same fate if you attempted it. Women die in childbirth, that is true, but many more live to watch their children grow and have children of their own." He removed his hand then spoke again. "Why would you not consider it for the two of you?"

"We have not discussed it. She never asked it of me."

"But if she did, would you?" he pressed.

I swallowed loudly, considering his question. I recalled my thoughts back in Trachis not long after Alexis and I met; when she spoke of her inability to carry a child for Basileios, I had almost told her if she still wanted a child, and I could provide it to her, I would. But I had not truly considered that, I had only wanted to take the pain of her past from her. Besides, what if I died? Alexis would have to raise our child alone. I did not wish to subject her to such a fate, just as I did not want to be without her if the situation was reversed.

"Have you not cheated death before?" Asclepius continued. "Have you not proven how strong you are?" I nodded faintly.

Gnosidicus had said I should not have lived after being speared when I first arrived in Trachis. The winters of training obviously held me in good stead, so perhaps it would for this too … Physically I was far stronger than Alexis so maybe it was what I must do for her. Perhaps it was who I must be *for* her.

"I have watched you from afar – you are confident, certain of your actions when it comes to so much," Asclepius noted.

"When faced with an enemy or given a specific task to carry out, I always know what to do, that is true. But this is so much … bigger," I countered.

"Bigger than remaining alive to face your next battle?" Asclepius asked with a grin.

I returned it but shook my head. "If Alexis asked me to carry a child for us, it would be so much more than what I believe I can do for her. It is instinct which guides me through battles or given tasks – it always has. But this is not something I can face the same way. Carrying a child, raising a child, is not a split-second decision determined by the actions you make as an enemy takes aim at you with his spear. It is ongoing, constant."

"Is it not an ongoing series of split-second decisions?" the god asked. "Do you not believe you could make them each time they arose?"

"I do not know," I murmured. Alexis believed that *I* could love a child that did not come from my body, but would she feel it was a failure on her behalf that she did not carry it? She too was fond of Hesper and Thaddeus' children, but she longed for one of her own.

Thaddeus. Would Alexis want me to lie with him? With another man? I would have to if I was to carry a child. I shivered despite the warmth of the evening. I had never allowed a man to touch me in such a manner. Had never wanted, nor sought it. Even with the slave girls and hetaerae I had never allowed them to enter me as I did them with the tools at our disposal.

There was a reason I chose women, even after what happened with Kuria. Their bodies, their touch, they were all I had ever wanted. There was much I would do for Alexis. But lie with a man, even just for this? I could not.

I shook my head and met Asclepius' eyes once more. "No. I cannot carry a child for the two of us. I cannot lie with a man to make it so." Asclepius said nothing, his intense gaze holding mine and I knew it was time to decide. Was I prepared to allow Alexis to be with another? Would I support her in her wish for a child?

I exhaled deeply then spoke. "If you can heal Alexis, if you give me your word that she shall be strong enough to bear a child, then I shall make peace with the knowledge that she must lie with Thaddeus to have what she desires. I say to you now that I want a child for Alexis and me. I ask you, great Asclepius, God of Healing, hear my request and grant it."

He tilted his head ever so slightly in a gesture that reminded me of Alexis. "You do not struggle with her desire for a child, just the manner in which you believe it must happen, is that correct?"

"Yes," I replied. Something deep within me shifted and in that moment I knew I truly wanted a child for the two of us, without question or doubt. I would support Alexis and protect her. Always.

"There are other ways to be gifted children if what you fear most about the process is having yourself or Alexis lie with another."

I frowned. "How?"

Asclepius only shook his head. "I remain here too long, I must go."

"Wait, please," I halted his departure, holding fast his arm. "Please go to Alexis. Heal whatever prevents her from carrying a child to term. I want this for us just as much as she does."

Asclepius smiled another of his kind smiles and lay his hand atop mine. "Sleep now, Skylar. The morning shall bring answers with it."

In a flash of light he was gone and I was left alone again, my body suddenly fatigued both physically and emotionally. I stretched out on the ground and closed my eyes. I repeated my wish to Asclepius, sending thoughts of the same to Alexis before falling deeply into Hypnos' realm.

# 13

A little after dawn the next morning I woke to find Deacon placing the coiled rope we had used to lead the ox to Epidaurus atop my bag.

"Apologies, I did not mean to wake you," he murmured when I pushed myself to my feet.

"It is time I greeted the day anyway," I replied, stretching my arms above my head. "Where is Alexis?"

"She remains in the abaton, but I am certain she shall join you here soon."

"Did Asclepius come to her?" I asked, casting a glance to the large building I had left my lover in the night before.

"She shall be along soon," Deacon repeated. "Safe journey to you both," he added with a smile before turning and making his way towards the Shrine of Artemis. I considered calling him back, demanding he tell me what had happened, but I feared what he might say and I prayed Alexis would return to me quickly to speak of it instead.

Whilst I waited, I put the rope and my sharpening stone back into our bag and checked our food and water supplies. We would need more if Alexis wished to sleep along the path again tonight. We could visit the agora in Epidaurus to gather them before we left the south. I was certain Alexis would want to see the seaside town, and perhaps compare their gulf to the Malian one at home.

I straightened, sliding my sword back into its sheath and turning my face upwards to catch Helios' rays. I closed my eyes as a gentle breeze lifted my hair and cooled the sweat that formed on the back of my neck. The heat of the day was not yet oppressive, and yet I was hot – no doubt a result of the apprehension I felt at what Alexis might speak of when she returned.

Despite my confidence last night that a child for Alexis and I was what I wanted, I remained concerned that Asclepius would not be able to assist us, or that Alexis would have to be with someone else. *There are other ways to be gifted children if what you fear most about the process is having yourself or Alexis lie with another.* I wondered again at his meaning.

I felt her presence behind me before she slid her soft, warm hand into mine. I blew out a long breath and turned my head, instantly lost in the green orbs I loved so dearly. Alexis smiled up at me. She appeared happy, but behind that lurked something else – apprehension of her own perhaps?

"Good morning," she murmured, pushing up onto her toes to kiss me.

"Is it?" I asked when we parted.

She nodded and placed her hand against my cheek. "I missed you last night," she said, pulling my face down to hers again. She brushed her lips against mine, her tongue darting out playfully.

"You seek to distract me from the questions you must know I have," I scolded even as my stomach fired.

"Perhaps," she replied, smiling again and pressing her body the length of mine.

"Alexis," I growled. "Please. Tell me of your night. Did Asclepius visit you? Did he heal you? Did he speak the words you wanted to hear?"

"He visited me," she offered, her hand skimming teasingly over my ribs and down my thigh, drawing the material of my tunic up.

I covered her hand, halting the movements. "Did he speak of us lying together this day, is that why you tease me so?"

"No. Today is for me," she replied and my eyes closed involuntarily as she dragged her teeth over my breast. "I recall the morning I first spoke of having a child with you and how you came back to our room."

"I remember," I breathed.

"You needed me then, to feel the strength of our connection, our love. That is what I want from you now. I need to revel in our togetherness." I stiffened slightly. I had used our insatiable lust for one another as distraction from my fears and thoughts, though it was true that I also wanted to feel the strength of our love. Did Alexis have words to say that she feared would hurt me? She raised her head, capturing my eyes with her own again. "I feel your hesitation and I know you have questions, but please, just love me," she pleaded, her hand balling into a fist beneath mine. "Make love to me. I need to feel you. Us." That was all it took to break my resistance.

I leant down and kissed her, taking her hand when I stepped back again. "Not here," I said, scooping my cuirass and bag from the ground, noting the extra weight and wondering what Alexis had added before she touched me. She nodded and allowed me to lead her back to the wooded grove we had passed through the day before.

Deacon was nowhere in sight and the other priests did not appear to have returned from Epidaurus yet. I led Alexis into the middle of the wood, leaving the path soon after and dropping the items I held. Placing both hands on Alexis' waist, I backed her against one of the tall pine trees, pressing my body against hers as I kissed her again. I was not gentle, I was not calm; I possessed her with my hands and my mouth until I felt her breath catch and her chest lifting in shallow pants. She slid her hands into my hair, her tongue moving inside my mouth with the same desperate desire.

I unclasped the pin at Alexis' shoulder and discarded the linen in one motion, a gasp escaping her as the air hit her skin. Just as it had been the day before, the grove was far cooler than the path outside had been and her nipples peaked before I had even touched them. I lowered my head to each, my tongue flicking across the hardness and shortening her breath even further. "Skylar," she whispered.

I straightened again and freed the sheath from my waist and the fibulae from my own shoulder, allowing my tunic to join her chiton beside us. I pulled her to join me as I knelt on the ground. Her knees touched mine and I slid my hand around her waist, settling it at the small of her back and closing the gap between us. Her breasts pressed against my chest, the soft hair between her thighs tickling my leg.

She moaned as my teeth found the flesh of her neck and I bit down. She ran her hand over my ribs, capturing my breast and squeezing hard. Desire raced down my spine and met the heat in my stomach. I separated our skin again and placed my hand flat against Alexis' chest, applying the barest of pressure. She understood what I wanted and lay back on our clothing, reaching for my hips and drawing me down with her. I lay in the vee of her legs and pressed my body into hers, eliciting another sharp intake of breath.

"Gods," she murmured.

"I love you," I whispered. Alexis smiled and drew my mouth to hers as we rode the exquisite wave of our union to satisfaction.

*

Alexis and I lay facing one another, our bodies entwined in the aftermath of our lovemaking. I drew my finger across her lips and she nipped at it with her teeth. "Now would you speak of what happened in the abaton?" I asked.

She nodded and released it again. "After you left last night, Deacon conducted a test of fertility." I grew still, but Alexis squeezed my hip, holding me against her so I could not move away. "It did not hurt and he did not touch me as you fear someone shall again." I attempted to calm the beating of my heart. Alexis spoke without hesitation and without a single hint of censure; I had to trust her words. "He said he needed to find out what was causing me to lose the children placed in my belly. He said it would aid Asclepius in determining a cure when he came."

"So what was the test? What did he do?" I asked, pleased my voice was steady when I spoke.

"He lit a bowl of incense and placed it beneath my chiton. I had to squat above it for a candlemark, the scent unable to escape, except through my mouth if it was going to." I frowned, but said nothing, allowing Alexis to continue. "It did not. I was closed."

"I do not understand," I said, my frown deepening.

"Neither did I, but Deacon said I must sleep so Asclepius could visit me. I did not think I would be able to sleep at all, but it was not long before I found myself in Hypnos' care and Asclepius came to me in my dreams. He appeared just as he did in the temple, bearded and with that same kind face, and a serpent was curled around his arm. He spoke in a quiet, soothing voice and told me not to be afraid, that the serpent would aid in what I sought from him. He then laid it on my stomach and it curled up, closing its eyes and sleeping. It warmed me and I felt as though you lay with me; your arms wrapped around me just as we sleep back home.

"Asclepius took my hand and sat beside me on the bed. We spoke of what I wanted and he spoke of you. He said you wanted a child for us. That you would be a wonderful mother, just as I believed you would. He said you told him that you wanted him to heal my body and asked if I wanted the same. When I said I did, he nodded and patted his pet that lay on me. Then he disappeared and when I woke again, Helios' light was greeting me."

"Asclepius came to me also, though I was not asleep," I admitted.

Alexis raised her brows. "So ... you *did* speak the words he repeated to me?"

I reached for her hand, drawing it to my lips and kissing her knuckles as I replied. "Yes. Somehow, I want to raise a child with you."

She smiled shyly and nodded, dropping her eyes. "Deacon asked what I dreamt of when I woke and I told him. He appeared pleased and said he must do another test. I did not have to remain sitting above the incense for as long this time – barely a quarter of a candlemark. He told me what the test was used for, and what it had meant the previous night.

"When a woman's body is open – or ready to receive a child in its midst – the smoke from the incense can travel from beneath her chiton, through her body and out her mouth for the healer, or in this case the priest, to smell. Deacon said it proves that the body is receptive and willing to accept a child for the couple. That it is their time and the will of the gods to allow them children. Last night that did not happen, but this morning, I could taste the frankincense as it filtered out of my nose and mouth."

I drew a quick breath. "You ... Deacon believes you shall be able to carry a child?"

She smiled and nodded. "Yes. He said that for whatever reason, Basileios and I were not meant to have children, but you and I are. That our united wish sees it so." She drew a breath, her grin fading slightly. "But there is more we must do before we shall be gifted with a child."

"Oh?" I frowned, my heart quickening again at the change in her voice.

She swallowed and dropped her eyes to our entwined hands before looking back to me. "Asclepius says we have to go to Corinth," she murmured.

# 14

I rolled onto my back, jumping to my feet and pacing across the cool forest floor. "No," I insisted, my heart beating painfully in my chest. "Absolutely not."

"Skylar," Alexis said quietly, joining me. "Please, hear what I have to say."

"I cannot return to Corinth. Please do not ask it of me."

She blocked my path, resting both hands on my waist as she forced me to look at her. "I know what happened there hurt you, that even now you feel responsible for actions you could not have prevented even if you had known of them. But it is time you faced what happened."

I stepped around her and gathered my tunic from the ground. "Do you not think I faced it when I spoke of it to you? Do you know how hard that was for me? To have you see me behave so cowardly before you. To *cry* as I shared the shame and guilt I feel over what happened to Kuria because of me?"

"Yes," she replied, ripping the tunic from my hands and throwing it to the ground before taking my forearms in a tight grip. "I know what it took for you to speak of it, to give your fear a voice. I know you held yourself back from me for a long time because you feared Melanthios may do the same to me. But you cannot remain lost in the past when your present, your future, is so very different." I opened my mouth to speak, but she pressed on. "You cannot keep punishing yourself for someone else's actions. Do not punish *me* over a woman I never met."

"Ale–"

"No, Skylar. The night you spoke of Kuria, you allowed me to know a deep, vulnerable part of you that you had not shared with anyone else. I did not run from you. I did not abandon you or tell you I could not be with you. Instead I held you, loved you with all I had. I could not bear to see you hurting so. I wished I could take away all your pain, as you wished to take away mine when I spoke of my mother's treatment of me. You did not deserve to be made to feel as though what happened to Kuria was your fault."

"It *was* my fault," I interrupted gently, watching Alexis' chest rise and fall quickly with the effort of her words. "I came between a man and his wife. If I had not allowed her to take me to her bed, then she would still be alive."

A tremor ran through Alexis as she shook her head. "No. Kuria's choice to ask you to remain was her own. You did not insist upon it, did you?" It was my turn to shake my head. "She would not have expected the severity of Stamatis' retaliation, but she must have known what his thoughts would be when she provoked him with her words. That is not on you. Neither are Stamatis' actions. Yes, it is sad and terrible what he did to her, but you cannot hold blame for it. He was a grown man, and you were only a child, with no prior knowledge of relationships between couples." She threw her hands up, starting to pace herself as she continued. "Gods, you were only just discovering your own body and what pleasures could be derived from it when you met them. How could you know how Kuria's words would anger Stamatis?"

"I should have known, I had been in battles before."

"That was not the same and you know it," Alexis snapped. "Your father ending Stamatis' life in such a quick manner was perhaps the only injustice that day, given what Kuria had suffered."

I drew a quick breath, surprised by the fierceness of Alexis' words, but feeling her love for me behind them. I put my hand on her arm, halting her steps and turned her to face me. "Alexis."

She shook her head, taking my hands in hers. "I wish you had never been there," she admitted. "But I cannot change that for you. If you allow us to return, we can stand together, face your past *together*. Please, allow me to help you to heal, just as you brought me here to Asclepius to have my body healed."

"I wish it was as easy as placing some incense beneath a chiton and having a serpent sleep on my stomach for those memories to be taken away," I murmured.

"Perhaps it shall be," she replied, taking my face in her hands and pulling me to her again.

"What if something happens to you whilst we are there?" I asked, sliding my arms around her waist, my heart still beating rapidly beneath my chest as

I allowed the question to hang between us.

Alexis pressed her body against mine, her arms tightening around my neck. "You shall always ensure I am safe. From the moment we met you allowed no one…" I attempted to interrupt but she pressed a finger to my lips. "*No one* to do me harm such as you had witnessed before. Corinth shall be no different." She pushed up onto her toes and kissed me.

"I would rather die than allow you to be harmed or taken from me again," I whispered.

"I know," she replied, laying her head against my chest and tightening her grip around my waist.

*

"We shall need more food for our journey. Do you want to visit the agora at Epidaurus?"

"No. Deacon provided for us. We do not need to delay our departure," Alexis replied, readjusting her clothing as I did mine.

"I suppose not," I mumbled. I could not deny that I would do almost anything to delay both our departure from Epidaurus and our arrival in Corinth. I could tell Alexis knew it as well when she ducked beneath my arm to stand in front of me.

"I know it is not where you would travel, given the choice, but I am grateful that for me you are willing."

"Only you could ask it of me," I agreed.

"Perhaps when we arrive we can secure lodgings with a warm bath and I can show you just how much I appreciate it," she smiled, pressing the lower half of her body against mine.

"The bath is tempting, certainly. But why wait for everything else?" I asked, returning her grin and reaching for the fibula at her shoulder.

She laughed and slapped my hand away as she shook her head. "It would do you good to have to wait. Perhaps I have given myself far too easily to you of late," she teased, walking backwards so only the tips of our fingers touched, her eyebrows high beneath her hair daring me to deny her words. "Indeed, I wonder if you could actually keep your hands from me until we arrived." I raised an eyebrow, worried thoughts of our destination all but disappearing with the hint of a game.

"Are you challenging me, Princess?"

She caught the look on my face and her smile widened. "Definitely."

"I do enjoy a challenge," I rumbled, stalking towards her. Alexis glanced behind her and I took advantage, grabbing her by the waist and trapping her against the nearest tree, just as I had earlier. I swept her hair off her neck and took the soft flesh between my teeth.

"I win," she murmured.

"We both win," I replied.

"Skylar," she groaned.

I slid a hand between us and pressed it against the heat that burned through her light chiton. "Tell me you do not want me to take you right here, that you want to wait until we arrive in Corinth," I drawled, dragging a finger along the inside of her thigh. She grunted and I could not tell if it was in pleasure or frustration, though the look on her face when she tangled her hand in my hair and pulled my head back suggested it was a little of both. "You truly want me to stop?"

"Never," she replied, tracing a finger over my lips. "But you prove my point; patience is not your strength."

"Hmm, true, though I have not heard you complain."

"No. But we should be on our way. How far is it to Corinth?"

I blew out a breath and leaned back ever so slightly as I thought. "We should arrive by sundown," I finally replied.

She nodded and threw me a cheeky grin as she placed her hands on my cuirass and shoved me backwards. "Should be an interesting day then, lover."

"A long day," I amended with a grin. I shook my head, gathered our bag and followed Alexis as she made her way back to the path and through the grove.

*

The heat of the day beat down onto my head and warmed my chest beneath my cuirass as I walked several steps behind Alexis. I found it was easier not to touch her if I did not walk directly beside her – and I suspected it was the same for her as well. The easy, familiar way she had always laid her hand on my forearm was too inviting for us both, so I hung back, keeping an eye on the path and plains around us as well as the graceful, sleek form of my lover.

Of course watching her walk ahead of me was a pleasant torture in itself. Though I could not see her shapely legs or the soft skin of her stomach and back, the curve of her hips was obvious in the fine linen she wore and I had begun to suspect that in the past half candlemark, she was aware I watched her and she held herself differently.

Alexis gathered the hair at the nape of her neck, lifting it to expose the light-colored skin beneath, and a drop of sweat, that slid down into her chiton. My breath grew shallow as Alexis' pace in front of me slowed, her hips very evidently being used to incite my desire as she turned to me with a grin. "Shall we stop for a little while?" she asked as she allowed her hair to fall back into place.

I swallowed loudly, balling my hands into fists and tucking them behind me so I did not reach out for her. "I do not believe that to be a good idea," I managed.

"Mmm. You appear flushed, is it the heat of the day o—"

"No," I cut her off, placing my hands on her shoulders and turning her so she did not face me. "Keep walking," I directed.

Alexis laughed, but started along the path again. "You have found some restraint, I am impressed, and a little disappointed," she said, watching me over her shoulder.

"As am I, believe me."

She laughed again. "You have lasted far longer than I imagined, we must be over halfway to Corinth already."

"Almost," I agreed, having successfully kept thoughts of our destination from my mind by thinking of Alexis and our night ahead with a heated bath.

"Perhaps you would tell me now of your time in Epidaurus."

I drew a deep breath, the flickering flames of desire in my stomach effectively extinguished by her request. "My actions there were far from noble," I murmured.

Alexis appeared to sense my sudden discomfort and slowed her pace until I was beside her. She threaded her fingers through mine, her thumb stroking my hand in comfort rather than caress. "It is not a tale you have shared with another, is it?" she asked quietly.

"No," I replied. "You and my father would be the only ones to know outside of myself and those involved."

"I promise to never speak of it, lest you should ask it of me," she replied genuinely.

I gave her a small smile and nodded. "I have found you are the only one I wish to share certain aspects of my past with."

"Have there been many who asked you of your past?" Alexis asked, her cheeks tinging when she spoke.

"Only one," I replied.

"Kuria," she ventured.

I nodded. "But I did not give her answers."

"Why?"

I shrugged. "She did not mean as much to me as you do, as you always have. From the moment we met I wanted to know you, for you to know who I was. The good and the bad. I have never felt that with anyone before."

Alexis smiled up at me. "Is it wrong to say I am glad?"

I stopped, pulling her to a halt beside me. "No and I would not have wished for it to be any other way." I leaned down and placed a gentle kiss on her lips.

"I win," she said with a grin.

"You took my hand first," I countered, though my own smile broke out.

"True," she admitted. "But would you share your story with me now?"

I blew out a deep breath. "Yes, but it begins in Anticyra, not Epidaurus."

"I hope it is a long story, for I enjoy listening to your voice as you speak. The night you spoke of how you came to have Skotos showed you have the same flair for storytelling as your father."

"He does enjoy sharing stories," I agreed.

"Especially ones that make you blush," Alexis said, her smile widening.

"Indeed," I replied with a nod, recalling the eagerness with which he had told Alexis and Hesper of the newlywed couple whose bath I had interrupted.

With my hand still in hers, Alexis turned back to the path, tugging gently on my arm until I followed.

# 15

"After I killed the mercenary and his men at Anticyra in my twelfth winter, Father took me into the nearby mountains and taught me to use spear and sword. He spoke words he had never shared with me before about where he was from; his tribe and his duty as a warrior for them.

"The day you brought me the honey-sweetened bread, you asked if Father and I were from Thrace, and that is indeed where he called home for many winters – until he met my mother and they left the north. His tribe was the Bessoi, who your father admires as the only Thracian tribe to have never submitted to the Persians. The two of them have spoken of much, including the ways of the Bessoi."

"They indeed became fast friends and have shared their histories," Alexis agreed.

I nodded before continuing. "From Anticyra, Father and I went north to Amphissa, whose fine horses rival even those of the northern town of Larissa in Thessaly, and he purchased Skaris. The Thracians worship the Sky-God Sabazios, father of their people and known to them as the Thracian Horseman. Father believed it was time he showed me how to handle Skotos not just for travel, but for battle."

"Sabazios is one of the Macedonian gods as well," Alexis said.

"Indeed?" I asked, raising an eyebrow. "Then it is no wonder you are such a competent rider – being in close proximity to Thrace I suspect Macedonians are as fearsome on horseback as the Thracians."

"Some. Though some of us ride for pure enjoyment," she replied.

I grinned, nodding again. "My father's tribe spent most time in the mountains, but still his skills would have matched even the finest of flat-plain riders. He taught me to wield a weapon and defend myself from atop Skotos, spending a number of weeks charging towards me, his spear thrusting at my body and head."

"Was he not concerned he would badly injure you?" Alexis asked, a deep frown creasing her forehead.

"Perhaps," I shrugged. "But his weapon found my skin only once, and even then it was just a passing glance. Twice I felled him from Skaris and he appeared cautiously pleased with my actions, satisfied that my display in Anticyra had not been sheer good fortune. I repeated to him that I wanted to defend innocent people who worked hard and deserved protection from mercenaries or those who sought to take what did not belong to them. Father was not so certain I was ready for such tasks, so we remained in Amphissa another moon and he taught me how to defend myself in close combat.

"It was then I first heard of Theseus. The Dioscuri, twin brothers of Helen of Troy named Castor and Polydeuces, were highly worshipped in Amphissa and the story was often told of the time they saved Helen from Theseus when he stole her away from Troy. Though it was not his most honorable deed, I soon learnt there was more to Theseus than that particular action; he was considered a great hero and helped many people. My father knew much of Theseus and his achievements and suggested we follow the hero's footsteps. He promised to tell me of the feats Theseus carried out when we arrived in the relevant town or plain.

"On our way south, Father took me to Mount Parnassos and Mount Helicon, teaching me to survive in the mountainous areas, how to find food and water from the plants, trees and streams. When we drank from the hippocrene – or horse-springs – on each mountain, Father spoke of another hero, Bellerophon, and the winged-horse named Pegasus he captured and rode during many great victories. It was said that wherever Pegasus struck his foot to the earth, a spring would erupt from the ground, giving great insight to those who visited. Athenian scholars still enjoy healthy debate as to which of the two mountains the Muses themselves call home, and even though I have visited both, I can offer no further answer as to which is most likely.

"My father said another spring was opened by Pegasus in Troezen, Theseus' home and the beginning of his journey, and I spent quite some time there when we arrived, asking for guidance to ensure I would always act in a manner fit to rival the heroes I learned of, no matter who, or what, I may face in my life … Why do we not eat and rest a while?" I asked, before Alexis could question me on my words.

She nodded in reply and we sought shelter beneath a large tree at the side of the path, Alexis taking food from the bag when I set it down.

"My father spoke of Theseus' life changing when he reached sixteen winters; his mother told him who his father was and encouraged him to go to Athens to meet him. Father firmly believes there are significant times in our lives that change the destiny intended for us. For him, it was when he fell in love with my mother and they left Thrace, only to have him lose her so soon after."

"He gained you," Alexis offered, reaching over to squeeze my arm.

I nodded. "He did, and that set him on a different path again – one of constant movement so my mother's family could never find us and take me from him."

"Did he cite your actions in Anticyra as that important time for you?" Alexis asked.

"Yes. I do not believe he had ever intended to teach me the ways of a warrior, though he had the skills. He did not want that to be my life. That being said, nothing I learnt helped when we reached Corinth three winters later. For all he taught me, there was still so much I did not know."

Alexis moved closer and slid her fingers between mine. "What happened there taught you much. It changed your path again. You closed part of yourself off, not believing you deserved to be loved or to love another in case they were harmed because of it."

"Yes. But I found myself changed again, for the better, when I met you," I added with a grin. "I wonder now if perhaps Father feels it is time for another change for him," I mused, looking up to the mountain range beside us.

"How so?" Alexis asked.

I returned my eyes to her. "There was a woman who travelled a while with us here in the Peloponnese; Father sent her to Konitsa to be safe, and now he too has gone there. Perhaps he wants to find love again after all these winters."

"I hope he can, for there is no greater feeling."

"Indeed," I agreed, placing my arm around Alexis' shoulders and drawing her close to press my lips against the top of her head.

"So, where did you go after the mountains? Directly to Troezen?" she asked, returning our conversation to its original path.

"No, from Mount Helicon we had intended to go to Marathon, where Theseus killed the bull which had been ravaging the countryside of Attica. But on the way, we met some other travelers who were going to Athens for the Panathenaic Games. They invited us to join them there, so we did."

"Are the Panathenaic Games one of the festivals you spoke about the day at the agora?"

"Yes."

"I recall much about that day," she smiled. I returned it, knowing it was the day we had shared our first kiss.

"The Panathenaic Games are held during the Panathenaea Festival every four winters. Only citizens of Athens are allowed participate and, though they are not as prestigious as the Olympic, Nemean, Isthmian or Pythian Games, travelers from all over Attica and the Peloponnese go to watch. Peisistratos, father of the Athenian tyrant Hippias, reinstated the Panathenaic Games about sixty winters ago. At the time, poetry and music competitions were only held during the Pythian Games, but Peisistratos added them to the foot and chariot races in Athens.

"From Athens we travelled north again, accompanying our new friends to Delphi for the Pythian Games, which are also only held once every four winters. After that we went south again, to Sunium, to celebrate the Festival of Sunium."

"It does not sound as though you found yourself following Theseus' path for quite some time," Alexis noted with a grin.

"No," I replied, my own escaping. "We spent five moons cheering on competitors, celebrating all manner of victories and giving thanks for sailing in safe battles we were not part of." I got to my feet, offering my hand to Alexis and pulling her up when she took it.

"I cannot believe your father would allow such lengthy frivolity."

"For the most part he welcomed it and insisted we attend when asked. I believe it was a way for him to forget what had happened in Anticyra for a time."

"Oh," she murmured.

I kept her hand in mine and, picking up our bag from the ground, started towards the path again. "After Sunium we went to Marathon, then Aphidnae where Theseus left Helen after he abducted her and the Dioscuri pursued him. We spent a moon in Athens and Father took me many of the places Theseus had visited or lived. After that we went to Phalerum which is the port Theseus sailed to Crete from to face the Minoan Bull. From Phalerum we travelled south and aided in mining silver from a recently discovered mine at Thorikos. We spent almost two moons in Thorikos and I learnt how the Athenians make their coins and how to craft bronze armor by mixing tin and copper together. Both those metals come from across the seas for the metalworkers to use."

"Did you make this there?" Alexis asked, tugging at the base of my cuirass.

"I did."

"It is well crafted, but how did you know the correct size? You were not as tall then as you are now, were you?"

"By the time we were there I had done much of my growing, and my father insisted I make it a little larger than I was at the time so it would fit me for many winters – we had not begun aiding cities or armies for coin then and I could not have afforded another so soon. I found I had a flair for the hard work of the mines and the crafting of armor, though far less time for the intricacies needed for coin making. After Thorikos we followed Theseus' path again, visiting the places I spoke of yesterday; Eleusis, Megara and the Isthmus. We reached Nemea in time for the Nemean Games, and we remained there for those before moving on to Epidaurus and Troezen, where our journey of Theseus ended, and his began."

"What happened at Epidaurus?" Alexis asked quietly, wrapping her hand around my forearm, her other still in mine.

I drew a breath. "When we arrived, I attempted to fit in with the girls of the town, but it proved difficult as I could not imagine how it was for them – they were expected to be betrothed by the time they reached fourteen winters, and they could not imagine how I could *not* be, given I was already of age. They asked me of the festivals I had attended when they overheard my father saying where we had been, but we quarreled when speaking of their roles during the festivals; their experiences of them so different to mine."

"How so?" Alexis asked.

"I had always joined the men and boys, not the girls, at the celebrations. My father wanted me close by in such crowds and as we had no allegiance to either Athenian or Spartans ways, I had not been taught what girls or women did specifically during them. The girls did not understand why I wore armor akin to their men. Their boys, who were training to be soldiers, did not wear armor until they were much older. I sought refuge with the boys as they practiced and trained with their weapons.

"I joined them each morning just after dawn on the plain between the city of Epidaurus and where the Asclepeion has been built. I had not exactly been welcomed by them, but they did not shun me as the girls had, not appearing to care what I wore, so long as I gave them fierce challenge with my weapons. I told them I knew the story of Theseus and how he had defeated Periphetes there. They were well aware of the hero's deed and boasted that they were just as good. Though they were my own age, their training had begun at seven winters, as all boys in Sparta's are, and their skills were more honed, their bodies more muscular than mine. It was then that things got out of hand.

"They challenged me to fight them for real, not with mock training or battles as we had been. I agreed, wanting to prove I could stand alongside them, to prove I was just as good as them, despite my lesser time with weapons. I believed one day I could be a great hero too and I had not had the chance to pick up a sword in such a manner since Father had tested me at Amphissa.

"The fight was set for the following morning and I snuck out before dawn with Father's xiphos and javelin, both sharpened to deadly points. When I arrived, they were waiting, all six of them with bronze-covered wooden clubs. They would not fall for the trick Theseus had used on Periphetes; they acknowledged what their clubs were made of and said they would not be offering them to me for inspection. I had to find another way to disarm them. Standing in a semi-circle, they did not intend to come at me one at a time – if I was to be considered successful, I would have to fight them all at once. They said that only when the last of their clubs found the ground, or I was too injured to go on, would they deem me done."

Alexis sucked in a breath, holding tighter to my arm, but I pressed on. "I squared my shoulders and held my head high, telling them I was not afraid and, with their clubs above their heads, they advanced. I defended their blows with my sword but had no sooner dispatched of one attack than two more landed against my cuirass or arms and legs, bruises immediately darkening my bare skin. After a candlemark there was only one boy and I left facing each other. Both of us were bloodied and tired, though neither would surrender until the other's weapon – or body – met the grass for a final time. The others stood nearby, their clubs back in their hands, shouting insults and goading me to give up, but none approached again, just as their rules stated.

"The final boy screamed and rushed forward, two clubs gripped tightly in his hands. I defended one of his attacks with my sword, but he brought the second club crashing into my cuirass, robbing me of my breath as it smashed against my side. I fell to my knees, but my sword remained in my hand. He laughed, his friends joining in as he pulled me up roughly by the bronze at my shoulder. He told me girls could not be soldiers, that though I had managed to disarm the others, they had gone easy on me. I would never survive in a real battle.

"I was enraged, not believing for a moment that their attacks had been anything but their best, and I told him so. He laughed again and landed another blow at my back, sending me stumbling forward. I drew in several deep breaths, the pain at my side becoming worse with each movement, but I faced him and dared them all to come at me again, to prove that I was better than any of them."

I paused. The intense heat of anger and quick beats of my heart resurfacing as I recalled their words and sneering laughter echoing across the plain that morning. The dew had been light on the ground, the grass dry where our tunics had met it and soaked up the moisture and I was certain I could feel the cool water on the back of my knees now.

"How badly did they hurt you?" Alexis asked quietly.

"Their weapons did not touch me again," I murmured.

"But … How?"

"A strange calmness, a certainty I would defeat them, came over me and I took to each with a fierceness and determination I had not felt since Anticyra. I fought them as though my actions were not my own. The pain at my side all but disappeared and I felled them swiftly, one after another, until there were none left. I stood above them, kicking at their injured bodies until they dragged themselves up to flee. The last one, the boy who had told me I was not good enough, could not run, the gash in his thigh from my sword preventing him from moving. I ... I ..." I paused, swallowing against the memory.

"Did you kill him?" Alexis asked.

I drew a deep breath and briefly closed my eyes. "No. But I have no doubt I would have, had my father not arrived at that moment." I heard Alexis blow out a breath of her own and I opened my eyes, seeing not the path in front of us, but the fear in the boy's eyes as I stood with my sword held high above my head, ready to drive it through his heart. I swallowed again.

"Father knocked the sword from my hand and pushed me to the ground, tending to the boy's wound. He picked the boy up and ordered me to follow with my weapons, and the remaining clubs that lay in the grass. He was silent the entire journey back to Epidaurus and made me apologize to the boy's parents, and to the boy himself. He said nothing as we gathered our few belongings and set out along the path, remaining mute until we reached our lodgings in Troezen and he took me to the baths to get cleaned up."

I paused, my chest tightening just as it had that day, not with anger now, but with shame and embarrassment. The look in my father's eyes when he saw me standing above the boy; I had never felt as small as I had then.

"As Father tended to my wounds, he spoke of his disappointment in me and in himself for having taught me to use weapons at all. He said that I was not ready for such lessons. I told him why I had been fighting the boys, what they taunted me with; telling me I could not be a soldier because I was a girl. He said I should not have believed them – I should know better. He told me that what I had done in Anticyra had been heroic, and for the right reasons, good reasons; to fight for someone who could not, that was admirable. But to pick up weapons just to prove I was better than someone else was not. I felt as though I had undone all the good I had done in Anticyra. I had failed him so badly. I did not ever wish to feel that way again."

"That is why you went to the spring in Troezen? To ensure you never disappointed him again?" Alexis asked.

"Yes. Though there have been times since when I have allowed others to goad me into similar actions, actions that force me to forget that I should not *enjoy* killing them when they have done wrong to me or someone I care for."

"Melanthios?" Alexis asked softly.

I drew a breath but faced her as I nodded. "Yes. I know I faced him, killed him, because I wanted to prove I was better than him. To have what was his."

"Me," Alexis nodded.

"Yes," I confirmed. I paused and placed my hand on Alexis' cheek when she stopped beside me. "But I would not change what I did. He killed Basileios for the same reason and his ways were not gentle, not what you deserved. I still fought for someone – for you – who could not fight for yourself. You would not have because you believed you must become his, no matter how it had come to pass."

"And that is why you must not blame yourself for your actions that day at the hot springs. You did what you had to, to ensure I was safe."

"But I enjoyed it," I admitted quietly, though I had told myself I would never speak of it with her.

"You … enjoyed killing Melanthios?" she asked, a frown marring her forehead.

"Yes," I answered, smoothing the skin at her brow. "I wanted him to suffer for what he had done to you."

"Did he?" Alexis asked, her voice barely above a whisper as she searched my eyes.

"Yes. I did not allow him to leave this world easily," I replied with a nod. "But I wanted him to regret he had ever been cruel to you. I wanted him to apologize for wanting to harm someone so beautiful, so precious."

"It is not how he saw me," Alexis said, bringing our hands to her lips and placing a gentle kiss on my knuckle. "But you did."

"I cannot believe I was the first to see it."

"Perhaps not, but you were the only one to speak of it to me, other than those who had vested interest to speak such words. But they were only words. *You* meant them. You love me as no one else ever has."

"As no one else ever shall," I amended. Alexis smiled and pushed up onto her toes to press her lips against mine. I released her hand and wrapped my arm around her waist, drawing her body against mine and deepening our kiss. "I love you," I told her when we parted.

"And I you," she replied.

"You know, when we met, you surprised me. You never questioned what I did or if I was skilled enough to do what I was there for. You just accepted I fought as men do, and that it had been that way for a long time. It did not scare or disgust you that I had killed, or would kill again. Instead you asked me what first led me to do so."

"If you were not talented in what you did, *my* father would never have sent for you," Alexis replied with a shrug.

I leaned back slightly and slid my hands to her hips as she knotted hers at the nape of my neck. "But you did not see me when I first arrived in the Spercheios Valley, before I was injured. And I was far from my best when I faced Melanthios at the baths. Had he not been halfway drunk that night, I doubt I would have overcome him so easily."

"I knew it was who you were, but there was far more I wanted to know about you. You being a warrior or a soldier was not what drew me to you, it was just the reason I was fortunate enough to meet you." I opened my mouth to speak but she placed her finger to my lips and I kept quiet. "You fascinated me as a person, not as a warrior. I mean I found that intriguing, but it was what you made me *feel* rather than what you did for coin that drew me to ask you about yourself. When we talked and you allowed me to get to know you, I found I wanted to be the focus of the intensity, the passion, with which your father said you did everything. That I saw you did everything with. I wanted to be that important to someone. To you."

I smirked. "You made me feel much also, and it was not because you were a princess. At the Spercheios Valley, I did not even know that was who you were, though your clothing was very fine, and fitted you well," I added, sliding my hands up either side of her body, my thumbs tracing the undersides of her breasts as I pulled her against me.

"You noticed my clothing the first time you saw me?" she asked, her breath catching as I touched her.

"I noticed how the design accented certain ... features," I acknowledged, my hands moving higher. She covered them with her own and took them from her body.

"I fear if we remain here much longer you shall lose the restraint you have shown."

"Would that displease you, Princess?" I asked with a grin.

"Displease? No. But I believe I have had enough of the outdoors and wish to find my pleasures with you beneath a tiled roof and in a far more intimate setting," she replied, separating our bodies and turning back to the path.

My own breath became hard to settle, but I balled my hands into fists once again so I did not reach for her. I would not lose the challenge she had set me. "You do enjoy teasing me."

Alexis looked back over her shoulder, her grin wide, and her cheeks tinged with pink. "You do not enjoy it?"

"Oh I do, though you push my powers of restraint to the limit. You always have."

"Good," she chuckled.

I shook my head and traipsed after Alexis, hoping we could find quick lodgings in Corinth and I could repay her for making me wait all day to have her.

Asclepius may have said we had to face my past together in Corinth, but it would not be tonight. Tonight I would forget where we were and would make love with Alexis until the dawn met the dark, longer if we could be so fortunate. I grinned and hastened my pace, passing Alexis so she had to keep up with *me* instead.

# 16

We were still a candlemark from the city of Corinth when we reached a monolithic mountain, on top of which stood the acropolis. Long shadows fell across fortifying marble walls by the towering temple that Kuria had worked at before her marriage to Stamatis.

Once again, I lengthened my strides along the path, relieved that Alexis either did not notice the top of the building above the wall or was too focused on our arrival to bother asking if I knew what it was. We would enter Corinth from the south, and for that I was grateful; the home that had been Stamatis' was on the north end and there was much I wanted to do before I saw that particular place again.

"Good day to you," a voice called. I turned, finding a girl waving in our direction. Her sudden appearance left me in no doubt that she had entered the plain from one of the gates in the wall, the patterns on her fine chiton marking her as a hetaira.

I hesitated, but when Alexis raised her hand in response and waited for the young woman to catch us up, I had to stop, placing my body slightly in front of her and resting my hand on the pommel of my sword.

Alexis reached for the water-skin in our bag and offered it. Now that she was nearer, I realized she was indeed just a girl, probably no more than fifteen or sixteen winters, her slender body mostly developed, though she held herself a little awkwardly. Clearly, she had not been at the temple long; she had not yet learnt to carry herself with the confidence the position required.

"Thank you," she said, accepting the water from Alexis and taking a long gulp before handing the skin back. "The day is warm and as you see there are few trees with which to find shelter here."

"Then why do you remain?" I asked, wanting to continue on as quickly as possible, before she spoke of where she was from.

"Is your home close by?" Alexis asked at the same time.

"I live at the Temple of Aphrodite, up there on the hill," the girl replied, keeping her eyes from me as she answered Alexis.

"Perhaps then it is time you returned," I growled, a frown creasing my forehead as finally she met my eyes.

"Sky—"

"I was told only to return when you arrived," the young woman said, lifting her chin.

"The two of you are acquainted?" Alexis asked, her own brow furrowing as she looked between the young woman and me for an answer.

"No," I replied.

The girl met Alexis' stare. "We have never met, though I was informed that you are Alexis, Princess of Trachis in the region of Thermopylae, and she," she paused and nodded in my direction, "is your lover, Skylar. The head priestess of our temple who interprets all from the great goddess Aphrodite, spoke of the two of you this morning. We have been expecting you."

"How could she know of us?" I asked before Alexis could speak.

"It is not for me to call into question my priestess. I only carry out the tasks she assigns me."

Alexis placed a hand on my arm, stepping between me and the hetaira and turning her back to the girl as she quietly asked, "Asclepius?"

I shrugged. "I do not know how often or even *if* the gods speak much amongst themselves, other than those who are lovers or friends. I have not heard of either between Aphrodite and Asclepius," I replied, keeping my voice just as low. "But the temple here ... it is not as the temple was in Epidaurus."

At the last of my words, laughter echoed off the rocks around us. Alexis jumped and spun around and once again I put my body between her and the newcomer. "Indeed it is not," the smooth voice confirmed. "Though I hear many prayers and words of thanks spoken following screams of ecstasy or by those passionately coupling." I began to draw my sword but the blonde woman laughed again, shaking her head and addressing the young hetaira. "Return to the temple Rhoda, you are required there more so than here." The girl's eyes widened slightly, before she dropped them to the ground and nodded, hurrying back along the path towards the nearest gate, never once daring to look back.

"Who are you?" I asked, noting the woman had the same perfectly chiseled features I had observed in Asclepius. Her long, blonde hair was slightly curled, and hung past her shoulders, reaching almost to her breasts, which were displayed admirably between the folds of her pale pink chiton.

She placed her hands on her hips and gave Alexis and me a playful grin. "Should I be offended you do not recognize the Goddess of Love?"

"Goddess of …?" Alexis began.

"Aphrodite," I breathed. She laughed again and held her hand out. Alexis slowly reached up to take it, but I threaded my fingers through hers, and lowered our arms to my side. "Why are you here?" I asked.

Aphrodite dropped her hand, though she did not appear offended I had not allowed Alexis to take it. When she spoke again, it was Alexis she addressed. "I am here to aid you of course. I have heard your wish to bring a child into this world with the one you love above all others. Indeed, I have heard much since Skylar arrived in your life, *your* desires most certainly." Alexis' cheeks heated and she dropped her eyes. "Asclepius sent you to Corinth, to *me*. Come to my temple and allow me to aid in what you desire."

"How?" I frowned.

"You agreed when Skylar said your temple was not as Asclepius' is in Epidaurus. What does that mean?" Alexis asked, her voice strong and once again overlapping mine.

"Though your blood is partly of Macedonian descent, I cannot believe that your mother or your young male friend never spoke of it. You have truly never heard of the Temple of Aphrodite at Corinth?" Aphrodite asked, her head tilted to the side. Alexis shook hers.

"There is no need to speak of it now," I rumbled.

The goddess continued as though I had not spoken. "Whilst it is forbidden to partake of pleasures of a sexual nature in temples, whether consensual or not, here at my temple it is not only welcomed, but encouraged and sought after." Alexis' brow creased and though I attempted to speak, no sound came out. "It is considered an act of worship and offering to me to partake of carnal coupling in this place. There are a thousand hetairai employed for such enjoyment and many a ship merchant, nobleman and … warrior … has been known to engage in such services," Aphrodite continued, looking to me as though daring me to deny her words.

It was no secret that both single and married men used the hetairai for pleasures of the flesh. For the married men it was often because they were separated from their wives by distance and found themselves in want of companionship during the long candlemarks of the night.

"You have been here before?" Alexis asked as her eyes found mine.

"No," I assured her, gripping her fingers between mine even tighter, glad Aphrodite had allowed me my words again.

"Unfortunately, we have not had the pleasure," Aphrodite confirmed, giving both of us another dazzling grin. "But today that shall change."

"It shall not. Unlike the men who pay coin for hetairai, Alexis and I are in no need of such services," I insisted. If thoughts of Alexis lying with a man gave me pause, they were nothing to imagining her with the hetairai of Aphrodite's temple. I had heard the rumors, known of men who had visited them and never returned home; their beauty and skill unsurpassed throughout Attica and the Peloponnese. I would not have allowed Alexis to be with the hetairai in *any* town or city in Greece, least of all the women there.

"Skylar," Alexis' soft voice drew me from my thoughts and I met her gaze. "Asclepius said you must face your past. Perhaps it was not only Kuria he spoke of. Perhaps we must ..."

"No," I said firmly. "There is nothing at the Temple of Aphrodite for us. We should continue into Corinth itself and find lodgings for the evening."

"You truly believe that?" Aphrodite asked, her head tilted to the side again, the taunting grin still on her lips. "If that is so, then why do you deny my offer? I know you have always enjoyed spending coin to have the very best bring you pleasure, and you must know that the women in my temple are more skilled than others. I ensure it is so. You do not wish your lover to experience the same pleasures you have so often partaken of?"

"We are not in need of such women," I repeated through gritted teeth.

"We shall see," the goddess replied, that self-assured grin mocking me. She offered her hands again and though I fought to keep Alexis' in mine, our fingers were separated, my hand treacherously lifting to take one of Aphrodite's as Alexis took her other. "Come, we have much to do before the dark greets us."

My arms and legs suddenly felt as if invisible strings pulled them towards the ground, though my feet lifted off the stony path and we flew upwards. The path, plain and mountain disappeared as we were plunged into darkness. I opened my mouth to question, to call for Alexis or Aphrodite, but my jaw remained as rigid as my limbs were against my body. The pressure around me grew and I closed my eyes against the wind that whipped through my hair, blowing it into my eyes and stinging me with its fierceness. A moment later I succumbed to Hypnos' realm, my last thought of Alexis.

*

I woke to find myself sitting alone in a cavernous room of what I could only assume was Aphrodite's temple. "Alexis!" I screamed. "Aphrodite, return her to me!"

Silence greeted my words as the echoing demand faded. There was a small wooden door set in the marbled wall and I stood and crossed to it. I pulled at the handle but it was locked; obviously from the other side as no timber sat in place on my side. I blew out a deep breath and ran a hand through my hair, turning around again.

I realized I must be in the entrance of the temple where, in other places I had visited for such a purpose, requests were made and coins exchanged. A double set of doors stood at one end of the room and when I opened them, they swung easily, revealing the mountain and a number of small houses nearby. The wall hid everything else, though the path Alexis and I had been following earlier ran away to the left and right when I pushed up onto my toes to look for it.

I closed the doors again and took in the stark, white room; there was no furniture, the only color coming from the lit torches and bunches of yellow and white narcissus flowers set at intervals along the walls. Incense permeated the air just as it had at Asclepius' temple in Epidaurus, the woody scent of the frankincense tickling my nose.

Three stone statues in a shade barely darker than the walls and floor sat against the opposite wall to the double doors and when I neared, I found them named; Aphrodite, Helios and Eros. Though I had never seen either of the other gods, the image of Aphrodite was frighteningly accurate, leading me to believe that their carvings would be as well. Eros, the God of Love, was to the left, a large bow held in his hand. The sun-god Helios was said to see all, including Aphrodite's affair with Ares many winters ago, and he stood between the other two, though why Aphrodite would want his statue in her temple I could only imagine.

Aphrodite's knowing grin and suggestive pose leered out from the white face and briefly I considered tapping the stone to see if it were solid or the goddess herself. "You may be a goddess, Aphrodite, but if she is harmed …" I warned, leaning close. The opening of the small door was my only answer, though it was neither Alexis nor the goddess who emerged. "Who are you?" I demanded, reaching for my sword and drawing it out of its sheath. "Where is Alexis?"

The young woman paused just inside the room, her eyes focused on the sharpened blade. "You have no need for weaponry here," she informed me. "We deal in love and pay with coin, not swords."

"Where is Alexis?" I asked again, stalking towards her, the tip of my weapon lifting her chin. "Where is Aphrodite? I demand to speak with her."

"Our goddess is always here, though she does not appear to us, save for when each of us arrives in her service. At that time we look upon her and she teaches us all we must know to carry out our duty in her name. As for your friend, she is being prepared."

"Prepared for what?" I scowled, lowering my sword ever so slightly.

"I have been sent to take you to the baths. You too must prepare yourself for the choosing."

"Take me to Alexis."

"I cannot. I do not know where they have taken her."

"Then find out."

"It is not my duty, that task belongs to another."

I pressed the blade against her neck. "Not good enough. Find Alexis and take me to her."

"Please, I ... I have my orders. I cannot incur my goddess' wrath."

"You shall incur *my* wrath if you do not aid me," I warned.

"You are a warrior and possess strength far greater than my own. I have no doubt you could harm me if that is what you intended, but I do not answer to you. I answer to Idylla and Goddess Aphrodite. Disappointing them fills me with far more fear than the threat of harm from you does."

"Does it?" I asked, lifting an eyebrow in challenge.

"Please. Your questions shall be answered in time, but we must make our way to the baths. You must look your best."

"Why?" I frowned.

She dropped her eyes from me then. "No one wishes to be overlooked when it comes time." My frown deepened, but she elaborated no further, keeping her eyes from mine. I began to replace my sword, then changed my mind. Reaching out, I grabbed the girl and drew her against my chest as I held the blade across her neck.

"Aphrodite! Show yourself or I cut her throat," I yelled.

"Please, there is no need for violence. W–" the girl's words faded out as a flash of light announced her goddess' presence.

"Skylar, Skylar, Skylar," Aphrodite grinned, crossing her arms over her chest. "You must trust me. Do you believe I knew nothing of your feelings for your princess as you attempted to deny yourself of them? I saw it all, every whim, every desire, every *action*, including the first in the bathing room at Trachis."

I released my hold on the girl and stepped towards Aphrodite, my sword aimed at her heart. "Take me to Alexis."

Aphrodite laughed, her fingers closing around my blade and pushing it aside as she approached. She raised her hand to trace the line of my jaw and though I attempted to lift mine to block her touch, I was once again unable to move.

"I know how much you care for Alexis, what lengths you would go to, to ensure she remains safe. You love her fiercely and deeply; your passion and desire for her as strong as only a few I have witnessed. Believe me when I tell you that you shall soon be reunited with your beloved. But before it is so, you must go to the bathing area and prepare yourself for her. Do it without incident, and without bringing harm to those who serve me here or I shall not look favorably upon the two of you."

Before I could reply, Aphrodite vanished in the same blinding light she had arrived in and I stumbled forward. I drew a deep breath, blowing it all the way out again as my arm obeyed my wish and I returned my sword to my thigh. I was silent a few moments more as I contemplated the goddess' words. If the only way to see Alexis again was to go along compliantly, then I would do so. For the time being at least.

I turned back to the girl. "Take me to the baths." She nodded once and led me through the marble halls.

# 17

I stood at least half a foot taller than the women on either side of me, needlessly adjusting my bronze cuirass and the crimson-colored tunic I wore beneath. My hair had been re-plaited and was kept up off my neck with golden hairclips. My feet remained bare, but the floor beneath was warm, as was the room itself. There must have been close to two hundred girls lined up either side of me and they wore simple white chitons with sparkling necklaces and anklets in gold, which matched the belts at their waists. None of them looked as out of place as I felt. They paid little attention to me now, but their eyes had strayed curiously over my outfit and muscular figure when I had first entered the room.

Kalika – the young woman who had met me in the entrance of the temple – had tended me at the bathing area. She washed the travelling dust from my body and hair and coated my skin with soft oil as an older woman prepared my cuirass and sheath in a similar manner, less the oil. Kalika spoke of why they prepared me as they did, and what she told me had me leaping clear of the bath and rushing out the heavy wooden door, calling for Alexis and cursing Aphrodite.

I did not get far before Aphrodite appeared, freezing my limbs, and returning me to Kalika, repeating that I was to do as instructed and bathe before going to stand with the other hetairai in the main room. She said if I refused to do as she requested, she would ensure I never saw Alexis again. I did not doubt her words, given the ease with which she had transported me twice, and allowed Kalika to clean and dress me without further outburst, the older woman returning my weapons and cuirass once I was dressed.

When it was time, I followed Kalika into the larger room and took my place among the women, waves of sickness passing over me as I thought of what was to come.

The hetairai whispered excitedly amongst themselves, speculating over who they waited for; the temple closed to all others this day. Was it a king? A prince? A rich nobleman looking for a lover he would lavish expensive gifts on? Perhaps it was a great hero to rival Heracles or Theseus. I remained silent, afraid I would lose the small amount of food Kalika had made me eat; knowing it was to be Alexis who chose from the gathered group.

Alexis and the woman she chose would be taken to a prepared room where they would remain until they grew tired of one another, at which time Alexis would be allowed leave the temple. I hoped Alexis had, at first, refused to go through with the choosing, but being that we were all now lined up, I had to assume Aphrodite had threatened her with never seeing me again – just as she had me – and Alexis had agreed to what the goddess asked of her to ensure that did not happen. At least I hoped that was why we were all now here.

The women around me passed skyphoi of opium to one another, each dipping a finger in and licking off the drops of juice. The drug was collected from the poppy flowers Kalika told me grew abundantly nearby for the sole purpose of enhancing the experiences of those who came to the temple. I had heard of the effects, though never felt the need to partake of it myself. A woman next to me spoke loudly of just that, stating that if she was fortunate enough to be chosen, the lover would not wish to leave without her. My fists clenched and I ground my back teeth together, my response silenced as a flash of light announced a new presence; Aphrodite. None of the women registered her appearance, though I had no idea how that was possible.

"Take the opium, Skylar," she said, indicating the skyphos Kalika offered. "It shall provide you with nothing but pleasure. It shall take away the pain and fear I see swirling inside you." I said nothing but slapped the skyphos from her hand. Though I knew Aphrodite spoke true, I wanted to keep a clear head. I had no intention of allowing Alexis to be with anyone else; goddess or not, I would find a way to deny it from being so.

"As you wish," Aphrodite laughed, disappearing again.

Kalika bent down and retrieved the skyphos, another woman stepping to her side to refill it before it continued down the line. "Skylar, please, do not be afraid," she said. "You and Alexis were sent to us for a reason, our head priestess …"

"How do you know we were sent here?" I frowned.

"Apologies, I speak out of turn."

I gripped her arms hard. "How do you know we were sent here?" I repeated.

She stuttered, unable to form the words until I shook her. "R-Rhoda, the girl who met you out on the path. She is my sister. We share all, even here." I released her again, knowing it was not Kalika I wished to take my anger out on. "You do not believe your lover shall choose you?" Kalika asked quietly.

I surveyed the women around us. They were beautiful and, though I was experienced, they were far more so. They were confident too, knowing how to wear the expensive material just as well as Alexis did, though that was not the talent which saw them so eagerly sought after, not what Alexis would choose them for.

I suddenly felt even more out of place in my armor and I dropped my eyes to my bare feet. How could I be certain she would choose me when we appeared to be at the mercy of the gods and what they determined our path to be at this moment? "I do not know," I finally replied.

The door at the end of the room opened and I raised my eyes to find another woman entering. "That is our head priestess, Idylla," Kalika whispered, the voices quieting around us.

I nodded distractedly, my eyes finding the elegant form of Alexis following the priestess. She wore a white chiton similar to the other women in the room, her hair kept from her face in a braid around her head in the same style Hesper had done mine the night of the banquet, a pair of leather sandals just visible beneath her clothing. She kept her eyes on the floor but paused when Idylla touched her arm and addressed the room.

"Ladies, I present to you a very honored guest; the Princess of Thermopylae." A murmur passed through the women around me, though it was not discontent they expressed, but eagerness as they admired Alexis' sleek form.

"The princess comes to us in the hope of new experiences, knowledge, and above all, enjoyment. Each of you shall be presented to her, and when she has seen you all, she shall speak of who she wishes to take to a private room."

A deep stab of fear pierced at my insides and I clenched my jaw. I attempted to step out of the line but was denied the action; Aphrodite appearing and shaking her head in a mock scold as she grinned.

"The coupling of the princess and one of the women here this day shall honor our goddess," Idylla continued, unaware of my attempts to move or speak. "Princess, I give you the finest two hundred hetairai of our temple. Allow us to begin so you may make your choice." Alexis nodded, finally raising her eyes to the long line of women. She focused only on the one in front of her as Idylla spoke the woman's name and gave Alexis reason to consider her.

My jaw tightened painfully when Idylla asked several women to disrobe, though Alexis touched none, even when Idylla suggested she could or should.

The hetairai were not shy in their presentations, especially those who shed their chitons, confident in their gifts as well as the desirousness of their bodies. Alexis looked over each, occasionally gifting one of them with a smile, though I could not read what was on her face; which of the women she had preference for, if any.

Finally, she arrived in front of me. I held my breath. Idylla spoke my name and, without thought of doing so, I stepped forward unimpeded as the others had before me. I swallowed loudly as Alexis' eyes met mine. Was this what Asclepius meant when he sent us here – was this what I had to allow Alexis to do – be with a woman as I had before we met? If I allowed it, would it then be easier for me to allow her to lie with a man and have the child we wished for gifted to us? I could not imagine it to be so and I had to work at controlling the shortness of my breath the thoughts caused.

"Do you wish to see this one naked?" Idylla whispered, leaning close to Alexis. She only nodded in reply. "Remove your weapon and armor," Idylla ordered.

I did as asked, laying my cuirass and sword on the floor beside me. When I straightened again, Alexis reached for the fibula at my shoulder and drew it from the tunic before Idylla had the chance. Her fingertips brushed the point of my collarbone, but her face remained impassive.

"A warrior. Strong of will and body. In her you shall find strength and tenderness at once," Idylla reported loudly for all to hear. "Passion and intensity encompasses all she does. A generous lover. Loyal. Willing to do whatever she must to ensure those entrusted to her remain safe."

I swallowed again as Alexis' eyes ran the length of my body, the dark centers growing large and overtaking the green. Just as I had been tracking Alexis as she neared, so too had the other women. They watched our exchange, several murmuring their appreciation at what lay beneath my tunic as I stood unclothed before them all.

When Alexis' eyes reached mine again she offered me a smile. I returned it tightly, my arms refusing to obey when I attempted to reach out and take her hand. I opened my mouth to implore her to choose me, but no sound came out and Idylla moved Alexis to Kalika beside me; the moment gone.

Without the ability to speak or move, other than to return to my place in line, it was another excruciating half candlemark before Alexis reached the end. Idylla had encouraged fifteen further women to remove their chitons, and though jealousy heated my veins as I watched my lover take in their forms, she removed none of them herself as she had mine.

Aphrodite remained in the room but did not speak to me and I refused to meet her gaze or the taunting smile I knew she wore. Idylla guided Alexis back to the head of the line, Alexis' eyes remaining on her feet.

"You have seen the finest we have to offer here. You have the name of the woman you wish to be with?"

"Yes," Alexis replied, her voice catching.

My breath refused to steady as I waited for Alexis to answer. I could not bear the thought of another's hands on her, of bringing her pleasure. Before me, no woman had touched Alexis. None had brought her the pleasures I had, that I wanted to, until my days in this world were done. With so many beautiful women, so many choices for her, why would she not want to experience passion and pleasure with one of them? But how would I touch her when she returned to me knowing that she had craved the touch of another? I squeezed my eyes shut, hot tears stinging the backs of them as my chest rose and fell sharply.

When I opened my eyes again, Alexis had leaned in close to Idylla, whispering the answer in her ear. Idylla stepped back, eyebrows raised. "You are certain?"

"Yes," Alexis assured her.

"Very well. I shall have a room prepared," Idylla nodded.

She caught the attention of a woman at the edge of the room before leading Alexis out. The hetairai who had discarded their chitons gathered them up again and made their own way out the way we had come in. I stood in place, unable to move, though I knew my limbs would obey if I asked it of them. I needed to know who Alexis had chosen. Who she had found desirable. Who she would allow to touch her so intimately. My voice refused to come out but when Kalika attempted to usher me outside I broke her grip, turning to Aphrodite.

"Who?" I demanded, in no doubt the goddess would know what I meant.

"Who do you address?" Kalika asked, confused.

"Leave," I told her.

"But, Skyl–"

"Just go," I repeated, shoving her towards the door. With another mystified look about the room, Kalika left, closing the door softly. "Who did Alexis name?" I asked again.

"Can you not guess?" Aphrodite taunted. "Of all the women here, you must know to whom your lover would be attracted to."

My jaw clenched as did my fists and I took a step towards her. "Alexis shall *not* take any hetaira to bed. Not today. Not ever."

"You cannot change what the princess has chosen." I advanced again, but Aphrodite waved her hand and I found myself frozen in place once more. "Return to the room where Kalika dressed you. When the time comes, you shall be sent for."

"Tell me who she named," I demanded. Aphrodite laughed and disappeared in a flash of light, my limbs unfreezing again. "Aphrodite!" I screamed, my words bouncing off the marble walls.

# 18

A candlemark later, I was back in the hallway outside the room I had dressed in. I had searched unsuccessfully for Alexis since Aphrodite disappeared from the choosing room, my anger growing with every step I took. "Aphrodite, show yourself!" I screamed. "You promised Alexis and I would be reunited."

"And you were; in the choosing hall," the goddess laughed as she appeared in front of me.

I raised my sword, the tip pressing against her throat just shy of piercing the skin. "I want to know where she is. We are leaving. Tell me now or I shall kill every hetairai in this place until I find her."

Aphrodite's smug smile faltered and a deep frown furrowed her brow as she disarmed me with a flick of her hand and stalked forward. She wrapped her fingers around my throat and picked me up, slamming me against the stone wall as she snarled.

"Listen to me, Mortal, there is much you do not understand. There are gods who favor you for talents you do not even know you possess yet but know this; if you harm even *one* of my girls you shall find yourself without your beloved forever."

"What talents? What gods?" I gasped.

"As with all, you shall learn of it in time. But I warn you; do not test my patience or threaten the women of my temple again." She released me and I dropped the short way to the ground, rubbing at my throat. Aphrodite retrieved my sword from the ground and relieved me of my cuirass before she spoke again. "Return to the room as I told you to or you shall never see

Alexis again. Do I make myself clear?" I nodded, fear now firmly replacing the anger. "Good," she murmured, disappearing again and taking my weapon with her.

My shoulders slumped and I reluctantly headed for the room, wondering how I could possibly remain there when Alexis was in another with someone else.

"Where have you been?" Kalika asked when I entered a moment later.

"Looking for Alexis," I replied quietly.

"You did not find her?"

"No."

"Good."

"Good?" I repeated in horror. "How is that good?"

"Alexis has chosen someone and neither of you can leave until the deed is completed. It is what our goddess wishes for." I squeezed my eyes shut, wishing that could block out the truth of it. "Come, Idylla seeks to speak with you."

"I do not wish to speak with her, besides, Aphrodite says I must remain here and wait."

"The time for waiting is now over. Kalika, you may leave us." I turned, finding Idylla in the open doorway behind me. Kalika lowered her eyes and, with a nod to her priestess, left the room without further words. "You have many questions, though I cannot speak of all you wish to know. There is much you must discover for yourself," Idylla mused, though I had asked her nothing.

"Who did Alexis choose? Who did you take to her room?" I asked.

"That is not for me to speak of. She shall do so when the time comes."

"Please. I believed I could stop Alexis from taking one of your women to bed. I know now that is not possible for if I attempt it, your goddess shall ensure I never see her again. But she belongs to *me* Idylla. I–"

"You speak of Alexis as though she is a possession. Is that how you see her?" Idylla asked, though she was not unkind.

"I ... no," I replied, exhaling a long breath. "I love her dearly, as she loves me. I am certain she would have spoken to you of that. Aphrodite is the goddess of *love*, why would she encourage another to come between us?"

The priestess regarded me a long moment before she replied. "Only *you* can allow another to come between the two of you."

"What do you mean? I would never allow it to be so."

"You already do."

"Do not speak in riddles. Tell me what you mean," I demanded, my anger returning.

Idylla did not reply, turning on her heel and leaving the room instead. "Come," she called when she realized I did not follow her. I blew out another long breath but left the room, the frown I wore etched deep into my brow. It appeared priestesses' were as cryptic as immortals. Idylla waited at the end of the corridor, continuing again before I reached her.

We saw no one as we travelled along the hallways and up numerous sets of stairs. Doors to rooms along the way were closed and no sounds came from within. I wondered how, in a place where a thousand women lived, it could be so quiet. After a while, Idylla stopped outside another closed door. I had been paying close attention to where we went as we walked, and knew it was not a section I had looked for Alexis in.

"This is where you are supposed to be," Idylla said, facing me again. "You must forget everything outside this room, everything that has happened this day. Now there is just the two of you. Give yourself fully to the woman you find inside. Allow yourself the pleasure she bestows in return."

"If Alexis is not inside then I cannot do that," I insisted.

"Be present in the moment. Do not waver or fear that this is not what is meant for you. Our great goddess is infinite in her wisdom. Trust her even if you do not trust my words."

"I cannot," I whispered. For me there would never be anyone but Alexis. She owned my heart and my soul and I would never kiss anyone else, let alone take them to bed.

"You must," Idylla replied, squeezing my forearm briefly before moving away again. "You cannot leave," she added, indicating the transparent wall which suddenly shimmered around me.

"What is this?" I asked, reaching out my hand, but stopping short of actually touching it.

"Go inside Skylar. Your time here at the temple should not be wasted," Idylla directed as she walked away.

I turned to the solid wooden door. Three strips of bronze ran across the top, bottom and middle; the same as the entrance doors at Agrias' palace and I wondered how much would have changed between Alexis and me by the time we returned.

I drew a deep breath. I placed my fingers on the handle and pushed open the door. The room was warm, a breeze blowing in through the open archway on the opposite side, shifting the light material which hung between the two areas, in turn hiding and revealing the outline of someone standing on the balcony. The sun was setting on the opposite side of the temple but bathed the room and balcony beyond in an orange glow.

A large bed stood to my right, a tall table between it and the wall holding a number of pyxides, amphorae and pleasure-enhancing items I recognized well. Another table stood against the far wall beside the arch and a second archway led to another room. I closed the door quietly and stepped through the billowing linen.

I took in the delicate form, blowing out the breath I had been holding as relief flooded through my body, loosening the knot in my stomach. She stood, a long, green chiton even finer than the one she had back in Trachis reaching past her toes to pool on the marbled ground beneath our feet. Her hands lay atop the stone wall level with her waist and she looked out over the city of Corinth and the gulf which lay to its north. The gentle wind lifted the hair at her neck and I caught her familiar flowery sweetness.

She did not turn as I approached, nor when I placed my hands on her hips. "Alexis," I breathed, pressing my lips against her neck and drawing in the spicy undercurrent of her favored perfume. There was no one else's scent mixed in with hers.

"You kept me waiting. Perhaps I did not choose wisely," she said, though I heard the smile in her voice.

"I … I … apologies," I stammered. "I did not know you had chosen me," I added in a whisper.

"For someone so smart, sometimes you can be so dense," she murmured, turning in my arms, her grin widening. Her eyes roamed over my face before dropping to the tunic I wore. "How could I not choose you?" she asked, twining her fingers with mine and drawing me even closer. "You were the most beautiful woman there."

"There were many beauties. You did not wish to experience them?"

"You would have wanted me to?" she asked, a sudden frown creasing her forehead.

"Never," I replied, smoothing the skin of her brow. "But … I… "

"I only want you Skylar. Forever. Even here where I had the choice of so many others, I chose *you* because for me there shall never be anyone else."

"Oh," I murmured. "For me as well."

She pushed up onto her toes and kissed me gently, her hands resting on my waist. "How could you doubt me so?" she asked, though her tone was not accusatory.

I drew a breath. "Sometimes it is hard to believe I am fortunate enough to have you love me. That someone could love me though I have caused them suffering so it could be so," I replied, tracing the line of her jaw.

Her face softened and she took my hand, kissing the palm. "You wanted me, fought for me. If suffering for a time led me to be able to have you, then I would gladly do so again."

"But you should not have to suffer for me," I insisted.

"Hush now," she said, placing her fingers over my lips. "It is time we prepared for the night ahead." I opened my mouth to speak again, but she covered my lips with her own, her hands pulling me against her body. I sighed as her tongue entered and mingled with mine. When we parted, she smoothed a hand over the fabric at my waist. "I knew a tunic in that shade would be perfect on you. I believe it is the same shade you wore to the banquet. The night you spoke of your love for me." She kissed me again.

"It is very similar," I agreed. "You look beautiful as well, you wear the color I most favor on you," I said, noting how the material accentuated every rise and curve.

"I know," she smiled shyly, her eyes dropping from mine. "Though if memory serves, you enjoy removing it from my skin even more."

"Indeed," I agreed with a grin, tightening my hold on her. "Perhaps the time for words is over."

"Not yet. We must make our offerings to Aphrodite," she replied, placing a hand on my chest, my heartbeat increasing beneath her fingers.

"She is not my favored goddess at this moment. She would not give me answers to anything I asked of her about where you were."

"I am certain she had her reasons."

I only grunted in reply as Alexis unwrapped herself from me and took my hand, her other drawing her chiton up so she did not trip on it. A pair of leather sandals peeked out from beneath the material as she led the way to the table just inside the archway.

A torch sat on the wall and Alexis lit it, pouring liquid from an amphora into the dish above the flickering flame. "What is that?" I asked.

"One of Aphrodite's favored scents. The incense combined with our prayer are to encourage and strengthen the love we have for one another, and to join us as we celebrate such love."

I leaned in close, sniffing at the incense. "I detect the hint of rose you wear, and the fresh scent of nardus as was in the incense at Asclepius' temple."

"Yes. Idylla told me they are coupled with sandalwood, bergamot oranges and basil. You find it pleasing?"

"I do," I replied, stepping back.

Alexis took a bunch of narcissus, lotus and rose flowers and began picking off a number of petals from each. I wrapped my arms around her waist again, resting my chin on her shoulder to watch as she worked. "Idylla told me a prayer we must speak when we add the flower petals to the incense."

"Shall I repeat it after you?" I asked, holding my hand out.

"Yes," she nodded, handing me a palm full and placing the stems aside on the table. "Ready?"

"When you are," I replied.

"O most beautiful goddess Aphrodite
Desired, loved and worshipped for your
Powers of wanton abandon and passion
We seek your guidance in aiding our expressions of love
With one another as well as grant us the power

To give and receive the love we both require
Accept our offerings of these flowers
And allow your love to fill our beings, though we are mere mortals."

I repeated the words, adding my petals to the ones Alexis dropped into the incense and watching as they shriveled in the heated oil.

Alexis turned in my embrace and laced her arms around my neck. "The adjoining room has a large bath which I had drawn for us, though being you took so long to come to me, I fear the water shall not be as warm as you would prefer," she grinned.

"If you are in it with me, it shall be more than warm enough," I assured her, leaning forward to kiss her soundly, allowing her teasing about my tardiness to slide. Deep stirrings of desire began in my stomach as Alexis' breath heated my mouth and my tongue explored in return. Her fingers stroked the exposed nape of my neck and I tightened my grip, feeling her heat radiate through the linen against my leg.

"I hoped you would say that," she smiled. "Come on."

"Wait," I grinned, grabbing her hand to halt her departure. "Allow me to undress you first."

"Gladly," she replied, returning my smile.

# 19

I took a handful of Alexis' chiton and raised it to expose her dainty feet, guiding her backward to the bed with my other hand against her hip. When the back of her thighs met the light blanket on top, Alexis took the length of material I held and kept it above her ankles as I dropped to one knee.

I slowly drew first one, then the other sandal from her feet. Sliding the linen higher, I pressed my lips against her calf, my tongue snaking over her knee. I felt the shiver run through Alexis and smiled, returning to stand before her. I took the hairclip from the back of her head, setting it aside on the bed and unravelling the braid from her brow, separating the strands until the soft, brown mass sat over her shoulders, a gentle wave through the normally straight tresses.

Brushing my lips over hers again, I moved down to the exposed flesh of her throat and the point that pulsed invitingly beneath the skin. Alexis removed the pin holding my own hair from my neck and wrapped her fingers around the nape, pulling my lips harder against her. My hands wandered up her sides and over the soft swell of her breasts, a solitary finger from each hand drawing a teasing line along her collarbones before meeting in the hollow between.

Alexis' chest rose and fell in quick succession as I pressed my thigh between hers, her eyes fluttering shut when I kissed her mouth. Her hands twisted in the fabric at my waist before searching for the ends of the short material and pulling it up so she could slide her hands beneath. I stepped away and her eyes flew open in consternation.

I smirked and lifted an eyebrow, my fingers tracing the line of her jaw and over her lips, which parted with a soft sigh. "It appears you are the one with little patience now," I teased.

"I have wanted you since before we arrived here, as you well know," she replied.

"I recall," I smiled. "Though it was you who denied me of your body, stating you wished to wait until we reached Corinth."

"And here we are and I would wait no longer," she growled, grabbing the front of my tunic, pulling me to her and straddling my thigh as she pushed herself against me.

"As always I am helpless to deny you of your every wish, my princess," I whispered, taking her bottom lip between my teeth and tugging ever so gently. "You wish to be free of your clothing?" I murmured close to her ear.

"No teasing … please. I need you. Right now," Alexis insisted, her fingers digging into my chest. Fire raced through my veins and I relented, ripping the fibula from her chiton and throwing it aside, not caring where it landed as I dragged the material down her heated body. My hands slid back up, my eyes following every inch of the way. I lifted her onto the bed, lowering myself on top of her.

"You wear too much," she complained, pulling at the pin at my shoulder. I pushed myself to my knees, stripping the material from my body. Alexis' hands instantly skidded over my stomach and hips and pulled me back down. I kissed her, driving my tongue between her lips and a thigh between hers. She arched beneath me, and I allowed her to set the pace of our lovemaking, my breath shortening each time her hot, wet flesh made contact with my own.

I knew she would not last much longer when she dug her fingers into my back and her movements quickened against me. I broke our kiss, her eyes opening and meeting mine as I pushed against her. "Skylar," she panted, her body soaring to its highest point, stiffening her back before sending her diving over the other side and into pleasurable oblivion.

She whispered my name and I pressed against her, knowing it would not take much for me to join her in the abyss that awaited me. As if sensing it, she reached between us, her fingers sliding through me and into the warmth she found. I gasped but pressed down onto her, calling out her name as I found my own release.

As my body relaxed in the aftermath, Alexis retrieved her hand, resting it at the small of my back. I remained where I was, keeping my weight from her by propping myself on my elbows. I kissed her again, slower this time, my tongue caressing her lips rather than possessing her as it had before. "You still wish for that bath?" I asked.

"Perhaps," she smiled, dragging her thigh against my still sensitized skin.

"Though I find I am most comfortable right here."

"Gods," I gasped, my eyes closing at the sensations she was creating within me again. "You are insatiable."

She laughed, exposing her throat to me and I leant down, catching the skin in my mouth and sucking gently. "You make it so. Are you complaining?"

I smiled and shook my head. "Never."

"Good," she whispered, placing her hand under my chin and drawing my mouth back to hers. "Then love me again."

"It would be my pleasure." I kissed her, my hand finding her breast, the nipple rising beneath my palm as I squeezed the soft flesh.

"Gods, yes," she groaned as I separated our mouths and slid down her body. I licked at the soft flesh between her stomach and hip, her breath shortening as her wetness found my chest. The pulsing between my thighs quickened when she tangled a hand in my hair and pushed me lower still, her hips lifted in offering. I dipped my head to taste her, working my mouth against her as I grinded the lower half of my body against the bed.

With my mouth I drove Alexis on, following her as she climbed higher, her hand tightening against my head as she peaked, repeating my name again and again. I moved against the bed, wanting to reach my own end, but Alexis touched my cheek. "Allow me," she said when my eyes met hers. We swapped positions, the rising pressure between my thighs threatening to erupt as soon as her mouth met my heated flesh.

"Oh gods, Alexis," I cried, holding tightly to her. "Please." She released me momentarily, a shiver of anticipation running down my spine before she drove her fingers inside and her tongue resumed its ministrations. I lost myself to the powerful spasms my lover drew from deep within and surrendered to the tightening of every muscle in my body.

When the last shudder left me, Alexis returned to my side and we lay face to face. "Do you know how hard it was not to reach out and touch you as you stood in that line?" she whispered, her fingertips caressing my neck.

"I wanted to take your hand," I replied, resting my hand on her hip. "But I could not move; Aphrodite kept me firmly in place."

"I believe if you had, I would have kissed you right there, the rules I was supposed to follow be damned," she smiled, sliding closer to nibble at my throat. I returned her grin, but Alexis spoke again before I had the chance to ask her about those rules. "And I was not the only one admiring the view."

"Indeed?" I murmured as her teeth grazed me.

"Oh yes. You are an impressive sight to behold when you wear your armor, but even more magnificent when completely naked. Had I not chosen you, I imagine there would have been many who requested your company this evening."

"I would not have done anything with them, I assure you. They hold no interest to me."

Alexis paused in her kisses, though her mouth remained where it was. "Am I enough for you?" she asked quietly.

"What?" I frowned.

She drew her head back so she could capture my eyes again, though they soon dropped to my neck. "Our relationship is new, but what if, in time, I am not enough for you? What if you crave to be with others as you have been before? Though you were just a child when you attended the festivals in Sunium, Delphi and Athens, you ... you partook of the specific ... er, *celebrations* which were offered, did you not?" I opened my mouth to reply, but she pressed on quickly. "It was no place for a child. To have you so near to so many drunken men was not right. You could have been hurt, they could have taken advantage of you, harmed you and scarred you and then you ..."

I reached up and took her fingers, squeezing them gently and silencing her words. "The men were strictly off-limits to me and I to them – my father insisted it be so and with his large frame, none dared defy him, and I certainly did not."

"And the women?" Alexis asked quietly.

"Them as well," I replied, lifting her chin so her gaze met mine. "When I found myself in the midst of those celebrations, I was the same age you were when you were first sent to Epirus. You would have had more experience than me by the time I was with a lover for the first time. But what would it have mattered if I had been with someone there?"

"They were strangers."

"How well did you know Basileios when you became his betrothed?" I asked, raising an eyebrow.

"That was different, he had been chosen for me. My father trusted that I would be safe with him," she argued, attempting to take her hand from mine.

"Your father had not seen Basileios in ten winters," I said, keeping hold of her firmly. "He could not know how you would be treated when you were in his home, in their village. His disposition could have mirrored Melanthios' after such a time. The same could have happened even if my father had allowed me to experiment with those who kept us company."

"It is not the same," Alexis insisted, and this time I allowed her to take her hand away and roll off the bed. "Basileios was my husband and you would have been with ..."

"Someone who was not, and never would have been, as with all my experiences," I finished, remaining on the bed but watching her closely. "You do not approve of the women I have been with, the slaves and hetairai? You must know they were not who I would have chosen during the festivals when I was fourteen winters old – I barely knew they existed at that time."

Alexis chewed at her lip, keeping her eyes from me and I blew out a deep breath, not wanting to fight with her. I got off the bed but did not reach out for her.

"Alexis, I had needs. Wants and desires, just as any young man or woman does. I am certain even *you* wished to feel the body of another against yours as you grew. But Kuria was my first experience with anyone. I had found myself attracted to girls previously, but after what happened to her I chose women because I believed them to be safer. Safer still was to only be with those I could pay for the privilege, who belonged to no one, who would never allow themselves to belong to anyone."

"The slaves would have belonged to someone else," she murmured, still refusing to meet my eyes.

I exhaled another long breath. "True, though not in the manner in which I speak of." I took her hand and pulled her closer. "And then you came along and turned everything upside down. I wanted to deny my growing attraction to you. I told myself I could not pursue you or spend time with you because I wanted to keep you safe. But I could not keep away or send you away when you came to me. I only wished that I had never known of what happened in Corinth. I wanted you to speak the words I so deeply wanted to hear and that we could be together without fear. I shall never need, or want, another, I promise you that. You broke me out of wanting those types of lovers. For me, you are all I shall ever need."

"I broke you?" Alexis asked, a grin sneaking out.

"You changed who I believed I was," I amended. "You challenged me to learn and embrace who I could be if I did not do what I always had, if I did not accept that being alone was all there could ever be for me. When Idylla brought me to this room tonight I did not want to enter. I did not want to be with anyone else. But she insisted I give myself fully to the one who waited here for me. I thought you would be somewhere else doing just that and I was devastated because it proved *I* was not enough for you."

Her face softened. "Skylar … That could never be so. You are the only one I shall ever want."

I leaned in and kissed her gently. "Good."

"Of course, we may not have had a choice. It is fortunate you were among those I had to choose from." I frowned, knowing that if Aphrodite had indeed wanted Alexis and me apart tonight, she would have.

I brought Alexis' hand up, pressing her knuckles against my lips in turn as I spoke. "If it had been so, and I had been made to be with another, my heart would not have been in it, I promise you that, sweetheart."

"I know. I am just glad it never came to be."

"Me too," I replied.

# 20

I sat in the bath, the water somehow still warm, which I guessed could only be courtesy of Aphrodite. Alexis was tucked in the vee of my legs and I drew a length of material across her shoulders and back, though neither of us were dirty; thanks to our baths before the choosing.

I placed a gentle kiss on Alexis' shoulder and set the linen aside, my hands playing over the soft skin of her stomach as she pressed herself back against me. "I am glad Basileios was kind to you, that he did not scare you when he came to you as your husband," I murmured.

"Until you, he was the only lover I had ever known. But you ... you have much more experience than me."

"Not with men. Does it bother you terribly that it is so?" I asked, my fingers making small circles across her ribs.

"No. But ... those implements on the table in the other room, you have used them before, with the women you have been with?"

My hands stilled and I hesitated, my eyes sliding through the doorway to the phalluses and belts which held them, before I replied. "Yes."

Alexis laid her head back against my shoulder, capturing my eyes with her own. "Did you enjoy using them?" she asked, her cheeks coloring.

I swallowed, uncertain where her line of questioning was leading, though I was given an inkling when her hand began to caress my inner thigh. "They were for the pleasure of the one I was with," I replied, attempting to keep my breathing steady.

"But you did not hesitate if their use was requested?"

"No."

"That is another area in which you are greatly experienced and skilled?"

"I suppose so." Alexis suddenly stood, stepping out of the bath and offering her hand.

"Why do you question me so?" I asked with a slight frown, taking her hand and joining her.

"It is a part of your past I want to know, to understand," she said, stepping forward to press her wet body the length of mine. "I want to experience the side of you they got to."

My frown deepened and I took a step back, unable to keep a clear head with her so near. "Why? There is no comparison between what you and I have and what I did with them. How I am with you is more than I ever gave to them. You know they never meant to me what you do. I did not love them, I simply used their bodies for release."

Alexis stepped towards me again, her fingers skittering over my stomach, an unmistakable heat beginning in my stomach. "I cannot imagine you made them feel used. I am certain you were a generous lover. They spoke often of enjoying what you did to them, did they not?" she asked, her fingers finding their way to my breast.

"Alexis." I gasped as she brought it to a point. "Why do you want to speak of this?" I put my hand on her waist and pulled her against me, her hand never stilling at my chest. I leaned close to whisper in her ear. "Those women are the last thing I want to think about now."

Alexis pushed her body against mine. "I believe they would have enjoyed their time with you, though *I* am fortunate enough to have you every night if that is my desire," she said quietly, her fingers tightening against my flesh again.

"You do," I breathed, feeling the pressure far lower.

She traced my collarbone with her tongue and I slid my hands to the small of her back as I began to move against her. "Tell me what you did to them," she pressed, her breath tickling my skin.

"Alexis," I breathed, further words refusing to come as she drew one of my thighs between hers.

"Show me," she insisted. "Use those things with me." She drew her head back to look at me. "Be inside me as you were with them. I want to feel you inside me in that manner." I regarded her silently. I could not deny I had always enjoyed the control I had had with those women. Paying for the privilege afforded me much of that of course, but the phalluses even more so. I had felt powerful. "Show me how you made them feel," Alexis added, tracing a finger along my bottom lip. "Be the powerful, sexy warrior I know you are. Own me."

A deep growl escaped my throat and I pulled Alexis' mouth to mine, driving my tongue deep inside with an intensity that lit the flames of desire warming my blood. I picked her up, carrying her to the bed and laying her on top of the covers without breaking our kiss. She wrapped her hand around the nape of my neck, urging me to follow her, but I resisted separating our lips and moving across to the small table instead.

Alexis' eyes widened as she propped herself up on her elbows, watching as I wrapped the belt around my waist and tightening it with certain fingers before attaching the leather piece in the groove designed for the purpose. I turned back to her, the pounding between my thighs heightening as her eyes roamed over my naked form and the attachment I wore. I reached into one of the dishes, coating my fingers with olive oil and applying it to the tip of the phallus.

Alexis moistened her lips with her tongue and I stalked around the end of the bed. Without warning I grabbed her ankles and pulled her down until her legs hung over the side. She gasped as I slid my hands beneath her back and pulled her up to sit before me, ensuring the phallus did not touch her. Yet.

I claimed her lips again, my hands at her breasts, stroking and teasing them as she had mine. With my knee I opened her legs, placing my palms on their inners as my tongue continued to possess her mouth, her hands at my neck and the side of my face, encouraging me on. I drew my fingers through her heat, feeling the moisture gathered there and groaning as it coated my fingers.

I leant forward slightly, guiding the phallus against Alexis as my hand had done, a moan escaping her when I pressed the tip inside. I broke our kiss, but moved against her slowly, her eyes finding mine when I pressed it inside her again.

"You are certain this is what you want?" I asked, the throbbing between my legs threatening to break the restraint I knew I needed to exercise.

"Yes," she breathed, her hands now both at the nape of my neck. "I want to feel you deep inside me."

I nodded, my fingers slipping in and drawing another gasp from Alexis. I drew out and repeated the action until Alexis' breathing shortened and her grip on me tightened. Keeping one hand at the small of her back, I guided the phallus inside with my other, pausing a moment to allow her to get used to the sensation. Her eyes widened slightly as they held mine but after a moment, they fluttered shut and she began to move, taking it the rest of the way inside her. I remained still, allowing her to control the rhythm, before pressing forward carefully when she lifted her hips.

"Skylar," she whispered, digging her nails into my skin as she wrapped her legs around my bottom.

As loathe as I was to take my eyes from her face, I wanted to watch as she moved against me. Alexis' back arched and she brought her body nearer to mine time and again, my own responding in kind. I closed my eyes, immediately wishing I had not: Melanthios inside Alexis as she cried helplessly, tied to the wood. *She enjoyed when I filled her and made her body tremble. She sought her end with me – her thoughts no longer with you or what you did to her.*

I opened my eyes again, my thrusts slowing. Did she truly yearn for a male lover? Had she enjoyed Basileios being inside her? Did she long for the times he came to her? Did she request it of him? Did he go to her often? I stilled, trying to dislodge the words that swirled tormentingly inside my head. Is it why she suggested Thaddeus aid us with a child, because she wanted to feel him inside her? *You believe you have won, but you have not. I have ruined her for you ... She shall never have your touch without thought of me.*

"Skylar?" Alexis' soft voice penetrated the images. "What is it?" Her movements slowed, then stopped altogether and I felt her wipe a tear from my cheek. I shook my head, pressing forward once more to drive the images away. "Skylar," she said again. I opened my eyes, meeting her concerned frown. "Stop," she insisted, softening the word by cupping my cheek. "Stop." I stilled. "Tell me what upsets you," she said quietly.

"I cannot," I whispered.

"Please. Did I hurt you? I do not understand how but ..."

"You did not hurt me."

She looked to the phallus between us, obviously attempting to find the source of my tears. "Then what is it?" Her eyes returned to mine as she unwrapped her legs and pushed me back ever so slightly. The phallus came free and only then did Alexis reach for my hand and draw me close again. Still I said nothing, Alexis catching another tear as it fell. "Skylar, please, you are frightening me."

I drew a shaking breath. I did not want to put words to what I feared. Would Alexis deny the enjoyment she had received from her husband, even though it would be a lie, or would she admit it was what she wished for, what she felt when I was inside her? I did not know which answer would be worse.

Alexis drew her legs up onto the bed and knelt before me, her eyes level with mine. "Speak to me," she pleaded, placing her hands either side of my face.

I drew another shaky breath. "I ... I am afraid it is not me you think of when I am inside you in such a manner." I admitted. "That you think of Basileios pleasuring you. That you want it to be him ... or even Thaddeus," I added in a whisper.

Alexis' mouth dropped open and I could see her struggling to form a response. Her chest rose and fell in quick succession as her brow furrowed. "I ... You ... No." Her hands tightened on my face. "No," she repeated, more forcefully. "No."

She released me, her hands balling into fists, and for a moment I wondered if she would hit me. I would not have stopped her. My stomach was roiling and I thought I might be sick if I moved or spoke. I wanted to take back my words. I wished I had the power to remove the thoughts.

Alexis closed her eyes and gathered herself as I stood motionless, waiting. When she opened her eyes again, she kept them on her hands. "Skylar, that … I cannot even …" She drew a deep breath and expelled it all the way out again. "How could you accuse me of that? Do you know how much it hurts to hear you say it?"

"I am sorry," I whispered.

"No. You do not speak now. You listen." She raised her eyes to mine, two dots of pink coloring her cheeks as her fists smacked against my breastbone. "Neither of us can change what is in our past; not who we have been with or what we have done with them. I accept that you have been with other women and you must accept that I was with Basileios, as was expected of me. As for Thaddeus, I have no desire to lie with him. None. I do not know how to make that any clearer."

"But to have a child …" I began, falling silent when Alexis' frown deepened and one of her fists hit me a little harder than before.

"If that is what must occur then I would take no pleasure in the act. It would be a means to an end and was all I could think of to gift us with something I wanted for you and me. How long is it going to take for you to understand, to *believe*, that I do not want anyone but you? You question me now, even when I chose you over all the others offered to me here."

"I am sorry," I said again. "I know you spoke the words earlier. I heard you. I did."

"Then *why* do you doubt me? When you were inside me, all I thought of was you, how it was an extension of you and how you loved me so deeply, so completely. When you filled me, I felt complete. Loved by you in a way no other has before."

"Really?"

"Yes," she replied, drawing my lips to hers and kissing me softly. "You are all I ever want. You are the only one I think of when we make love." She kissed me again, her hands sliding across my shoulders and down my arms.

"You are all *I* ever want," I breathed.

"You have me. But if you *ever* accuse me of thinking of someone else when I am with you, I shall … I shall … well I do not know what I would do, but you would not enjoy it," she promised. She drew her fingers lightly across my chest, her lips following. "I never want to be with anyone else. Never. Do you hear me?"

"Yes," I murmured as the slow fire began in the pit of my stomach.

"Good. Then allow me to prove it, to make love to you as you were to me."

Her hands went to the belt at my waist and through the haze of my renewed desire came a sudden stab of fear. "Alexis, I ... wait," I stammered, covering her hands.

"What is it?" she asked.

"I ... I have never ..." I fell silent again.

"You never allowed anyone to be inside you in that way?" she guessed.

"No," I agreed.

"Why?"

I shrugged. "I never asked it of them. I never wanted to be with them in that way."

Alexis straightened, placing her hands either side of my face again. "Then allow me to be the first. I want to be your first."

I raised my fingers to trace the line of her jaw, her words touching me deep inside and chasing away a fraction of my fear. "Yes," I managed, swallowing loudly.

Alexis' hands returned to the belt, but her eyes never left mine as she untied it. "Help me?" she asked, holding it up.

I nodded and she handed it to me as she stepped down off the bed. I tightened it at her hips and allowed her to push me gently backwards until I sat on the edge of the bed facing her. Another flutter of nerves gripped me. Alexis found my hands balled up tight on top of my thighs and opened them, drawing my palms to her lips and kissing each tenderly before placing them at her waist. "You made the first time we were together so special," she whispered. "It was new to me but I feared nothing because I knew you loved me. You would never hurt me. Allow me to return the favor." She opened my legs to stand between them and leaned forward to kiss me, her tongue languidly tracing my lower lip and sending pleasant sparks through my blood to gather and fire at the pit of my stomach.

She pulled back so our lips barely touched. "Allow me to love you as you love me. Completely. Passionately. Fiercely. Allow me inside to touch every part of you."

"How could I deny you when you ask it of me in such a way?" I smiled, sliding my hands from her waist up to her ribs and over her breasts.

She returned my grin almost shyly and placed another kiss on my lips. With only a single finger, she traced my collarbone and each breast, in turn teasing and caressing before continuing down my stomach to the top of my thigh.

My heartbeat quickened, the sound loud in my ears as Alexis dipped her head, her tongue following the path her hands had made down my body. She spent little time at my chest, concentrating instead on my stomach and the skin just above the dark hair between my legs.

I closed my eyes as her fingers made their patterns on the tops of my thighs, the intensity of my earlier desire flaring when her thumb brushed the space between. Alexis brushed the back of her hand over me and I groaned, lifting myself from the bed. She kissed the skin of my inner thigh, a solitary finger slipping through the wetness it found and I dropped my head back, my mind devoid of thought other than the feelings her touch inflamed.

Alexis' mouth began its return journey up my body and I slid my hand beneath the hair on her neck when our lips met again. "Are you ready for me to love you?" she asked when we parted. I swallowed but nodded.

"You shall need some oil on it," I directed quietly, my words wavering ever so slightly. Alexis nodded. I released her, resettling my hands beside my legs as she reached across to the small dish, immersing her fingers in the syrupy liquid and coating the phallus as I had.

With her other hand at my shoulder, she pushed me back until I lay flat on the bed. Her eyes remained on mine as she followed, lowering herself so our skin met. The feel of her excited my already heated body, and the soft leather of the phallus was warm and not entirely unpleasant as it pressed against my inner thigh.

Alexis put a hand between us, dragging her short nails up the inside of my thigh and through the lips at the apex, causing me to widen my legs beneath her. I drew in a deep breath, taking a fistful of the light blanket beneath as Alexis repositioned her body and pushed the phallus slowly into me as I had done to her.

"I love you," she whispered, holding my eyes. I nodded in return, unable to speak as my heart pounded wildly in my chest. "I belong to you. In your bed, at your side. There is no one between us, no one else in my heart just as there is no one but me in yours." I swallowed and nodded again. "I am going to love you for the rest of my days. I want you to feel how deeply."

I nodded a third time, inhaling a deep breath as she pushed into me slowly. She paused momentarily, her hand finding my breast and drawing her thumb over my nipple, sending a sudden jolt of pleasure lower and as I gasped with the sensation, she entered me further.

"I love you, Skylar," she whispered again, her hips rhythmically moving against me as mine began to do the same beneath her.

Releasing the blanket, I placed my hand at the back of her head, raising mine to kiss her as I settled the other on her bottom, drawing her even further into me as I wrapped my legs around hers. "I love you more," I murmured when we parted, the delicious beginning of my release snaking along my spine.

"You choose this moment to reassert your competitiveness?" Alexis grinned.

"Yes," I smirked, tightening the hold I had on her with my legs and rolling her over, my arms holding me above her as I pressed down. She placed her hands on my back, pushing up into me with each downward thrust I made.

"Feel me," she urged, reaching up to grab the skin of my shoulder in her teeth.

"Gods, Alexis. I do," I panted as my muscles tightened.

I gave myself up to the sensations having the phallus deep inside me created. I called her name as I fell over the precipice, the heat of her breath at my shoulder an anchor in the storm of emotions which crashed over me; joy, wonder, love, contentment, satisfaction.

As I regained my breath, I lifted myself from Alexis. She quickly undid the belt at her waist, throwing it aside and drawing my thigh between her own. I gasped at the heat and wetness, my eyes finding hers as I grinned. "My turn," she demanded before I found a suitable remark, thrusting my hand between us and groaning as I drove it inside her.

"My princess," I whispered before claiming her lips. Her body writhed beneath me as I loved her more entirely than I ever had before. She stiffened as I brought her closer to the end she so desperately sought until finally she fell against the blanket, her hand on mine loosening.

As her breathing slowed, I kissed her gently, rolling off her and out of the bed. "What are you …?"

I just smiled and kissed her again as I slid my arms beneath her body and lifted her up. She wrapped her arms around my neck as I pulled the covers back, placing her down again and crawling in beside her, drawing her against my chest and resettling the blanket over us.

"My warrior. My love," she whispered, placing a kiss on my chest.

I smiled and hugged her closer to me. "Always," I promised, closing my eyes as the first rays of dawn lit the balcony outside our room. Before Helios' light joined Eos' dawn on the marbled floor, I had slipped into Hypnos' realm, my mind devoid of dreams as I enjoyed the deepest and longest sleep I had had since Alexis and I left Trachis almost half a moon ago.

# 21

"When are they going to be done?" Ares complained, crossing his arms over his chest as he leant in the archway of the room.

His Chosen One lay on the large bed, the princess straddling her thighs, a seductive grin on her lips as she held up a rope, her eyebrows raised both in question and challenge.

"You know how it is with new love; you cannot get enough of one another," Aphrodite reminded him with a laugh. The goddess came in from the balcony, joining him in the doorway and sliding her hands over his shoulders to caress the coarse hairs on his chest, watching the two women.

"Besides, do we not still take to one another at every opportunity with the same fervor?" she asked, pressing her lips to his neck. "You notice the princess grows bolder in this place and your Chosen One does not appear to mind," she added, grinning as Alexis tied the rope first around Skylar's hands, then to the base of the metal torch holder on the wall above the bed.

"She allows much from her companion," Ares smiled, taking one of Aphrodite's hands and kissing the palm. "But honestly – a week? At this rate they shall not be able to travel from their constant … exertions and I am eager to have them on their way. I grow impatient to have my battle with Father."

"Trust me; their time here has been well spent, as I knew it would be when I suggested it."

"How could you know they would speak of everything they have?"

"Asclepius was not the only one keeping close watch on them in Epidaurus. I saw the depth of their love, their devotion to one another. I knew then that Alexis would, without a doubt, select no one other than Skylar if she was presented in a ceremony with other women. I have to admit though, the incense I had them prepare was more potent than I intended; I did not expect them to speak of their fears or past lovers their very first night.

"But Skylar's strength for who you need her to be can only be achieved with Alexis at her side, not apart as you first suggested. Somehow, I knew if I placed them together and created the right atmosphere they would speak of what they kept inside, that what they feared most would arise as they enjoyed the pleasures of one another's bodies ... and of course I gave them the tools and desires to bring about such conversations."

Ares grinned. "You certainly did. The phallus, the rope there," he noted, indicating the items. "You ensured they were in here so Alexis would ask Skylar about them, about her past and those she had been with? To share that part of herself with her new lover?"

"Yes, and in return, Skylar had to accept and believe once and for all that Alexis loved her, no matter what or who her past held. She had to have Alexis show her, prove it in a way no other lover had."

"She appears a little uncertain about letting her princess hold her captive in such a manner," Ares smiled, watching as Skylar struggled in the restraints, her eyes never leaving Alexis' hands as they caressed her own breasts and stomach.

"Just wait," Aphrodite grinned.

As the immortals watched, Alexis' touches moved lower over her body, her eyes fluttering shut as they reached the apex of her thighs and she lifted herself ever so slightly off Skylar's legs. Skylar's breathing matched the princess' but before Alexis could bring herself to her end, Skylar wrenched her hands free of the bindings and pulled Alexis down on top of her, taking her lips in a crushing kiss.

"Your Chosen One does not remain out of reach of her beloved for long," Aphrodite laughed.

"Indeed," Ares agreed. "Look out!" he added, grabbing Aphrodite by the waist and dragging her out of the way.

Skylar, with Alexis wrapped around her upper body, crossed the room, placing Alexis' back against the stone wall beside the arch as she pressed into her.

Aphrodite drew her lover's face from the couple to meet hers. "I shall appear to them in the morning and tell them it is time to leave. In the meantime, why do we not enjoy our own delights far from here?"

"Another perfect idea," Ares said, placing his hands on her hips. "One more night for them in this place shall not matter." He drew Aphrodite against his body, taking her lips as the two disappeared from the room in a flash of light unseen by Skylar and Alexis.

# 22

"Time to wake up. Now."

I frowned and opened my eyes to find Aphrodite seated on the end of the bed, the sun already lighting our window. Alexis was beside me, an arm around my waist and her head on my shoulder. "What do you want?" I rumbled as Alexis stirred.

"It is time you took leave of my temple and Corinth itself. You have not left this room for a week and I grow tired of needing to replenish your bowls with food," the goddess complained, indicating the few remaining figs on the table near the archway.

"Mmm, we certainly have feasted," I murmured, grinning cheekily down at Alexis, whose sleep-filled eyes met mine.

"That we have," she agreed with a laugh, her cheeks heating with her words.

"I am well aware, but your journey is not yet at an end. What you have faced here, what you have spoken of has built on the strength of your relationship, but it is not all that is required for you to have a child."

"What are you talking about?" I asked, my tone turning serious.

"Coming to Corinth was never so you could return to Kuria and Stamatis' home and recall the new and disturbing experiences you had, Skylar. It was always about what the two of you could endure when faced with truths of the past. If you could forgive yourself and allow yourself to be loved, if you allowed Alexis to know all of you, then you would have what you required to move forward."

"And we have done so?" I asked.

"You have," Aphrodite nodded.

"What must we do now? Where are we to go?" Alexis asked, holding the light blanket to her body as she sat up.

"To the Peraea of Corinth," Aphrodite replied.

"What is that? Is it in the city of Corinth?"

I shook my head in reply to Alexis' question, but it was Aphrodite who spoke first. "Peraea relates to stretches of coastline, in this case, the land directly across the Gulf of Corinth. The Peraea of Corinth includes the whole land northwest of the Isthmus where the Geraneia Mountains dominate much of the area."

"There is a small town called Thermae on the southeast tip, Peraia Chora is a town within the mountains themselves and is also known as 'the land on the other side'. Lake Eschatiotis is to the west of Peraia Chora, and there is also a small harbor about twenty-five itinerary further on where I believe the Heraion of Peraea is located." I added.

"You speak with truth, and much knowledge, though with your constant travel and your father's wish to educate you in so many matters, perhaps it should not surprise me so," Aphrodite said with a nod.

"You have been to those places?" Alexis asked.

"No. I have only heard tales of past deeds at the temples at the harbor – they are dedicated to the goddess Hera, are they not?"

"They are," Aphrodite acknowledged. "The Hera Akraia and the Hera Limenia are the temples you speak of. And that is where your journey sees you onto."

"How far is it?" Alexis asked.

"As the weather is favorable, it should be a half day's walk. Your friend Thaddeus shall accompany you there. He waits for you outside," Aphrodite replied.

"Thaddeus?" I yelled, jumping out of the bed. "No. Absolutely not. Asclepius sa–"

"Calm yourself," Aphrodite insisted moving to my side just as swiftly. "Asclepius spoke words of finding a way of creating a child in a manner acceptable to you, but it is not possible with *just* the two of you. Thaddeus *must* accompany you." I said nothing, my jaw clenching painfully. "Have Asclepius or me given you any reason to doubt that we do not wish for you to receive a child? Have we not ensured Alexis' body is ready to receive such a gift, or your coupling the strength to bear it?" Again, I said nothing.

"Skylar," Alexis said quietly, the light blanket still held against her body as she crossed to me and lay her hand on my arm. "She speaks true. The gods thus far have only aided us. I believe we can trust her in this too." I blew out a deep breath as I met Alexis' eyes, but did not speak.

"Go to our queen's sanctuary. She is the only one who can gift you with what you seek," Aphrodite advised.

"Fine," I muttered, holding Alexis' gaze. Without another word, the Goddess of Love disappeared in her usual burst of light and Alexis and I were left alone to ready ourselves to leave her temple.

*

A candlemark later, having enjoyed another warm bath, and a bowl of fruit and fish, Alexis and I said goodbye to Kalika and Idylla and set out across the lush grass from Aphrodite's temple to the surrounding wall and the small gate which would put us back on the stony path towards Corinth. As the wood closed behind us, a familiar voice called and Thaddeus, atop his horse, Darko, came trotting over.

He dismounted and set aside the shield – my shield – he held and took Alexis in a warm hug. "I cannot believe it, but I thank the gods we are reunited," he murmured.

"It is good to see you again," Alexis said, accepting his embrace. "Have you been waiting long?"

"I have been in Corinth almost three days yet have no idea how it came to be so. A number of lovely young women kept me plied with food, wine and a comfortable bed, though this morning they sent me on my way, insisting I wait out here; that the two of you would come along and we would travel together again," he replied, offering me his arm.

I hesitated, but Alexis' eyes found my own, imploring me to trust, and to accept what must be for the moment. I took his outstretched limb and gripped it tightly, as he did in return.

When he stepped away again I noticed a second horse beside his; Skotos. I frowned, but Thaddeus grinned. "When I found myself here, I had both steeds, my weapons, and your shield. I was most grateful for familiar items when so much was unknown." I bent down to retrieve my shield, but Thaddeus shook his head, a slight red marking his cheeks.

"Er, no, that is mine."

"But it has ..." I began.

HE smiled again, rounding Darko and untying a second shield from Skotos, which he handed to me. "Moeris and I have placed your design on our shields, as have a number of the other ephebes including trainees such as Brygos."

"Why?" I asked as I took it from him.

"King Agrias has never favored a design of our own, but now you are here, we want to. We share your wish to keep safe those who cannot keep themselves safe – whether that is our own families, or strangers we have just met. It is an honorable notion and we believe a fitting way to welcome you into the barracks, and as the lover and protector of our princess."

"Oh," I murmured, uncertain what else to say, though I was touched by his words.

"Agrias also speaks of having you lead our soldiers alongside Moeris, if you are agreeable to it."

"Me? What about you – is that not a position you wish to occupy?" I asked, an eyebrow arched.

Thaddeus smiled and shook his head. "No. My duty is to my King, my dearest friend. I am his primary guard and though I train with the other soldiers, I would only join in battle if he did. I protect him, the queen, and the princess when she is at Trachis ensuring they are far from harm's way when the need arises. Though I know I failed in that duty the night Alexis was taken by Melanthios," he added after a short pause.

"You know I place no blame with you for what happened," I said.

Thaddeus only nodded in reply as Alexis stepped closer and threaded her fingers through mine. "It is a great honor to lead the soldiers," she murmured, smiling proudly at me. "I am not surprised my father suggested it, or that Thaddeus and the others have crafted their shields to match yours. You have impressed more than just me since you arrived."

"I did not realize it to be so," I mumbled, embarrassed by her words and the actions of men I barely knew. I raised my eyes back to Thaddeus. "You say Brygos has adopted my design as well?"

"Yes," he replied with a nod.

I nodded, though it was more to myself than him. "The day I sparred with him I was not a good teacher. Moeris said he was still learning his craft. I should have taught him how to defend my attacks … I should not have attacked him at all."

"Brygos understands your anger was not directed at him, he holds no ill-feelings. Indeed, I believe your fierceness spurs him on to better himself; to learn and become as good of a soldier as you are."

I gave Thaddeus a tight smile. "I thank you for your kind words. I shall consider the request. When we return to Trachis I shall speak to King Agrias and give him my answer."

"Very good," Thaddeus smiled. "And now that you and Skotos are reunited, our journey home shall be faster, and I imagine travelled with less aggravation being you do not have the ox as well."

Alexis laughed. "Oh yes, but the week it took for us to get from Trachis to Epidaurus would have felt far longer had we had to keep the two of them from nipping at one another."

"Perhaps we could have tethered the ox to Skotos with a length of rope and just allowed it to run behind," I mused with a grin.

"It would have to have been a *very* long piece of rope, for it did enjoy poking its horns into Skotos when you first introduced them. Travelling behind Skotos could have been too much of a temptation."

"True, though perhaps our journey would have been made in only two days instead," I laughed, Alexis and Thaddeus joining me.

Thaddeus untied Skotos from Darko and handed me the reins. "May I ask of your time in Epidaurus? Was it fruitful?"

I drew a deep breath as Alexis replied. "We believe so."

"Come, there shall be time for conversation as we travel, though we are not returning to Trachis yet," I said, tugging gently on Skotos' reins and taking the lead.

"Where are we headed?" Thaddeus asked.

"To a temple dedicated to the goddess Hera on the southern end of the Gulf of Corinth," I replied.

"I presume you were given explanation as to why I was to join you," Thaddeus said. Alexis fell into step beside me and took my hand, squeezing briefly. When I met her eyes, I nodded. She returned it and addressed her friend again, telling him of our time in Epidaurus and the conversation with Aphrodite earlier.

"Why does Aphrodite not simply transport us all to the temple if that is where we are to go?" Thaddeus asked.

"Perhaps she had other more important matters to attend," Alexis replied.

"Perhaps," he agreed. "The gods are capable of much, but to gift you a child without us lying together is that even possible?" he murmured, catching my eye and attempting to gauge my reaction. I gave him a shrug. I had no idea how Hera intended to do so but for now, I would just place trust she could.

I re-tied my shield at Skotos' side and helped Alexis up onto his back, pulling myself into position behind her as Thaddeus mounted Darko. "Come, we do not have to travel through the city of Corinth itself, we can go around, meet up with the gulf and travel along the peninsula to the Heraion," I said as we set off along the path. "Unless you wish to go there," I added, hoping Alexis did not answer in the positive.

"We can go around," she replied quietly, and I exhaled the breath I had been holding.

"Your father says you have spent much time in the Peloponnese. He said you had followed the path of our great hero Heracles when you were the same age as Agrias and I when we left Macedonia," Thaddeus said. "Perhaps you would speak of it as we ride?"

"Thaddeus," Alexis began, but I tightened my arms around her waist.

"I do not mind speaking of it," I murmured in her ear. "Though I had so recently disappointed my father with my behavior in Troezen, I learnt much and enjoyed our travel throughout the region. I shall share the story with him, with you both."

"Are you certain?" she asked, half-turning to look at me.

I gave her a smile and pressed my lips against hers. "Yes." I looked up at

Thaddeus, who kept his eyes trained on the path ahead, rather than us. I raised my voice as I addressed him again. "I am certain Alexis shall speak with you of the journey Father and I took along Theseus' path also one day, I shared it with her as we travelled from Epidaurus."

"You have indeed travelled in the footsteps of the greatest of heroes, it is no wonder you are so heroic yourself," he said, his face lighting as he met my gaze.

"Er … thank you," I muttered.

# 23

"We had been following Theseus' path and when we reached Troezen, my father decided to teach me of another hero – Heracles, and the Labors he was set. Being that Heracles is known in Macedonia, I am certain you know the act which saw him sent to his cousin Eurystheus in Mycenae?"

"Of course," Thaddeus nodded. "Hera sent a fit of madness to him and he killed his wife and children as they slept, knowing only of his terrible deed when he woke the next morning to find them slain, and himself covered in their blood, knife still in hand."

"Indeed," I agreed.

"But do you know what led Hera to send such a punishment to Heracles?" Thaddeus asked with a grin.

"I do," I replied. "Before either Heracles or Eurystheus were born, Zeus decreed that the next born descendant of Perseus – of which Eurystheus and Heracles were both great-grandsons – would take the title of King of Mycenae and become the favored hero. Zeus' choice was obviously his son Heracles, whilst Hera chose his cousin Eurystheus. Hera successfully delayed Heracles' arrival and caused Eurystheus to be born early. But without the immortal blood running through Eurystheus' veins, he was far inferior to his cousin and never reached the heights of fame and adoration Heracles did.

"Unable to allow Zeus his victory, Hera plagued Heracles throughout his life, eventually sending a fit of madness down onto him and ensuring his atonement be spent in the service of Eurystheus carrying out impossible tasks. The goddess and Heracles' cousin intended for Heracles to be killed in the attempt. Unfortunately for them, he was not and his fame only grew from his feats."

"Much can be overcome if the reasons are important enough; if we believe the cause or what shall come next to be great enough," Alexis murmured.

I tightened my grip on her and placed a light kiss on her shoulder. "Yes, it can," I agreed.

"We mortals are often the subject of jealousy at the hands of the gods, though we are taught to worship them without question from the time we are born," Alexis said, louder this time to include Thaddeus in her musings.

"Yes, often we are their playthings, subject to their cruelty and petty spats through no desire of our own," Thaddeus nodded.

"Stories of our heroes prove that is sometimes the case. It is true that the gods can be frustrating, we do not always understand their intentions at first, but sometimes they aid us in what we seek and for that, we must be grateful," I said. For all the secrecy, worry and anger Aphrodite had put me through at her temple, it appeared her intention had been to aid Alexis and me in strengthening our relationship and put behind us what hindered us to move forward.

"Skylar speaks the truth," Alexis agreed. "Though Asclepius and Aphrodite's ways differed, both gave aid, and now we seek Hera for the same."

"We must not allow stories of others' experiences with them to color our own. If Hera can aid us then, no matter what she did to our hero Heracles, those deeds were between them and have no bearing on what we seek her for," I added.

"The two of you are far better judges than me, for I only have the stories of our heroes to go by, but if Hera – and by extension, I – am to aid you in having a family I shall show her nothing but the utmost respect if I am fortunate enough to meet her as you have Aphrodite and Asclepius."

"I suggest that is wise for they have far worse punishments, and far more power, than we mortals can inflict on or over one another," I nodded.

"Indeed. Would you now speak of your time following Heracles' path?" Thaddeus asked. "Did you visit each place in the same order he performed his feats?"

"No, we had travelled to Elis in the west of the Peloponnese with a number of athletes who were to participate in the Olympic Games, so we visited the site of Heracles' fifth task first," I replied. "It was the Augean Stables of Olympia which, in Heracles' time, had not been cleaned for thirty winters. After the Games, we escorted one of the victors back to his hometown, and he showed us the place at Stymphalos where Heracles defeated the Stymphalian Birds."

"We heard they were man-eaters with beaks and feathers of bronze and sacred to Ares, the Greek God of War," Alexis said.

"I heard the same," I nodded. "And if that is true, then I cannot imagine Ares was too pleased when his brother, Hephaestus, provided Heracles with the rattle that scared the birds away from their swamp. The two gods have held no love for one another since Hephaestus caught his wife Aphrodite in bed with Ares; acts akin to this one with Heracles only continuing their animosity."

"It must have greatly injured Hephaestus to find his betrothed so unfaithful to him, especially with one so close to him," Thaddeus murmured, his eyes finding, and holding, mine.

I drew a deep breath, my fingers tightening on Skotos' reins. "Such a betrayal would weigh heavily on any husband or wife who suffered the same." I felt Alexis stiffen and she covered my hand, pulling Skotos to a halt before turning to face me.

She placed her hand against my cheek, encouraging my eyes to meet hers instead of Thaddeus'. "Skylar," she whispered, a hint of worry crossing her face.

I swallowed and gave her the barest of nods before looking back to Thaddeus. "Though they were brothers, Hephaestus and Ares were never close, and from what I have heard of the God of War, if there is some battle he wants to influence or a territory he wishes to see gained, not even his father, Zeus, can prevent him from ensuring the deed is carried out on his behalf," I said.

"A formidable enemy," Thaddeus acknowledged.

*As I would be* I thought, though I did not speak the words aloud. "One of many," I responded instead with a nod. Alexis' fingertips tightened at my cheekbone. I drew another breath and released Skotos' reins, turning my eyes to Alexis and covering her hand with my own as I placed a kiss on her lips. "Though the words I speak are true, my thoughts no longer hold fear that you wish for another to warm your bed," I said quietly.

"They had best not or perhaps you shall discover just how formidable *I* can be," she said, gripping the top of my cuirass and taking my mouth in a hot, hungry kiss, as though to remind me of what I would be missing.

My stomach instantly heated with her fierce possession and I could not help sliding my hand over her ribs and down to rest atop her thigh, my fingertips easing the material higher in search of her naked skin.

Alexis groaned but covered my hand, stilling my movements and breaking our kiss. Her chest rose and fell as my own did and her eyes were darker than they had been a few moments ago. "Gods, I wish we were alone," she murmured, tracing a finger along my lips.

"We are not?" I whispered with a grin.

"Skylar," she groaned, half a plea, half a warning.

"Yes, Princess?" I drawled, sending my fingers higher as I kissed her again.

"Shall I go on ahead, and give the two of you some privacy?" Thaddeus asked, and I heard the grin in his words.

"Yes," I replied immediately, taking Alexis' bottom lip between my teeth. Her breath caught as I found the flesh beneath her chiton.

He laughed as Alexis halted my hand once more. "Where did you and Leandros journey next?" she asked loudly, steering our conversation back to its original path.

"I am not certain your warrior recalls what we were speaking of before you kissed her in such a manner," Thaddeus supplied, still laughing. "You make me miss my beloved Hesper with such displays."

"Sometimes such distractions are warranted," Alexis insisted, her eyes remaining on mine as if in challenge.

"Mmm ... such a pleasurable distraction," I murmured, lowering my lips to her neck and feeling a shudder run through her.

Her hand atop mine loosened and I skittered my fingertips closer to the heat calling so seductively to me. "Skylar, please," she whispered, and this time there was no doubt it was in warning; her restraint was waning.

Thaddeus cleared his throat and I chanced a glance in his direction – he had returned his eyes to the path, clearly allowing us time to compose ourselves.

I removed my fingers from her leg, though not before I swept them higher, causing Alexis to suck in a quick breath. I placed another kiss on her lips, ensuring it did not deepen, though I was sorely tempted to, if only to find out how far she would allow us to go with Thaddeus so near. "Perhaps it is time I found my way by foot," I grinned, sliding from Skotos' back in an attempt to quell the fierce beating between my legs.

"And continuing your tale," Thaddeus smiled.

"Of course. Now, where was I? Oh yes ... so after Stymphalos, Father and I spoke of travelling across the sea to the island of Crete where Heracles captured the Cretan Bull and brought it back to Greece." I took Skotos' reins in my hand and gave him a gentle tug to follow. "Are either of you aware that it was the same bull Theseus later slew at Marathon?" I added, looking to both Thaddeus and Alexis.

"Is that really true?" Alexis asked.

"It is," I assured her. "The two heroes never met, and yet they were connected by more than just the heroic deeds they carried out."

"I suspect had Heracles known of the damage the bull would do at Marathon, he may have killed the beast himself, rather than allowing it to roam free upon his return," Thaddeus mused.

"Perhaps," I agreed. "Father and I journeyed to the town of Hermione in the southeast of the Peloponnese to find a boat to take us to Crete.

Hermione is known for its skilled shipbuilders and their boats sail to Rome in the west and Troy in the east, further even in other directions. Being a trade port, many of the boats bring rare goods for the Greek agorae in return for our own exports." I reached over and placed my fingertips on Alexis' knee as I spoke again. "It was in Hermione I first learnt of perfumes."

"They make them there?" she asked as I removed my hand again.

"No. While we were waiting for a ship, I met a trader on his way home to Crete. He had visited many trading ports and agorae across Greece, purchasing new ingredients and selling the perfumes he had already produced before he arrived there. We spoke at length of his favored scents and he taught me to recognize the individual elements and what aromas work best together."

"Did you enjoy travelling across the waters?" Thaddeus asked. "Though we live so close to the Malian Gulf, I have never been on a boat."

"We never ended up going to Crete; until Father and I travelled to Stratos eight moons ago, I had never stepped aboard one either. But I can tell you that I did *not* enjoy the experience of travelling over the water."

"Why not?" Alexis asked.

"The constant movement as we rose and fell with the waves upset my stomach. I spent the best part of seven candlemarks with my head over the side of the vessel, returning the fish I had consumed for breakfast to the waters of the Corinthian Gulf below," I replied.

A laugh burst from Alexis and she clamped her hand over her mouth to hide her wide grin. "Apologies," she managed as Thaddeus began to chuckle as well. "I cannot imagine you enjoyed feeling so poorly – you were a terrible patient for Gnosidicus."

I narrowed my eyes as another laugh escaped her. "I do not believe *you* would have fared much better, Princess. The waves which buffeted us around were higher than your head, not to mention the pouring rain and high winds!"

"Apologies," Alexis said again, still grinning. "It does not sound as though it was a pleasant journey at all. Was there nothing you could do to prevent it?"

I attempted to keep the stern frown on my face, but my own grin escaped. "Apparently there is something called ginger that you can eat to settle your stomach, though I did not learn of it until after we were on dry land again. I found another way to take my mind off it – I fought with one of the Spartan soldiers we were to aid in Stratos."

"You trained to take your mind off your stomach?" Thaddeus asked. "Given the sailing conditions you describe, that must have been challenging."

I looked across to him, shaking my head. "Lykaon and I did not spar for amusement. When he commented loudly once too often on my inability to stand upright on the ship, I threw him overboard."

"Truly?" Thaddeus asked, smiling.

"Truly," I repeated, recalling how satisfying it had been to wipe the smug look from Lykaon's face. "He did not make mention of it again."

"Was he lost to the sea?" Thaddeus asked.

"No, unfortunately. He managed to grab hold of one of the oars and was hauled back in."

"So why did you not travel to Crete as you intended?" Thaddeus asked.

"Two days before we were due to set sail, another boat arrived in Hermione from Miletus in Persia. Among the usual crew and traders who disembarked, a woman named Nasrin and her daughter, Ava, also came ashore. Nasrin had been enslaved in the court of Darius, the King of Persia, and sought refuge far from his reach. When she spoke of what she had endured there, Father and I quickly agreed to aid them, and we continued our travels in the Peloponnese with them."

"What caused Darius to enslave her?" Alexis asked. "Did he conquer her home and take her as a slave? Where was she from?"

I smiled as always at Alexis' thirst for knowledge. "Nasrin was born in Babylon. When Ava was eight winters old, Darius became King of Persia and the Babylonians revolted against him. Darius himself led the Persian soldiers at Babylon and as bounty, took Nasrin and Ava back to the capital. Nasrin was treated very poorly but made friends with a Greek physician in Darius' court named Democedes. It was Democedes who orchestrated Nasrin and Ava's escape from Darius' palace and organized safe passage for them from Miletus to Hermione. Nasrin and Ava joined Father and me as we visited more of Heracles' Labor sites in the Peloponnese."

"Your father did not wish for all of you to go to Crete?" Thaddeus asked.

"No. Nasrin did not want to be aboard a boat again so soon," I replied. "We made our way north to Mycenae instead, where Heracles learned of the twelve labors he had to carry out. From there we travelled to Nemea, where Heracles faced the Nemean Lion. It was said no arrow could penetrate its skin, but Heracles stunned the animal with his huge club before finding its weak spot and killing it."

"I heard Heracles returned to his cousin wearing the skin, but how could that be if its pelt was impenetrable?" Thaddeus asked.

"And where was its weak spot?" Alexis added.

"It was weakest inside its mouth," I replied, smiling at the two of them. "While the beast lay stunned, Heracles drove his knife up and into its head, killing it."

"He used his knife to cut it apart from the inside?"

"No, he used the lion's own claws to remove the skin."

"Smart," Thaddeus noted.

"Effective," Alexis agreed.

I nodded. "We also travelled to the swamp near Lerna where Heracles slayed the Hydra which grew two heads in place of each one he cut off."

"Alexis always said it was Hera who made the heads regenerate, but I often think of it in comparison to the flowers Hesper grows in a corner of the courtyard garden; when she cuts them back after they have flowered, they return twice as dense the following winter," Thaddeus mused.

I smiled, surprised he would notice such a thing and his cheeks colored when he saw my grin. "Perhaps both answers are true," I offered. "We went to Ceryneia and Mount Erymanthus too, where Heracles captured a deer with golden antlers and hooves belonging to Artemis and the Erymanthian Boar. We made our way to Megara at the Isthmus afterwards and Father and I left Nasrin and Ava to their journey north."

"Why?" Thaddeus asked, slowing Darko so he walked beside us. "If your father was so fond of Nasrin, why did he allow her to go without him? Why did the two of you not accompany them?"

"I cannot say for certain, though perhaps it was because it would have taken us so far north, and so close to his home of Thrace, where he had not been for many winters."

We were all quiet a long moment before Alexis reached down to touch my shoulder. "You found yourself in Corinth soon after, did you not?" she asked when I met her eyes.

I nodded. "The following moon."

"Corinth?" Thaddeus queried, a slight frown across his brow. "If you permit me the question, what happened? It sounds as though it was important."

The tall walls of the named city loomed large on our left and I could not help casting my eyes to them as we continued along the path. The thick wooden doors opened as we drew level with the entrance and a large number of slaves and traders made their way out of the opening, hurrying to carry out their assigned tasks or continue onto their next destination. Some took the path towards the Isthmus while others headed off into the plains either side.

Behind the merchants came a long line of soldiers – a familiar figure leading the men in all their red finery. Our eyes met, and I raised my hand in acknowledgement, the leader's face splitting into a wide grin as he called my name and hurriedly led the soldiers towards us. I returned it and reached for his outstretched arm when he arrived, grateful for his sudden appearance, which ensured Thaddeus' question remained unanswered.

# 24

"Hello, Cleomenes."

The Spartan King ignored my offered arm, pulling me into a crushing hug instead. "It is wonderful to see you again, my friend," he said, slapping my back hard before releasing me, his eyes sliding behind to take in Alexis and Thaddeus. "Your father does not travel with you? I hope you shall not tell me of an untimely demise?"

"No, Father is quite well and would certainly wish me to pass on his regards," I replied.

"We shall go on ahead, King Cleomenes," one of the soldiers said. Cleomenes only nodded in reply and I took the opportunity to step around Thaddeus, who was dismounting from Darko, and assist Alexis from Skotos.

"This is Thaddeus, favored guard of King Agrias of Trachis, in the region of Thermopylae," I said, indicating the named man. "And this is the Princess of Thermopylae, Alexis. I give you both, King Cleomenes of Sparta."

"King ..." Thaddeus began, dropping his eyes to the ground before offering his arm.

"It is an honor to meet you, King Cleomenes," Alexis murmured, inclining her head as well. "Skylar has spoken of your victory in ousting the tyrant Hippias at Athens."

Cleomenes grasped Thaddeus' arm briefly before turning his attention, and a wide smile, to Alexis. "Without Leandros and Skylar's aid, I am not certain it would have been so, did she speak of that also?" he replied, taking in Alexis' elegant form with interest before his eyes returned to her face.

"She did, though humbly. Skylar does not gloat of her involvement in battles, she fights and kills when she must, but is known to possess a softer hand when it is called for," Alexis replied.

I raised an eyebrow, but the Spartan King spoke before I could make comment. "You speak true, for I have witnessed both sides of the warrior and she is more than proficient whether wielding words or weapons."

"You do not appear to have suffered permanent damage from either of my weapons," I quipped.

He laughed, rubbing the tiny scar I had given him at his temple as he shook his head. "No. My healer saw well to me and by the time I was reunited with my wife, there was but a scratch."

"You did not join us at Stratos as expected, you decided to return to Sparta instead?"

"Not immediately, I found myself enjoying Cleisthenes' entertainments too much. I am certain you recall how fine they were." I nodded but did not offer further comment and thankfully Cleomenes continued before either Alexis or Thaddeus found voice for their own questions. "I was in my wife's arms when I heard the Epirotes had been defeated in Stratos. I offer my thanks once again for your assistance there. Shame about Lykaon."

I only grunted.

"Lykaon – the man you threw overboard?" Alexis enquired.

"Yes," I nodded, directing the rest of my speech to Cleomenes. "Perhaps if he had put as much effort into fighting the Epirotes as he did me, he would have returned to your homeland with his shield."

"I believe it to be so. Demosthenes spoke of your disagreements," Cleomenes acknowledged.

"Does Demosthenes travel with you now?" I asked.

"No, but he shall join us in due course. Family matters keep him in Sparta for the time being. But come, the rest of my men wait for us beneath the trees up ahead. Allow us to share a meal and provide your horses with water whilst we speak of other more pressing matters."

Cleomenes held his arm out for Alexis to take, which she did after a brief look in my direction. I gathered Skotos' reins as Thaddeus took Darko's and we followed the king towards the gathering of trees and Spartan soldiers on the higher ground to our right.

As Cleomenes gave the order to his men to share food, Thaddeus tethered our horses to a shady tree and set down a large bowl (also provided by the Spartans) for them to drink from.

"Where are you travelling today?" I asked as I seated myself beside Alexis on the short grass.

Cleomenes took half a loaf of bread from one of his soldiers and pulled a chunk for himself before offering it to Alexis. "Back to Athens," he replied.

"Oh? For what purpose? Hippias remains expelled. We heard he travelled north and finds himself in King Darius' court in Persia."

"He does, and I too heard of Hippias' alliance with the Persians. He is not my concern. Cleisthenes has been archon for some time and another has emerged to challenge him for the title."

"Oh?" I asked with a raise of my eyebrow.

"Yes. His name is Isagoras and I stayed with him when I first arrived in Athens. He is well respected and hails from another rich, aristocratic Athenian family. The people of Athens shall have a difficult decision as to who should lead them into their new era, though Isagoras wishes for me to stand beside him, rather than his rival."

"You intend to do so?"

"I am interested to hear what he has to say, as his name was spoken with eagerness at the agora before I left. Though Cleisthenes ha–" His words were cut short, eyes widening as his gaze fixed over my shoulder.

"Run!" another of the soldiers cried. Men jumped to their feet around us, the bread quickly forgotten. Reaching for Alexis, I too sprang up, dragging her with me as I spun around to see what the danger was.

"What is that?" Alexis asked, her eyes finding what mine had.

"Wild boar," I replied. "Thaddeus! Take Alexis into the trees, climb them if you have to."

"What about the horses?" he asked.

"Untether them, encourage them to join you in the dense wood, but if they do not, drive them away, we shall chase them down later," I replied, taking my sword from its sheath.

"Consider it done," he said, crossing to Skotos.

"Skylar," Alexis began, her hand tightening on mine.

"Go with Thaddeus. All shall be well."

"Here," Thaddeus said, returning to our side and holding out my shield. I nodded and took it from him. "Come," Thaddeus added, taking Alexis' hand from mine.

"Be careful," Alexis said, reaching out to lay her hand on my arm, her voice shaking.

"I shall. Now go," I insisted, pushing her towards Thaddeus.

She nodded and allowed him to lead her into the trees – our horses, thankfully, no longer in sight. The boar was gaining quickly, though with the disorganization of the running soldiers, it appeared uncertain who to attack first. I gripped my weapon and charged forward.

"Cleomenes, call your men to formation!" I yelled.

"What?"

"Have them stand in a line behind me. When the boar charges, form a ring around us. Plant your shields on the ground and stand behind them, leave no room for the boar to drive its tusks into your legs."

"Understood," the king acknowledged. "Spartans! Bring shields and swords behind the warrior. Do not break formation!" The soldiers were well drilled and obeyed their King without hesitation.

The boar was less than a hundred feet from us now. I cast a quick glance behind me. Cleomenes' men were in position. I planted my feet and raised my shield and sword, a single, still target for the boar to turn its attention to. It quickened its pace, bearing down on me. Its sweat-stained hide glittered in the sun, nostrils flaring and mouth open as it expelled great snorts of breath. Its hooves clattered against the ground, the thunderous vibrations reaching me long before the beast did.

"Skylar?" Cleomenes called uncertainly.

"Hold formation," I commanded, never taking my eyes off the approaching animal. The boar reached me and with a leap, threw its head about wildly, hoping to engage its tusks with my flesh. I turned at the last moment, bringing my shield up to crash against the side of its head. It dropped back to the ground, stunned, but kept its feet. "Form the ring!" I shouted, pleased when Cleomenes and his men immediately complied.

The boar took a step back and shook its head, its eyes finding the shields of the Spartans now blocking any attempt at escape. It pawed the ground, its breaths coming in harder pants. The boar and I circled one another, its beady eye watching me as I watched it. I could only hope I would recognize the signs for how it would next attack.

"Press in closer," I ordered, still watching the beast.

With a clang of metal, the men tightened the ring. The boar gave another snort and threw its head up again, the soldier behind flinching when the tusks neared his shield.

"Remain still," I said, glancing up at the young man. He could not have been more than sixteen winters and I saw the fear in his eyes as he fought to remain where he was; it appeared this was the first real battle he had been involved in. Still, his panic surprised me – had he not been training since he was seven winters old?

I returned my eyes to the boar, knowing I could not lose focus in case it sensed my distraction and took advantage.

"What do we wait for? There are twenty of us here, allow us to take our swords and run the beast through," a voice behind me said.

"We shall, but we must tread carefully, unless you want to find its tusks lodged in your flesh," I replied. "Move in closer. Do not allow it room to flee."

"King Cleomenes, you are closest, drive your sword through its neck," the soldier spoke again.

"We wait," Cleomenes replied.

"I shall not give it the chance to harm any of our men, we need everyone with us when we arrive in Athens."

"No!" I cried, but the soldier had broken rank to my left. I threw out my arm, catching him across the chest with my shield, the hilt of his sword slamming against the top of it and falling to the ground. My momentary lapse gave the boar the chance it needed, it backed up until its tail hit the Spartan shield behind it, then rushed forward, leaping into the air. Its hooves crashed into my chest and knocked me to the ground, robbing me of my breath as I hit the hard surface, the weight of its body pinning me to the grass.

I lay completely still for a moment, attempting to catch my breath before I slammed my shield against the boar's side; the action inciting the animal to jab at me with its deadly tusks rather than remove it from my chest. I threw my head from side to side to avoid the long pieces of bone being thrust in my direction and the hot, smelly breath choking me. I whacked my shield against the beast's side, but it remained solidly in place and I knew I would have to use my sword instead to free myself. I hoped I would be able to get enough power behind the action.

Holding tightly to the handle, I let out a yell and drove my blade up into the boar's ribcage at the same moment as Cleomenes slammed his sword through the boar's neck from above. His weapon slid straight through the animal and I only just managed to get my head out of the way, the steel tip glancing my arm before lodging itself in the ground.

The boar crumpled sideways, releasing my sword as it fell, and spurting blood across my cuirass and the flattened blades of grass around us. Several soldiers came forward and nudged the beast with their sandals, clearly relieved when it did not rise again.

"Return home, Acayo. You shall not join me in Athens. You disobeyed a direct order and almost got Skylar killed. You shall not serve beside me again until you have learnt the error of your ways. Tell Leonidas of your deed. I shall ensure he sets a fitting punishment."

"But King Cleom—"

"Go! Before you find yourself at the end of my sword rather than the end of my patience." Acayo — the soldier who had rushed forward to end the boar himself — opened his mouth, then, thinking better of it, closed it again, gave a curt nod and turned on his heel. "Gather wood for a fire and take the beast. We shall dine on its flesh," Cleomenes directed the rest of his men. "Apologies for my man's behavior, and my own reckless strike," he said, offering me his arm.

I left my sword where it was and took Cleomenes' arm, wincing when he hauled me to my feet. I surveyed the wound as I spoke. "It is not deep. Some herbs and time shall see it healed, and I am certain Acayo shall not disobey you again."

"Not if he wishes to remain in my army."

"Skylar! You are injured," Alexis cried, skidding to a halt beside me, one hand circling my upper arm as she looked over the bleeding gash. I took her other, pressing my lips to her knuckles.

"It is nothing," I assured her.

She raised her eyes, taking in the blood on my cuirass before meeting my eyes. "This blood ... is not yours?" she asked, releasing me to wipe at a spot on my chin.

"No," I replied, stroking her cheek. She held my gaze a moment longer, swallowing loudly before she nodded. Thaddeus joined us, leading Skotos and Darko, and he picked up my weapons, holding each out for me to take.

"Thank you," I said with a nod, re-sheathing my sword. "Can you wipe down my shield and attach it to Skotos again? He does not care for blood and I do not wish to frighten him anymore than he already has been today."

"Of course," Thaddeus replied, taking the named weapon.

"Come, I must clean your wound, though I do not have herbs for it," Alexis said.

"We do. Tell Macrobio what you require," Cleomenes offered.

"Thank you," she replied. With my hand in hers, Alexis led me back to the edge of the trees, settling me on a large rock before gathering a water skin and material from our bag. She spoke quickly to Macrobio, who provided her with several items and returned to me.

"You frightened me," she whispered.

"I am sorry. I believed I had the situation well in hand. I would have, had Cleomenes' men *all* obeyed the orders their king issued."

"We could not hear what was being said, but we saw one man rush from his position and then the boar charged you."

"Yes. But do not be concerned; the beast is dead and I shall heal quickly," I replied with a small smile as she wet the linen and began to remove the blood around my wound.

"You are as brave, and as reckless, as I recall," Cleomenes noted, dropping down beside us. "You have obviously faced such beasts before, or you would not have believed your plan would work."

"I have never been faced with a wild boar," I replied with a shrug, hearing the gasp from Alexis. I placed my finger beneath her chin and raised her eyes until they met mine, grinning. "But someone once told me I possessed the correct amount of stubbornness and arrogance and I applied both to this situation."

She shook her head as Cleomenes laughed. "Oh yes, you certainly have both those qualities," he agreed.

"It does not mean you have to place yourself in danger," Alexis scolded.

"I placed myself between an attacker and those who required protection," I amended. "I would do it again without hesitation if the occasion arose."

"I know," she murmured. "And that is what scares me. I want you to remain in this world with me for many, many winters."

I drew my thumb across her lips and gave her another smile. "I shall. I give you my word."

"Perhaps before any further danger seeks to separate us, I would take the opportunity to speak of a proposition with you," Cleomenes said as Alexis returned to the task of cleaning my arm.

I raised an eyebrow and settled my gaze on him. "I well recall the last time you offered a proposition. I did not accept it then, and I hope this one does not mirror the sentiment."

"This is not the same sort of suggestion, I assure you," Cleomenes grinned.

"What was it?" Alexis asked.

"It is not important," I murmured.

"I wanted to betroth Skylar to my brother, Leonidas," Cleomenes said at the same time. "I believed then, as I still do now, that the match would be beneficial to all, but she would not agree to it, nor would her father."

"You know why I declined it," I insisted before Alexis could speak again.

"I do – I believe your exact words were that your tastes for kings and men differ from those of most young women," he grinned. "Our host in Athens certainly provided … inviting entertainment, which you enjoyed once again in Sunium if I am not mistaken?"

"Reminder of what Cleisthenes provided is not required. I have not forgotten the entertainment or hospitality he showed," I said tersely.

"Good. Perhaps then we can turn our thoughts to him, and you shall consent to the proposal I have. As I told you earlier, Cleisthenes fights for the crown of archon with Isagoras and though Isagoras sent word asking for my support to aid him in being victorious, so too has Cleisthenes. I travel to Athens to meet them both and shall favor one with my assistance in his campaign for victory."

"You bring with you part of your army. Why? Do you intend to kill whoever you do not stand beside? Has one threatened to do harm to the other to call themselves victor?" I asked.

"Not at all. Neither man has given the people of Athens cause to believe they would be anything but fair and just rulers. But I know how such situations can turn quickly and I do not wish to be caught unawares should I find myself in danger. Besides, I am quite flattered both men have asked for my backing and believe that no matter who calls himself archon, our two great cities could unite and put behind past spats. If you would agree to join me there and provide your own alliance, I am certain that Cleisthenes or Isagoras would provide you with whatever you asked for in return. A certain woman of their house perhaps?" he added with a grin.

"A woman?" Alexis asked, her eyes back on my face.

"Such pursuits do not interest me any longer," I assured him though gritted teeth.

"Indeed?" Cleomenes mused, eyebrows high beneath his hairline.

"Indeed," I repeated firmly.

"How so? For when I mentioned my brother Leonidas a moment ago, it did not appear you had wavered on your intentions with him either."

"My time in Trachis saw me defeat more than the enemies we had been requested for," I replied, my gaze finding Alexis. "I lost my heart to the princess and no longer wish for any other to warm my bed now, or in the future." Alexis grinned as she wound a long piece of material around my arm; I had not even felt when she applied the herbs.

"I see. Well, that is happy news. It appears Alexis gives you what Leonidas could never have."

"As no other ever could," I confirmed, rewarded by Alexis pressing her lips above the bandage she had applied.

"Well, if your princess and guard are not in a hurry to return home, would the three of you consider accompanying me to Athens? Have you ever visited?" he asked, addressing Alexis.

"No," she replied, turning as she shook her head. "But Skylar has told me much."

"Perhaps you could send word to your father and ask if he too would be prepared to back the man Skylar and I choose? Perhaps he would come to Athens and meet the men I speak of?"

Alexis raised her eyes to mine, but I saw no hint of wish behind her stare, and I was in no doubt of the answer *I* wanted to give. "King Agrias has his own matters to attend at home and would not want to be away at this time," I said, my gaze shifting back to Cleomenes. "I believe that my time to give you aid has also passed. It is *you* the two men have requested and I am confident you can make your own decision once you have heard both their intentions for Athens. I wish you victory in the man you decide to place your faith in but cannot join you, though I thank you for the offer."

"Bu–" he began.

"I would ask you to pass on my regards to Cleisthenes and ask for your understanding in my decision. Alexis, Thaddeus and I are on an important journey of our own to the Heraion of Peraea, one which is of far more standing to me than who is ruler of Athens. To delay it would not please any of us; we wish to return home as soon as possible, Thaddeus especially, for he has a wife and three children who long to see him again."

Cleomenes looked between Alexis and me for several moments before finally nodding. "I see you are not to be dissuaded. When one finds themselves upon a certain path, it is a brave man who would stand in their way. But would you stay a while longer and enjoy the flesh of the beast you bested? My men should have it well cooked by now."

"We could do so," I replied as Alexis slipped her fingers between mine.

# 25

When we had finished as much meat from the boar as we could fit, Macrobio halved what was left to share between our two groups. As we were all headed in the same direction for the time being, I suggested to Cleomenes we travel together, which he happily agreed to. Thaddeus walked with our horses at the back of the pack, speaking with a few of the soldiers, as Cleomenes kept Alexis' attention with stories of old kings of Sparta and tales his brother Dorieus sent back from the colonies across the seas.

Two candlemarks later we arrived at the Diolkos; the stone portage road which cut across the Isthmus from the Gulf of Corinth to the Saronic Gulf. I had briefly spoken of it with Alexis when she and I travelled over it on our way to Epidaurus, but now entertained our party with what I knew of Periander – once the tyrant of Corinth – and the man who organized its construction.

"For many winters, Corinth has held a uniquely powerful trade position by both land and sea. Access to both gulfs, by way of the ports of Lechaeum on the Gulf of Corinth to the west and Kenchreai on the Saronic Gulf to the east, as well as the Isthmus land itself between Attica and the Peloponnese, has seen much of the pottery the city is famous for reach many far-off destinations. Much of the plain we have just traversed is the site of the potter's clay for the items, and the fertile soil of the area also produces good grain and some of the finest grapes for wine," I told them. "Lechaeum lies twenty itinerary to the west of Corinth, joined with the city by a pair of long walls. Cleomenes, I am certain you and many of your soldiers have attended, if not competed in, the Isthmian Games held in the area," I added, looking across to the king. He only nodded in reply. "Then you would have visited the city of Isthmia and the sanctuary dedicated to Poseidon, God of the Sea. Three itinerary south of that sanctuary stands the city of Kenchreai with its port."

"I recall looking down onto its shores, but have never ventured into the place myself," Cleomenes replied.

"Periander wanted to cut through the Isthmus to give trading ships easier and faster access to and from the gulfs either side of the land. He undertook much research, and indeed attempted to dig part of it himself so he could determine how long it may take, and how costly it would be. He soon abandoned the idea, building instead the stone roadway you see before us, where ships are pulled overland on rolling logs beneath the boat's bows.

"The tolls he imposed on the captains wishing to extend their exporting distances by using the Diolkos, quickly paid for the labor of the slaves he employed to carry out the task, and the materials needed for its construction. When it was finished, he used the coin he continued to receive from ship merchants for use of the roadway, to build temples, other public buildings and to promote literature and the arts within his city for those under his rule."

"He sounds a fair ruler, but you spoke of him as a tyrant. Those deeds do not suggest it was so," Alexis said.

"According to many, he *was* a fair and just ruler who worked to ensure wealth was distributed to all in Corinth, not just the nobles or those from rich families, though others tell of a different man; a cruel and harsh leader, sparing not even his own family from his firm hand." Alexis opened her mouth, the many questions she had for me written across her face, but it was Cleomenes who spoke first.

"As much as I wish to hear more of Periander and his feats, I am afraid this is where we must go our separate ways." I smiled and squeezed Alexis' hand, a silent promise I would speak of it again once Cleomenes and his men had departed. "As always, your knowledge impresses me and I hope in time our paths may cross again, and you shall join me as I request, or I you if that is to be the way of it," the Spartan King said.

"Perhaps we shall see a day when it is so," I grinned.

"On your way to the Heraion of Peraea, you shall pass the town of Thermae, ensure you partake of their thermal springs – your arm shall thank you for the attention. My soldiers and I often rest there on our return from battles and I can attest to their aid in recovering from wounds sustained in such fighting."

"Could we?" Alexis asked, her eyes bright with the thought. I grinned and nodded.

"Do you know the tale of how the spring is able to remain warm?"

Cleomenes added.

"I do," I nodded. "But I suspect my friends have not and though you spoke of leaving us, it appears you are eager to tell it, so please, go ahead."

Cleomenes turned to Alexis with a large grin, a similar one mirrored on her own face. "It is said that beautiful Artemis, Goddess of the Hunt, passed through this area one day and was so taken with the beauty around the spring and the warmth of its water, that she stayed for a number of days, inviting her nymphs and brother Apollo, God of the Sun to join her. Apollo too, was impressed with the site and basked in the water even longer, blessing the spring and ensuring his sun forever shone down on it, no matter the season."

"How did the spring come to be so warm before the immortals arrived?" Alexis asked.

"I am afraid I do not know," Cleomenes replied. "But perhaps when I am in Athens I shall find a learned man and ask him for his thoughts on the subject."

"Perhaps it shall be a similar story to the one of how the hot springs in Thermopylae became such," I offered.

"How was that?" Cleomenes asked.

"You know of it?" Alexis asked, turning to me and smiling.

"I do. The day I awoke in Trachis after I was injured in the Spercheios Valley, Father was speaking of it to me, though he was not certain I could hear his words."

"You were injured?" Cleomenes frowned. "Badly?"

"I have never seen anyone – soldier or otherwise – survive such an injury, indeed many men have fallen with lesser wounds," Thaddeus replied before I could wave away the king's question.

"She did not wake for almost a week," Alexis added. "Our healer did not expect her to last the night."

"Indeed?" Cleomenes murmured.

"Do you wish to hear the story of Thermopylae's hot springs or not?" I asked impatiently. I preferred not to think of that particular time – knowing if I had not recovered, Alexis would find herself now betrothed to Melanthios, her world a far darker place.

"Go ahead, go ahead. I see you still struggle with patience," Cleomenes laughed.

Alexis joined him, leaning in close to the king as she said, "I have not found patience to be her strongest trait."

"Alexis," I groaned. Cleomenes, and a number of his soldiers sniggered, and I felt the heat touch my cheeks. "The hot springs in Thermopylae may not have been blessed by a god or goddess, but the half-immortal hero Heracles turned the waters hot when he jumped into the river," I said loudly. "He was attempting to rid himself of the hydra's poison infused in

145

the tunic he wore. The river bubbled and heated and has remained so ever since. Though the hero died from the poison."

Thaddeus regained his composure first, his smile replaced with a faint frown. "Heracles bathed in *our* spring? But how can it be? You speak as though Heracles died in Thermopylae, and I have never heard such glory bestowed on the land. The story we were told as children had his wife Deianira unwittingly sending him a poisoned tunic whilst he served a punishment in the lands of Euboea, across the Gulf. I believed *that* was where he met his end."

"I heard it was the Dyras River, north of Trachis, which saw Heracles wash the poison off, though it did not remain heated afterward," one of Cleomenes' men offered.

"There are many versions, I am certain," I nodded. "But the one I heard was this: Heracles' wife – Deianira – feared she had lost him to Iole, daughter of King Eurytus, though Iole was from Thessaly, not Euboea. Several winters before Heracles died, the centaur Nessus attempted to steal Deianira from the hero. Before Heracles killed Nessus, the beast gifted Deianira with blood and told her that if she ever doubted the depth of her lover's feelings for her, she should place the blood on a garment and present it to him as gift. When he put it on, his heart would return to her and she would never lose it again.

"Nessus told Deianira to keep the blood out of Helios' light and Hephaestus' fire, and so when she placed it on the himation she did so in a dark place, wrapping it in thick wool for its journey. Her messenger had been gone several days when Deianira found a single piece of wool with a drop of Nessus' blood on it. She thought nothing of brushing the wool aside until a slant of sunlight hit it and the wool burst into flames, reducing it to fine pieces of ash.

"It was then, Deianira realized that Nessus had tricked her. She ran, weeping to find her son, Hyllus, speaking of her ill-fated gift and urging him to send someone to bring word of his father in Thessaly. She then took to her room and drove a sword through her chest as punishment for her actions against her husband.

"Hyllus meanwhile, had barely gathered men to accompany him when others arrived, carrying a litter with Heracles lying atop it. He was still alive, though the pain of Nessus' blood had robbed him of much of his strength and when the healers attempted to remove the himation, it drew away flesh, leaving his bones exposed.

"Heracles woke briefly, and Hyllus told him of his mother's error, and her own death. Heracles let forth an angry tirade at the long dead Nessus before asking Hyllus to build his pyre at the peak of Mount Kallidromon and take him there. Hyllus did as asked, his friend Philoctetes lighting it when the time came, as the boy could not bring himself to do it, so overcome was he with grief at losing both mother and father on the same day."

"Was that the same Philoctetes whom Heracles entrusted his bow and arrow to, and later killed Paris with at the battle of Troy?" Cleomenes interrupted.

"So it is told," I nodded.

"It would appear that each man was the other's downfall, and with poisoned blood no less," Alexis noted.

"Ah, yes," the king acknowledged. "I believe it was Heracles' … second labor which saw him face the hydra. When he had severed the final head, he dipped his arrow into its poisonous blood and used it to rescue his wife from Nessus, the poisoned tip killing the centaur."

"That is true," I nodded.

"Your tale does still not explain how the hot springs in Thermopylae came to be so," Thaddeus said. "I believed Heracles' father – Zeus – ensured his son ascended to the realm of the gods on his death, and if that is so, then was his mortal flesh not burned away, leaving only his immortal side, at which time his father took him to Olympos?"

"It is, though as Hyllus and Philoctetes prepared Heracles' pyre, the healer of Trachis settled Heracles in the nearby spring. He hoped to remove the poison from the hero's skin and relieve him of his pain and the himation, and perhaps stave off his death for another day at least. When the poisoned blood met with the water, it bubbled and boiled, turning the water hot, but the tunic remained firmly attached to Heracles' body. When the pyre was ready and the three attendants took Heracles from the spring, the water stayed hot, as it does to this day," I replied.

"Oh," Thaddeus murmured, nodding slowly, though it was more to himself than anyone else.

"After such a time, there is no way to know for certain the truths of the story, though I would consider your homeland blessed if indeed the hero called it home at one time," Cleomenes said with a grin. "And now I believe it time we took our leave and left you to speak amongst yourselves about the tales of the heroes who have walked these paths before us and debate the truth of such words."

"Indeed," I agreed.

"Apologies again for Acayo's foolish behavior, perhaps quick recovery would see forgiveness granted," Cleomenes said, offering me his arm.

"There is no need for forgiveness, I hold no anger with you for his actions," I assured him, taking it and gripping him firmly as I nodded. "Perhaps now we shall consider ourselves even."

"Very good," the king smiled as he released me. Cleomenes offered his arm to Thaddeus and they shook before Thaddeus turned to the other soldiers and did the same. Cleomenes opened his arms to Alexis. She wrapped hers around his waist and they hugged briefly.

"Take care of the warrior, and remind her that sometimes patience brings welcome reward," he said just loud enough for me to hear.

"I shall," Alexis laughed. "I hope one day, if your journey should find you nearby, that you would visit us in Trachis. You would be most welcome, your wife also."

"Thank you for the invitation, I shall keep it in mind. I offer the same in return should you ever find yourself in the great city of Sparta."

"Thank you," Alexis replied.

With a final nod in my direction, Cleomenes released Alexis and turned, leading his soldiers east towards Megara, and further on to Athens as Alexis, Thaddeus and I headed west to Thermae.

# 26

After parting ways with Cleomenes and his men, Alexis, Thaddeus and I re-mounted our horses, arriving in Thermae less than half a candlemark later, our discussions on the accuracy of the stories we had heard on Heracles' final resting place helping pass the time.

We bathed in the bubbling thermal springs before heading down to the beach, finding several fishermen casting their lines into the rolling waves. The water was clear and a number of shades of blue, the sand littered with smooth pebbles and larger rocks, one of which held a man standing precariously atop it as he drew his string – and a fish – in through the crashing waves. Several other men cheered his success and he returned to the sand, picking up more fish and making his way towards a fire burning further up the bank. He waved us over and I raised my hand in reply, leading Alexis and Thaddeus, the horses trailing us unhurriedly.

"Good day to you," the fisherman said, taking a knife and gutting his catch.

"And to you," I replied, Alexis and Thaddeus offering their greetings as well. He added the fish to the pile beside the fire and I noticed they were all the same with bright silver scales turning almost gold at the tops, their size the only difference.

"Poseidon has been kind to you this day," I said, indicating the pile. "May I?" I added, reaching out for one of his pre-gutted specimens.

"Of course," he replied, passing it to me.

It was not particularly heavy; only one or perhaps one-and-a-half mina, oval in shape, thicker through the middle before tapering to a thin tail. The dorsal fin ran the length of its body from head to tail and had a combination of twenty-five sharp and soft points. A shorter row ran under its tail, though there were only about fifteen fins there, and only three of those were sharp. Another five soft and one spiny ray covered the two ventral fins beneath its stomach. The pectoral fins were long and the forked tail fin mirrored the tip of a spear where the point met the body. I opened the thick lips at its mouth and the gums beyond showed eight large teeth in both the upper and lower jaws. Behind those were two more rows of wider teeth, reminding me of the back teeth in mortals.

"I know this by the name of the Sargos, is that what you call it also?" I asked, carefully running my finger along the exposed rows.

"Sargos, yes, or sea-bream," he answered. "You do not appear a slave who frequents the fish markets, your father or husband taught you of fish?"

"My father, yes. When I was very small he showed me how to catch them with a line as you do, and by hand, at the water's edge of streams and the beach. Possessing such a skill ensures you never fall hungry if you find yourself far from an agora, or with no coin to purchase items."

"Indeed," the man agreed. "Would you care to taste some? It is always best when eaten directly from the fire's heat."

"We would be most grateful. We have fresh meat from a boar we can share with you in exchange," I offered.

"Splendid. I very much enjoy the fish I catch each day, but never pass up the opportunity for other meat. Was it the animal who caused the injury on your arm?" he asked, nodding in my direction.

"It was."

"I am Sophos of Thermae," he said, reaching out his arm to me as Alexis retrieved our bag from Skotos and brought it back to the fire.

"Skylar of Trachis and these are my companions, Alexis and Thaddeus, also of Trachis," I said, introducing them.

"Trachis ..." Sophos frowned momentarily before taking Alexis' arm in his and smiling widely. "Ah, yes of course – you speak of the town in Thermopylae; the Hot Gates. Our areas share much in common, though yours is far more known for its springs than its excellent fishing."

"It is," Alexis said with a grin. "And your springs were extremely welcome when we found ourselves enjoying them earlier."

"Best springs this side of Mount Geraneia. Your friend's wound should heal faster now you have dipped it in the healing waters."

"One can only hope," I murmured, though I would not be surprised to find it so as my arm hurt far less than before I had immersed it.

"You have called this area home for many winters?" Thaddeus asked, taking Sophos' arm.

"Many," he replied with a nod, releasing Thaddeus and drawing a long stick from its holders above the flames of the fire. He held up the dark

Sargos skewered along the wooden length. "Please, sit and allow us to share food and words."

"Thank you." Alexis divided the boar between us all as we joined Sophos. "We seek further answers, if they are within your knowledge," I said.

"Ask away," Sophos replied.

"We travel to the Heraion in the Peraia Chora region. I understand it is within the mountains of Geraneia, near Lake Eschatiotis. The fastest route would be to follow the water's edge from here to the lake, and then beyond, would it not?"

"There is no doubt it would be, but I am afraid it is not possible."

"Why not?" Thaddeus asked before I could.

"The path you speak of is extremely rocky; the steep ridges of the mountain rise directly up from the Gulf of Corinth, making the area almost impassable. The sides of the valleys between are almost as sheer. If you intend to take your horses, you shall find it even more hazardous for them."

"How can we get to the Heraion then?" Alexis asked.

"There is an inland route which would take you through the mountains. It is longer, around four candlemarks or so would see you there, but the terrain is not as difficult or as sharply steep where the path cuts through."

"Four candlemarks? Helios' light is already halfway across the sky, if we continue on today, do the temples at the Heraion provide adequate shelter to house us for the night?" I asked.

"Yes, there are several buildings, not just the temple, I do not expect you to have trouble finding somewhere comfortable to slumber. Forests occupy the south and west of the Geraneia Mountains at a height of between thirteen hundred and twenty-six hundred feet. Barren land lies to its center, though you shall not traverse that area, nor the grasslands or further bushland in the northwest. You would take the north path around the lake, where the cliffs overlook the water."

"After we have finished our business at the Heraion, we intend to return to Trachis. Must we return to Thermae and travel across the Isthmus or is there a path to see us home to the north or northeast?"

"There are paths certainly, they are not as worn as the one from here to the Heraion, but it is possible to traverse them and it would be the shorter trail. When we finish our meal I shall take you to my home – I have a map of the area I would be happy to gift you to see you safely to your lands again."

"We would be most grateful," I said, finishing the food.

"Before you depart the Heraion, take some time to explore the area – the cliffs towards the headland beyond the harbor are known to be excellent for jumping from."

"People go there to throw themselves to their deaths?" Alexis shivered.

"No, no," Sophos laughed, shaking his head. "To swim. If the day is very hot, there is nothing better than to climb the rocks and jump or dive head-first into the cooling water below."

"There are no rocks at the bottom?" Thaddeus asked.

"No, or if they are, they remain far below the surface. It is quite safe and fun, though it is many winters since I partook of such ventures myself," he added with a grin.

"Oh," Alexis murmured, her face showing doubt she believed it was a *fun* activity.

"It is not for all of course," Sophos winked, patting Alexis' shoulder. "But for those to whom it holds appeal, it is a fine way to pass a summer's afternoon."

*

Two-and-a-half candlemarks later, the mountain flattened out to the valley that would see us around Lake Eschatiotis. Thaddeus and Alexis had ridden the horses most of the way while I remained on foot ahead of them, watching for dangers or steeper parts of the mountain, alerting them when they needed to dismount and lead the horses through particularly thin tracks or over large boulders.

Though the paths were reasonably well worn, just as Sophos had said, the sides were slippery with small pebbles and larger rocks protruded through the compact ground between the trees and shrubs. I found a large, flat rock to sit on beneath a tall pine tree as I waited for them to catch up, their voices not far in the distance as they chatted.

"Is everything well?" Alexis asked when they arrived a short time later.

"Yes. We have left behind the mountains for the time being, so I thought we could travel together to the lake."

Thaddeus dismounted and I crossed to Alexis, helping her off Skotos before retrieving the waterskin from our bag and taking a long drink. "Sophos said Lake Eschatiotis was salt water, so we shall have to wait until we get to the Heraion to refill the skins. How many more have we got?" I asked.

"Four," Alexis replied, taking the waterskin from me when I offered it to her.

"That should be more than enough," I nodded. "We should be at the lake in another half candlemark, the Heraion another candlemark after that. Once the sun begins to set, the heat shall not be as intense." I gathered Skotos' reins, pulling him along as we began to walk, side by side, across the short grass.

"We were just discussing the trees here. The pines and oaks are similar to those which grow in the Othrys Mountains in the north of the Malis region," Thaddeus said. "Though others I do not recognize at all."

"I would only recognize rosemary or olive bushes if there were any here. I do not know the names of many trees, and none of the ones here are the same as the ones in Trachis," Alexis added.

"No, around Trachis there are laurel trees but there are none of those here, only the pines and oaks Thaddeus mentioned, along with some firs. Did you know the resin from some trees – pines included – can be found in the frankincense used in perfumes or incense?" Alexis shook her head.

"Indeed?" Thaddeus asked, his brows raised.

I nodded. "Come, I shall show you," I led the two of them to a small cluster of trees. Handing Skotos' reins to Alexis, I took my sword and made a small hole in the trunk of the closest pine with the tip of my blade. Almost immediately, thick sap began to ooze from the hole and I allowed a small drop to coat the end of my weapon before turning back to Alexis and Thaddeus and holding it out for them to see.

"When a living tree is cut, it leaks this substance, just as we lose blood when our skin is pierced. But the resin works to protect the tree, hardening and filling the gap where the cut has been made, whereas we must hold a hand or cloth against our cuts to ensure too much blood does not leave our body. Feel the resin on my sword," I offered, holding it closer to them.

Alexis raised a tentative hand and pressed one finger into the sap, which had already started to set. "If I had not seen the liquid form it took before, I would not have believed it could be so," she murmured, moving aside so Thaddeus could feel it as well.

"Amazing," he agreed. I grinned and lowered my weapon, wiping it against the grass to remove the resin.

"How did you learn of it?" Alexis asked.

"When I received this," I replied, running my finger over the scar in my right eyebrow. "Oresinios, the healer at Eleusis, used it to seal the wound. He told me he used the resin just as the trees use it – to hold deep cuts closed so they have the chance to heal without illness getting into them. I heard of its other use in frankincense when I met the perfume merchant from Crete.

"I spoke with Gnosidicus when I was first injured in Trachis, he had heard of the practice of using resin, but prefers to trust in the gods and the herbs he prepares. When Melanthios and I tussled at the baths, I again attempted to convince Gnosidicus to apply it, but he did not have any and the nearby laurel trees do not produce it."

"Do you believe it to be a successful method of healing, say for soldiers stranded on remote battlefields without herbs?" Thaddeus asked.

"It could be, though I have never attempted to use it in such a manner," I shrugged. "I suppose if you could find it nearby, it may help, but I do not know how successful it would be for major wounds."

"You should mention it to Moeris as well, in case you or the soldiers ever find yourselves in such a situation," Thaddeus said, nodding. "I can see why Agrias wants you to lead our soldiers on your return; you hold knowledge of more than just battle. The men who teach my own children could learn much from you."

I shrugged again, but did not make reply.

"Thaddeus speaks true," Alexis agreed, slipping her hand into mine. "There are many positions you could hold in Trachis if leading the soldiers was not the one you wished for."

I grinned and leaned close. "There are many positions I wish to explore in Trachis, though none akin to the ones you speak of now."

"Skylar!" she scolded, slapping at my arm as Thaddeus laughed and shook his head. I laughed as well and straightened again, clutching her hand tighter as we began to walk.

When we reached the lake, Thaddeus tended the horses, ensuring both had enough fresh water to drink from our water skins before tethering them to a low branch. I shed my cuirass and tunic, taking a number of quick steps towards the water before launching myself into the clear, calm surface, my arms stretched out above my head. I kicked strongly through the warm saltiness, breaking the surface again quite a way from the bank where Thaddeus and Alexis stood.

I could hear Alexis' laughter, and Thaddeus appeared to find his sandals more interesting than the lake before him. "What is it?" I asked, stroking back towards them.

"Nothing, all is well," Thaddeus replied, keeping his eyes downcast.

Alexis laughed again and turned her friend so his back was to the two of us. "Your sudden nakedness causes Thaddeus embarrassment," she replied, reaching for the fibula at her shoulder and shedding her chiton.

"I did not take you to be shy, Thaddeus," I called, grinning.

"Not shy exactly. It only served as reminder that I travel with women, neither of whom is my wife. I would not wish to offend nor make you feel uncomfortable by me seeing you unclothed," he replied.

My gaze followed the lines of Alexis' naked form as she waded into the water and across to me, the shimmering water hiding her features the closer she got. "I appreciate the sentiment and if you intend to free yourself of the sweat and dust from our journey, I promise our eyes shall remain as far from your form as yours remain from ours," I grinned, sliding my arm around Alexis' waist when she arrived in front of me.

From the corner of my eye I saw Thaddeus reach down to remove his sandals. "That would be much appreciated," he replied.

# 27

After a short while we left the salty lake, pulling ourselves back out onto the shore and sharing one of the fish Sophos had given us to replace the boar we had shared with him. Now that I was fully clothed again, Thaddeus came to sit beside me on a nearby rock, the reflected heat drying the water from our legs and arms in no time as Alexis chose one opposite us.

As she went to seat herself, I realized it was not a rock she was about to sit on. I grinned and nudged Thaddeus, nodding in Alexis' direction and attempting not to alert her. He snorted, covering his sudden outburst by pretending to choke on his food. I slapped his back, feigning concern for him as I wiped the grin from my face when Alexis looked to us.

"What happened?" she asked.

"Sucked in a bone. I am well," Thaddeus finally replied, tears rolling down his face, though he still wore the hint of a smile when he caught my eye.

We watched Alexis as she settled herself on the foot-long black and yellow tortoise. She had barely touched it when it stirred, pushing up onto its feet and unbalancing her. She squealed and jumped off, spinning around to see why her rock had suddenly moved. Thaddeus and I burst out laughing.

"What is …? You knew?!" she cried, her fright masked by indignation. "Why did you not warn me?" Thaddeus and I continued to laugh, tears now streaming down my own face as Alexis looked between the tortoise, as it moved away slowly, and Thaddeus and I in disbelief.

"Apologies," I finally panted, wiping at my cheeks. "I should have warned you, but ..." I began to laugh again as Alexis planted her hands on her hips in a gesture I was well familiar with.

Thaddeus made his way to the tortoise, picking it up with some effort. "Apologies to you as well my friend, I am certain you were not expecting a giant to come sit on you as you warmed yourself in the summer sun," he told it.

"A giant?" Alexis asked, staring her friend down. "I am hardly such, though if it was unfortunate enough to have been sat on by Skylar, well that description would be well warranted."

"Me?" I asked, arching an eyebrow high on my brow as I stood. "Careful now, Princess or this giant may just steal you away," I threatened, stalking towards her.

"Ah ... Skylar?" Alexis asked uncertainly, dropping her hands from her waist and backing up a number of steps.

"Yes?" I smirked. She continued to retreat and when her eyes darted to the left, I grabbed her, lifting her up and throwing her over my shoulder as I headed for the lake again.

"Skylar!" she squealed, taking hold of the back of my tunic. I stepped into the water, attempting to lift her up and dump her back in, but she was securely attached to my clothing. I wriggled and turned in three tight circles, her fingers gripping tighter the faster I went until I became dizzy and stumbled forward, submerging us both as Thaddeus' laughter was lost above the surface of the water.

Alexis freed herself from my grip as we sunk lower, kicking strongly upward. I followed quickly, grabbing her by the ankle before she could get out again. Through the density of the water I heard Alexis' cry of surprise and I gave her a tug before darting past and breaking the surface a moment before she did.

"You shall pay for that," she warned, wagging a finger at me.

"Promise?" I challenged, swimming over and sliding my arm around her waist again. She splashed a handful of water in my direction, breaking my grip and heading back to the bank as I wiped my eyes and face. I laughed and followed her.

"You have improved immensely since I last saw you attempt to swim," Thaddeus noted as I pulled myself out of the water again.

"Alexis has taught me well," I replied with a grin. Alexis had taken me to the Melas River most weeks after she found out I could not swim, making it her personal mission to ensure I learnt. She claimed it was essential, given her penchant for needing saving so often since I had arrived in Trachis, but I suspected it had more to do with her enjoyment that she was more skilled at something than I was.

"I barely gave her four lessons before she was swimming as well as you or me. It is disgusting how easily she is able to turn her hand to so many skills," Alexis scoffed. I grinned, sticking my tongue out, recalling how scared, and yet perfectly calm, I had been under her guidance the first day when she had taught me to keep myself afloat by kicking strongly beneath the water.

"You are only jealous you have not fared as well under my javelin training," I shot back.

"Perhaps it has less to do with the student, than with the teacher?" Thaddeus offered with a grin.

"You want to take another swim?" I challenged, raising an eyebrow.

"You would not subject our animal friend here to the water, would you? He does not deserve such treatment," Thaddeus asked, holding up the tortoise.

"I would disarm you beforehand," I promised, still smiling.

"Perhaps it is time we made our way to the Heraion, we do not want to lose our way in the dark," he suggested hastily.

"We still have at least two candlemarks until we lose the light but yes, we do need to get going. Now put that poor creature down already."

"I am old enough to be her father, and yet she speaks to me in such a manner; what is to be done about it?" he asked the tortoise, heading towards a few scrubby bushes.

Alexis wrung her hair out and took a step forward. "Not so fast, Princess," I said, taking her hand and halting her progress.

Casting a quick glance in Thaddeus' direction and finding his back still to us as he chose the perfect spot to release the animal, I drew Alexis' body against my own and claimed her lips in a hungry kiss. She groaned, tangling a hand in my hair as she pressed herself even closer, the feel of her nipples hardening beneath her tunic firing my blood.

"Gods, I love it when you kiss me that way," she breathed when we parted.

"Mmm ... me too," I purred, nibbling at the flesh beneath her ear. "You taste salty," I added, licking down her neck until I reached her collarbone.

"You have to stop," she whispered. "Thaddeus ..." her words halted as I caught the flesh of her neck between my teeth.

"I am certain he would go on ahead if I asked it of him. He could be in charge of the map."

"You would give up the power of it?" she smiled.

"I have it memorized, I could see us there by only the slightest sliver of the moon," I assured her, sliding my thigh between hers and feeling the heat gathered there.

"Why does that not surprise me?" she laughed, putting her hands flat against my chest and pushing me away ever so slightly. "But we should all continue on together. The sooner we get to the Heraion and find out what awaits us there, the sooner we can enjoy one another as we did at Aphrodite's temple."

"A quick diversion would not be unwelcome, would it? And it *would* be quick," I smirked, pressing into her.

"Gods," she pleaded as her hands tightened on my arms.

Thaddeus cleared his throat and I turned a lazy eye on him, noting my cuirass and our bags in one of his hands and the horses' reins in the other. "You two appear to need another moment of privacy. I shall begin around the lake and meet you when you have ... er ... when you are ready, shall I?"

"Yes."

"No," Alexis replied at the same time, her voice firm. "Aphrodite said we must travel together. There shall be time for ... more later on."

"I do not mind," Thaddeus grinned.

"I do," Alexis said, removing my hands from her body and taking my cuirass from Thaddeus, holding it out for me to take.

I hesitated then grinned, placing my hand against Alexis' cheek as I drew her forward, kissing her thoroughly again, my tongue skimming her bottom lip. "Later," I promised when we parted.

She only growled in reply, shaking her head as she drew in several deep breaths in an attempt to compose herself.

"Come on, Warrior, to tease the princess any further would just be cruel," Thaddeus laughed, handing Alexis the bags when I took my cuirass from her. I laughed as well, sliding it over my head and settling it in place.

*

We led the horses up and over the cliffs to the north of the lake, reaching the other side a little over half a candlemark later. Our vantage point revealed the flat valley between the mountains and we headed in that direction, the last of our journey to be travelled across non-mountainous terrain.

"Perhaps Skotos and I can challenge you and Darko to a race when we reach the valley," I grinned over at Thaddeus.

"Absolutely, I am certain the horses would welcome the chance to stretch their legs in such a manner."

"And where shall I be whilst the two of you are doing that?" Alexis asked, hands on hips once again.

"Tucked safely in my arms and holding tightly to Skotos' neck of course," I replied, squeezing the hand of hers I held.

"Not a chance," she said, shaking her head.

"You do not trust me to keep you safe ... and win?" I asked, tilting my head to regard her.

"Oh, I have no doubt you would win, but without knowing the terrain, or possible hazards, certainly it would not be wise to attempt such a run?"

"Father and I raced from the Evrytania Mountains through the Spercheios Valley before meeting you outside Trachis, and we were no more familiar with that territory than I am with this. No harm came to us then."

"You are well aware the Spercheios Valley has far fewer trees, rocks or cliffs and valleys than we find here, the chance of injury was much less," she reasoned.

I pouted slightly though I knew she spoke true. Alexis squeezed my hand and took a quick step, placing herself in front of me so I could not continue. She gave Thaddeus a brief grin and he continued on ahead as she pressed her length along mine.

"If you intend to have your way with me when we reach the Heraion, I am certain you would not wish to be injured," she teased, her words quiet.

"Hmm, perhaps your words have merit, I shall consider them seriously," I grinned.

"A wise choice," she agreed, pushing up onto her toes and pressing her lips to mine. She returned to my side and we began to walk again. Thaddeus remained a number of paces ahead, the distance increasing the further down the slopes of the cliffs we travelled towards the valley. Birds called from the trees around us, and though I kept my eyes out for more tortoises, we saw none. Every now and then, the bushes at the edge of the path would shake as a small animal sought shelter further back from our footsteps. We saw none of them either, but I kept my palm on the pommel of my sword just in case – Sophos had spoken of animals as ferocious as boars frequenting the mountains and I knew I would have to be ready if one crossed our path.

The frequency of the movements in the brush began to increase as Helios' light travelled further across the sky on its downward journey and I hastened Alexis and Skotos until Thaddeus and I walked shoulder to shoulder, he on my left, Alexis my right.

A louder, prolonged movement caught my ear past Thaddeus, and he too slowed his pace when I nudged him and nodded in that direction. I released Alexis' hand and drew my sword as Thaddeus did the same, both of us waiting as the sound drew nearer. I tightened my grip as it grew closer. Suddenly, a hare burst forth through the shrubbery, bounding past, barely noticing us on its journey. I lowered my sword slightly with a grin, quickly raising it again as the bushes continued to tremor. Obviously it was not *our* presence which had caused the hare to rush from the bushes.

Ensuring I was between Alexis and whatever was about to emerge from the trees at the side of the path, I squeezed the handle of my sword, keeping my body poised for fight or flight. Thaddeus caught my eye and nodded, waiting until I had returned it before settling his gaze back on the bushes. Barely a moment later, the leaves parted and a long, grey serpent slithered forward, its tongue flickering out to taste the air. It had to be three or four feet long with bright reddish-brown spots edged in a deep black along its body.

It stopped when it caught sight of us, but when Darko saw it he reared up onto his hind legs with a cry. Thaddeus fought to hold onto his reins as the snake also raised itself up into an attacking position, exposing its black and white stomach to us.

"Darko, no!" Thaddeus cried, fumbling to re-sheath his sword and hold Darko at the same time.

"What is it?" Alexis asked, from behind me.

"Take Skotos and retreat along the path a few feet," I replied, stepping forward to draw the serpent's focus from Thaddeus. Turning its attention to me, it shook its tail, spurting some sort of liquid from its rear end onto the leaves and ground behind.

I took another step forward and it extended itself in my direction, fangs bared, though it was still at least four feet from reaching me.

Thaddeus continued to struggle with Darko who pawed the ground, snorting loudly and shaking his head as though attempting to dislodge the reins from his neck and Thaddeus from the end of them. The snake slid forward, still upright, and darted towards me again. I slashed at it with my sword, its fangs finding the tip. I backed up as it came again, but before it had the chance to strike a third time, I sliced its head from its body, both halves dropping to the ground with barely another twitch.

I turned from the serpent as Thaddeus cried out; Darko had managed to free himself and was racing wildly in my direction. I threw my sword down and grabbed for his reins, pulling him up short, still snorting and bucking.

"Thaddeus!" Alexis called.

I picked up my sword and dragged Darko behind me as Alexis rushed forward to where, only moments ago, Thaddeus had stood.

"What happened? Where is Thaddeus?" I asked. I pushed my sword into my sheath and tethered Darko to the nearest tree, crossing to Alexis' side. I wrapped my arm around her waist as she held tight to one of the trees and leant forward.

"He went over the edge. Down there!" she shouted, leaning out even further as she pointed at the scrubland below. "Thaddeus!" she called again. Between the pines and oaks, I caught sight of Thaddeus' white tunic, and a growing red stain beneath his dark hair. He had to be at least sixty-five feet down and was not moving.

"I see him," I nodded, hauling her away from the edge and setting her back on the path. I ran back to Skotos, taking the length of rope we had used to lead the ox to Epidaurus (and for far more enjoyable pursuits at Aphrodite's temple) from our bag. Returning to the tree line, I quickly wrapped one end around the largest trunk near the edge, shaking it so it uncoiled. The other end snaked its way through the bushes, coming to rest on top of a small purple-flowered bush. "Stay with Darko and Skotos away from the edge. I shall get him," I directed.

"Do you think …?" Alexis began.

I placed a hand on her shoulder. "He shall be fine. Just please, remain here so I do not have to worry about you as well," I replied, hoping I spoke true. She nodded and I placed a kiss on her forehead as I took off over the edge, barely gripping each trunk as I slipped my way down the cliff towards Thaddeus' motionless form.

I reached him without incident or injury, bar a few scratches from low hanging branches, and crouched beside him. His eyes were closed and he did not answer when I said his name. I brushed aside the hair at his forehead and wiped the blood away with the end of my tunic, finding the gash to be fairly shallow. I pressed my hand against his chest.

"Is he …?"

"His heart beats strongly," I cut her off, relief flooding through me. "Thaddeus?" I asked again. Again, he did not answer, but his eyelids twitched, as did two of his fingers.

I made a quick check over the rest of his body, noting the odd angle of his left leg. It was not a pleasant injury to have – I had seen similar when soldiers fell from their horses in battle, and their screams spoke the words their mouths could not. I would be able to do more for it when I got him back to the top of the cliff. Satisfied the rest of his wounds were only superficial, I drew my sword.

"I did not intend to have to use the sap when I spoke of it," I murmured, driving the tip of the blade into the nearest pine tree. Sap immediately leaked from the hole and I placed my fingers beneath it for a number of long moments, allowing the thick substance to coat them before smearing it across the line on Thaddeus' forehead. I wiped what was left on my fingers on my tunic, though most of it remained where it was, and put my sword away again.

Taking both of Thaddeus' arms, I hauled him upright, bending my knees until his chest was at the same level as my shoulder and throwing him over, much as I had done to Alexis at the lake. I tottered unsteadily for a few paces before finding my balance and starting back up through the trees, tightly holding to each I passed and pulling us upwards.

I reached the rope I had thrown down, able to grip it in both hands and ensuring our return was quick. When I got to the top, Alexis rushed forward, one hand at my elbow, the other around my waist as she aided me onto the path. She checked Thaddeus' head for herself before allowing me to set him down on the ground.

"You used the resin," she noted.

"Yes," I replied. "Horses have an aversion to blood and I did not want to scare them."

"I did not know that," she murmured. "Does he have any other injuries?"

"His leg is broken, but once I get a splint on it and he wakes, he shall be able to travel with it. He shall be in pain for a time and he needs rest more than anything else, but he shall be well again soon enough."

"You have seen the injury before?"

"Yes," I nodded. "Can you find me another tunic in his bag?"

Alexis nodded and fetched the item. "First a boar, now a serpent, what other surprises have we to endure this day?" Alexis muttered as I set to work slicing Thaddeus' tunic into strips.

"Hold this and do not watch," I told her, ignoring her musing and handing her the remains of the material. Without question, she turned her gaze from me and I took Thaddeus' leg in my hands; one at his thigh, the other at his shin. With a quick flick of my wrists and a sickening crack, I returned his leg to its correct position and took his sword from his waist.

I wrapped one length of tunic around the blade and placed it beneath the damaged limb, the hilt mid-way between his knee and groin. With three more lengths, I ensured the sword held his leg in place, briefly wondering how we would transport him. Alexis had obviously been wondering the same and questioned me.

"When soldiers are injured, they are laid face down across a horse's flank, but with the angle of his leg, I do not know if it is possible," I replied.

"You could not carry him as far as the Heraion?"

"Perhaps, but it would be faster if we could all ride. Bring Darko closer." Alexis did as directed and we allowed the horse to sniff at his master's head and face before I slid my hands beneath Thaddeus' legs and shoulders and lifted him off the ground. If the path narrowed on our way to the Heraion we may not be able to get through but placing Thaddeus over Darko's back as I had mentioned was not an option. "Stand Darko beside that rock," I said, nodding in the direction of a stone roughly a foot high.

Alexis led him over and I stepped up onto it, the bottom of Thaddeus' body now level with Darko's back. The steed remained still as I lifted Thaddeus and lay him so his spine met the horse's; his injured leg a reasonable distance from the edge of the animal. I gathered the rope from the tree at the edge of the cliff and threw it over Thaddeus and Darko. Ensuring Thaddeus was firmly bound, I tied off the ends.

"You and I can ride Skotos," I told Alexis, walking back and untying my horse from where he had remained calmly. I attached our bags to his rump, giving him a pat on the nose before holding my hand out for Darko's reins. Alexis passed them over and I knotted them with Skotos' before helping her astride my horse. I jumped up into position behind her and tightened my thighs against his flank to encourage him forward.

He stepped over the body of the beheaded snake and Darko fell into step beside us, the path more than wide enough for both steeds to walk side by side, and ensuring I was able to keep a close eye on Thaddeus' sleeping form.

Alexis placed her hand above mine on Skotos' reins and leaned back, her forehead level with my chin. I turned my head, kissing her gently as she exhaled a long breath. "He shall be well, when he wakes he shall tell you himself," I said quietly.

"Yes," she nodded. "I just ... I..."

"What is it?"

"Sometimes I wish I knew as much as you do about the world. If you had not been here today, I cannot bear to think what would have happened to Thaddeus, or with that boar."

"If I had not been here today, then neither would the two of you," I countered. "Do not waste time thinking of it, consider instead what awaits us at Hera's temple. Thaddeus shall wake and we shall receive answers as to how we can have a child."

Alexis nodded again, but did not reply, nestling against me further as I turned my hand beneath hers and threaded our fingers together, also intent not to dwell on what could have happened outside Corinth with the beast.

# 28

We arrived in the Heraion Valley without further incident as the sun cast long rays in brilliant pinks and oranges across the waters of the Gulf of Corinth. Thaddeus had not woken and I was fairly certain Alexis had nodded off as we travelled, though I did not bear either of them ill-will for it – gods knew I was eager to have something to eat then find a place to rest my own weary body as soon as possible.

Sophos had not spoken specifically of bedding or klinai, but had said that whatever was required by those who travelled there, was provided. I believed him, for as we approached the first of the buildings, I swore I could smell cooking meat wafting out to greet us. "We are here," I murmured into Alexis' hair. I was rewarded with a smile and sleepy eyes when she tilted her head back and they met mine. I leaned forward again, pressing my lips against hers.

"Thaddeus?" she enquired.

"He has not woken. But his breathing is strong."

"Thank the gods," she said, casting a glance in her friend's direction. "Do I smell food?" she added as her stomach rumbled.

"I wondered that too," I grinned, dismounting from Skotos before helping her down. "Perhaps it comes from the building up ahead?" I added, nodding in the direction of the peak-roofed structure.

"Do you think there are others here tonight, or priests such as at Epidaurus?"

"Perhaps," I replied, resting my hand against the pommel of my sword. Though Aphrodite had sent us here, she had not said we would be the only visitors and with the day we had had, I would not be unprepared should we find foe rather than friend to greet us.

Leading both horses, I kept my eyes on the dusty ground for signs of anyone else. There were a few small footprints, but I could not tell how recent they might be given their light impression. There was nothing to suggest mercenaries or heavily armed soldiers had arrived before us and no hoof tracks, apart from the ones Skotos and Darko made.

The structure was rectangular and roughly eighteen feet along the solid east wall which faced us. We continued around to the north-east side, finding a set of stone steps and taking them up to the three rooms. Darko and Skotos remained outside as Alexis and I entered the first room; it was empty and there was no south wall, the side simply left unbuilt and revealing the harbor of the Gulf of Corinth and a drop to the rocks below. The second room again had no rear wall and housed only a massive bronze statue of a bull, which dominated most of the space.

"Among other animals, cows or bulls are sacred to Hera," I told Alexis when she caught sight of the statue.

"This is the temple we are supposed to visit then?"

"I do not believe so," I replied. "If it was a temple of Hera, I would expect to find a carving of her as well, and an altar outside."

"Perhaps they are in the next room?" Alexis ventured. I shrugged and led her next door. There was no statue, only a hearth with a thick length of wood supported either end above it; an object I knew as a spit. Normally, an animal such as a boar or ox was set upon it and roasted in the same manner as Sophos had cooked his fish on the beach, and this one was no different – a deer cooking above the flames.

"The source of the smell," Alexis noted, her stomach rumbling again.

I grinned and nodded, not surprised to once again find the south wall an open void to the view beyond. "We should find out who else is here, hopefully they shall be kind enough to share their meal," I said, leaving the building and taking Skotos' reins again.

We descended the stairs and I noticed a spring to the left. Several libation vessels lay scattered about and when I crouched down to look into the clear water, I could not make out the bottom. I dipped the tips of my fingers in, tempted to clean the dust and sweat from my face in the cool water. I did not – knowing better than to bathe uninvited in waters which could be considered sacred, thereby risking offence to the goddess we sought aid from.

I returned to my feet and led Alexis to a second building, a little further to the west towards the harbor, but still constructed close to the edge of the cliff. It again had three rooms, though was set out differently to the first, with walls on all sides broken up only by the opening in the north side for the entrance. It was almost square rather than rectangular, and the initial entrance room was bare. The two south rooms contained eleven dining couches as long as I was tall built against the wall with seven small rectangular tables in front of them.

"It does not appear anyone has claimed use of this room for their meal, we should put Thaddeus here," I said.

Alexis nodded and we made our way back outside. At the doorway I stopped abruptly, causing Alexis to bump into me, her head hitting the bronze of my cuirass. "Ow!" she gasped. "What is it?"

"Apologies," I whispered, not adding anything further as my eyes settled on the old woman patting Darko.

She turned at Alexis' cry, a warm smile splitting her face. "Welcome, welcome. The Queen of the Gods has been awaiting your arrival," she said, bustling over and holding out her hands. Tentatively I raised my own to meet hers and she gripped me strongly. "It appears your journey has not been without its challenges," she remarked, her eyes straying back to Thaddeus' prone form.

"A serpent startled his horse in the mountains. He fell over the cliff edge, saved from a longer drop by the trees on the hillside," I replied.

"A fortunate blessing," the old woman remarked.

"Indeed," I agreed as she released my hands and took Alexis'.

"You must be hungry and tired. Put your friend in one of the rooms beyond and settle yourselves in the other, I shall bring food for you."

"We would be most grateful," Alexis said with a smile.

"May our horses drink from the spring?" I asked, nodding in its direction.

"Of course, but I shall tend them for you," the woman replied.

"I am happy to do it, after I set Thaddeus inside," I insisted. I crossed to Darko and untied Thaddeus from his back, taking him into my arms. I could not say why, but I did not believe that the old woman was simply just that.

"We would be grateful if you could assist us with our animals," Alexis said, laying her hand on my arm to halt my progress with Thaddeus, and any objection I might have. "We are weary from travel."

"Very good. It is no trouble for me. Eat and rest. Tomorrow shall bring you the answers you seek." She led our steeds to the spring as I headed for the rooms.

"You do not trust her?" Alexis asked quietly, her pace matching mine as we entered. She moved the table in front of the first couch and I lay Thaddeus down, ensuring his leg remained straight and protected from further injury.

"When Jason was on his way to Iolkos he met an old woman who asked him for aid. He carried her across the river, losing a sandal in the process, and fulfilling the prophecy that the future king would arrive wearing only one sandal," I said.

"Jason?" Alexis asked. "I do not understand."

"Of the Argonauts," I replied, frowning slightly as I straightened again. "It was not merely an old woman he met, but the goddess Hera disguised as such, though he did not know it. I did not expect we would meet an old woman here, a priest or priestess perhaps, but not her."

"You do not believe she is a priestess?"

"No. She does not wear clothing, or insignia, to claim such position and given the remoteness of the place we find ourselves in, it cannot be safe for an old woman to be here alone."

"Perhaps it is the remoteness which gives her protection, along with favor of the goddess she serves."

"Unless she is Hera," I muttered.

"You believe it to be so?"

I shrugged. I had heard too many tales to know all may not be as it appeared – especially where Hera was concerned – and we found ourselves squarely in a vicinity dedicated to her worship.

"Does it matter who she is?" Alexis asked holding her hand out and leading me to the second room when I took it.

"If she *is* the goddess, I would prefer she appear to us in that guise just as Aphrodite and Asclepius did."

"Why?" Alexis asked, yawning as she crawled onto the first klinai inside the door. I shrugged again and released her hand, settling along a second couch so our heads almost touched.

"With so much in our journey still unknown, I want to know who it is I deal with. She did not even offer us her name."

"Perhaps she has not used it for many winters, and cannot recall it?" Alexis mused, yawning again. I grinned as I watched her lay her head on her arm, propping my own on my hand as I stretched along the soft fabric.

"If that was so, I am certain you would find a way to get her to speak of it."

"It would be an interesting tale, I am certain of it," she agreed. "I am glad we have finally arrived."

"As am I. I am also glad I do not have to find, kill or cook anything to be fed tonight."

"Would you teach me to catch something as we journey home?" Alexis asked, tilting her head back so our eyes met. "We have been fortunate enough so far to be gifted with enough food to see us to our next destinations, but I would welcome the opportunity to learn that of your past also. Was it only your father who taught you?"

"It was. Sometimes we fished, other times we found small animals or birds, though I admit, until today I had never killed my own boar to eat."

"Perhaps we could begin with something a little smaller," Alexis grinned. "With less deadly claws and teeth."

"Deal," I replied, leaning over and kissing her. The old woman returned as we parted, setting down an amphora and two skyphoi before handing each of us a terracotta bowl of steaming, delicious smelling roasted deer, a ring of red-seeded fruit at the edges of the dishes. "Thank you," I said, sitting up and taking the offered food.

Alexis repeated the sentiment and did the same, shoveling a handful of the meat into her mouth with a barely disguised whimper. I chuckled and helped myself, though showed a little more restraint as the woman poured rich, red wine into the skyphoi.

"I have sent prayers to goddess Hera for plentiful rest for you and your friend. You may sleep as long as you all require. You shall not be disturbed."

"Wh–" I began.

"It is appreciated," Alexis cut over me, her mouth full as she raised her brows in my direction. I hesitated but gave her a small nod. Alexis spoke true; it did not truly matter if the old woman was Hera in disguise or not. We had arrived, though not as unscathed as I wished, and when morning greeted us we could ask the goddess for aid.

"Thank you for this," I said, raising my bowl momentarily as I reached for the wine. The woman only nodded in reply, leaving the dining structure again, her sandaled feet making barely a sound across the dusty ground outside.

When Alexis and I had finished our food, I set the bowls aside, checking on Thaddeus and the horses before stripping off my cuirass and tunic, as well as Alexis' soft chiton, and drawing her against me to sleep.

"Skylar?" she whispered after a few moments.

"Mmm?"

"Do you think we shall have to wait until Thaddeus recovers before Hera aids us?"

"I do not know. Probably."

"How long until his leg heals?"

"A moon, maybe more."

"Oh. But you believe Hera shall still help us? That Thaddeus shall still be willing to aid us in having a child?"

"It is only his leg that is injured, the rest of him is fine. It shall be sore, but I am certain he shall want to do what he came with us for. Now, go to sleep."

"You do not wish to finish what you began at the lake?" she asked, and I heard the smile in her voice.

"Definitely, but I am too tired."

She chuckled. "I think I am glad for I am exhausted as well. I love you."

"I love you too," I replied, hugging her closer as Hypnos claimed me moments later.

# 29

I woke early and dressed, taking a handful of figs from the bowl on the table before heading out to the horses. I led them over to the spring, where they drank the cool water greedily. I leant against the trunk of a large willow tree beside them and took in the other buildings of the Heraion, which were on a lower level to where I stood. There was a gentle slope to take me down there and I intended to do just that once the horses were finished. The harbor lay to the southwest past the few buildings, and the tip of land that Sophos had said separated the Gulf of Corinth from the Halcyonic Gulf.

When the animals were done, I re-tied their reins to the tree that would shelter them from the heat of the sun later in the day. I looked in on Alexis and Thaddeus, both of whom still slept, and decided to leave my cuirass and weapons in the room as I followed the path to the lower level.

The sheer rock face accompanied me unbroken on my right as I descended, but on the left, where, at first, it had been just a steep drop to the ground below, a building began to appear – its patchy, thatch covered, high-peaked roof close enough for me to touch from the path. When I reached the bottom of the slope, I found I was at the back end of the building and that it was far older than the ones up higher. Most of the roof on the side closest to the harbor was missing; some of it scattered outside, some inside on the dirt-covered floor when I stepped in, the rest gone altogether.

Where the other structures had been roughly uniform in their size and the number of rooms, this one was only a single space, with a small opening on the east end, and a solid, curved end on the west. The shape reminded me of the hairpins Alexis often wore, and which Hesper had put into my hair the night of the banquet. It bore no windows and nothing inside, but when I exited, I saw a stone altar directly to its south. It was probably the original temple of the area.

I walked across to the altar, which stood eight foot wide on the end closest to the old temple and stretched thirteen towards the water. Eight Ionic-style columns stood at intervals either side, their inclusion adding another few feet to the entire stone structure. They bore similarities to the fluted Doric columns at the Temple of Asclepius in Epidaurus; comprising of three sections – the base, the shaft and the capital – which tapered upward with parallel concave grooves. But, the Ionic columns astride the altar were more slender than the Doric ones and had twenty-four grooves along their fluted shafts, rather than twenty. They also sat on a stepped platform at ground level. At the top, the columns tapered but between the capital and shaft was a wide, plain collar, and the capital itself did not flare out, housing instead a spiral ornament with four scroll-like flourishes which reminded me of ram's horns.

Where Asclepius' temple had been decorated with metopes and triglyphs *above* the columns, here they were displayed on each side of the altar between the base and top. The pattern was the same though – the flat panels of the metopes between three black, carved upright bars of the triglyphs the entire way around.

A newer building stood nearby, its north and south walls almost one hundred feet long, and its roof made of marbled tiles rather ceramic ones or thatch. I was surprised there were no triangular pediments or corner sculptures on the building as there were on the two buildings in Epidaurus, though this structure still held metope and triglyphs above the four Doric columns at the east entrance.

Unlike some of the others, the building was well tended with a garden along the south wall and two smaller ones in front of the Doric columns of the porch. There was little room between the north side of the temple and the cliff face, but what area there was, was taken up by a tree which had taken root partway up the cliff and overhung towards the entrance. I recognized it as a pomegranate – the fruit the old woman had brought us with the deer meat last night and as I looked up through its lower branches, I saw several more of the fruit hidden between the narrow green leaves and big flowers with bright red petals and yellow cores.

The marble edges of the garden beds either side of the entrance were built up about two feet. They held clear, still water filled with bright yellow flowers growing on long, tubular stems above rounded, green leaves which floated on the surface. Their presence suggested that perhaps the building was the temple we had been directed to visit by Aphrodite – water lilies were often attributed to Hera and offered to her with prayers and sacrifices in Greek homes and temples alike.

I entered the long, narrow room known as the cella. It was divided by two walls, making three aisles, which was quite an unusual design, and one I had not seen elsewhere. The walls were only as high as my hip, but six Doric columns rose up from them to meet the roof above. Towards the west end, between the solid wall on the north side and the first columned section, was another cross wall, and standing in front of that was a large statue. I made my way over, confirming when I saw the bronze statue that I was indeed in the temple dedicated to Hera – the Heraion.

I nodded to myself, satisfied I would know where to come and what I would find when it was time for Alexis, Thaddeus and I to go there. I left the temple again and headed towards the harbor and the open area beyond. I would hardly have deemed it a harbor, more an inlet, as I doubted that no more than three small boats would have been able to anchor on the shore at once.

To the extreme south-west of the entire area was a dusty, odd-shaped space. The western end was carved into the rock of the cliffs above and at its base ran a wooden bench about twenty-five or thirty feet long. I walked back to the water's edge and kicked off my sandals, immersing my toes in the soft sand. The clear water shimmered in the morning light, revealing large, flat rocks akin to those I had only ever seen in rivers, beneath its surface. The water that lapped over my feet was warm; about the same temperature as the air I stood out in. I stripped off my tunic and waded in, diving under an incoming wave when I was in as deep as my waist.

I swam out, following the land around the far end of the Heraion. When the temples and inlet were mostly hidden from view, I stroked across to the black rocks and pulled myself out of the water. They were smooth to the touch and almost square, stacked on top of one another so it was easy to find footing as I climbed them. Small ridges made it easy to curl my fingers in and pull myself up to the next level, and I was surprised to find they were not slippery at all, even with my wet limbs.

When I reached the top, I found the slab of stone extended only a foot or so back before it disappeared beneath thick shrubs and grasses. From where I stood, I could not see how quickly the rock may fall away on the other side, but it possibly extended as far as thirteen feet before dropping to the odd shaped area and wooden benches below.

I looked back to the water, noting how clear and clean it was and guessing I was probably fifteen foot above it; higher than I had realized when I decided to climb up. Regardless of the knowledge I had just swum through it, and that my feet had been far from reaching the bottom, I still searched the depths for hidden rocks or other dangers. I was keen to attempt the cliff jumping Sophos had told us about and wanted to experience the sensation of falling from heights when it was of my own choosing rather than by accident.

I tightened my toes against the edge of the rocky outcrop, my calves resting against the final half-foot of rock before the flat top. I drew a deep breath, rocking on the balls of my feet and feeling the solid stone at the back of my legs, the barest of breezes sliding between when I moved forward. The water below was calm and I concentrated on watching it as I inhaled again. I exhaled and pushed forward, launching myself out over the side.

Sophos had instructed me to keep my legs together and my arms across my chest, with one holding my nose closed. I barely had time to do it all before I hit the water. I sank for a few moments before kicking up strongly, a wide grin and a whoop of delight leaving my chest as I broke the surface. I swam back to the rocks and pulled myself out once more, racing to the top and jumping off without hesitation.

I repeated the process again and again, interested to note that I did not feel as if I was falling from a great height – that perhaps it was not high enough to be of true challenge. I wondered if there were other places I could cliff jump from. I knew the waters along the Malian Gulf were too dangerous with the rocks which lay at the bottom, but I was certain that somewhere in Greece would provide the same clear waters as I found at the Heraion, and I intended to seek them out when I had the opportunity again.

# 30

Aphrodite lounged on a klinai at the abaton of Epidaurus, a simpering smile plastered to her face. "I know you are here Asclepius, show yourself," she ordered.

The god appeared in a flash of light, arms folded across his chest as he regarded the Goddess of Love. "What is it you seek me for?" he asked, no hint of warmth to his question.

"The mortal who visited you here, Alexis. You sent her onto me just as Ares asked. In turn, I sent her and her lover to his mother so she may gift them what they seek. Another joins them and he is instrumental to the success of it, though he is deep within Hypnos' realm, injured and useless. I wish for you to go to him, heal his injuries so the child can be created."

"I am aware that Thaddeus joins them at the Heraion. It appears young Skylar finally accepts it is how it must be. But what is the urgency for him to recover? The more time the three of them spend together speaking of all they have kept inside can only strengthen their bond when the time comes."

"I do not owe you explanation, and it is not just I who wishes for the child to be created sooner rather than later."

"Oh? I can only assume it is your lover who wishes for it, for apart from Ares, you care for none more than yourself and would petition on behalf of no other."

Aphrodite dropped all pretense of civility, on her feet with a swiftness which surprised even the other god. "You and I have not favored one another in all the winters we have existed, and though it pains me to have to seek you at all at this time, if you would heal the boy as I ask, perhaps I shall consider putting behind us the part you played in that unpleasant business with Hippolytus and Artemis."

Asclepius laughed. "You must indeed have great stake in the child to speak of such an offer ... I could consider seeing it so," he shrugged, considering her a moment longer. Aphrodite ground her teeth together but said nothing. "Perhaps in the future, should I require *your* aid, you shall favor me without threat or cross words. Hmm?" Aphrodite only nodded once in reply. "Good. Do give my regards to Ares when you return to his side." Still Aphrodite said nothing, afraid she would undo what she had been able to achieve if she opened her mouth. She disappeared from the temple knowing Ares would be pleased his wishes were progressing as planned.

# 31

Quite some time later, as I sat on the shore with my feet in the water and my tunic back on, I heard the unmistakable sound of footsteps crunching over gravel. I turned my head, finding Alexis making her way down the slope from the upper level. I waved and she smiled as she returned it, joining me at the water's edge.

"Good morning," she said, sitting down beside me and offering her mouth.

"Morning," I replied, obligingly pressing my lips against hers. "You slept well?"

"Very. I am not surprised to find you down here, though I prefer to see you when I wake. Have you been up long?"

"Since Helios' light greeted Eos," I replied. "The water is lovely and warm. Can I interest you in a swim … or perhaps another pleasurable activity?"

"Oh yes," Alexis grinned, reaching for the fibula that held her chiton together.

"Allow me," I offered, covering her hand with my own.

"Gladly," she murmured, placing both of hers on the sand behind her and leaning back. I smiled, kneeling as I faced her and drew out the bone implement. "What have you been doing whilst I have slumbered this morning?" she asked as the material fell from her body.

"Looking around," I replied, my eyes going immediately to her exposed breasts.

"Find anything interesting?"

"An altar. Some buildings. One I believe is the temple Aphrodite spoke of us visiting." I ran my tongue over my lips, my eyes meeting Alexis' again and I noted the dark centers larger than the green around them.

"Indeed?" she breathed. I only nodded in reply, leaning in close and kissing her, my tongue sliding the length of her bottom lip as her own brushed against mine and I inhaled sharply with the contact. With a hand on the nape of her neck I drew her forward, not breaking our kiss as I pulled her to her feet.

"I also attempted the cliff jumping Sophos spoke of," I said when we parted.

"Was it not dangerous to do so by yourself?"

"No."

"You enjoyed it?"

"Very much," I grinned. "Allow me to introduce you to the warm waters of the Corinthian Gulf then I shall show you," I murmured, placing my fingers at her waist.

"I believe I shall enjoy them," she smiled, removing the fibula on my tunic and pushing the material to the ground.

"Me too," I replied, returning her grin as I wrapped my arm around her waist and lifted her into my arms, wading into the warm water until it reached my underarms.

"Then we shall go to the temples you found?"

"Yes."

Alexis nodded and settled one arm around my neck, her other tracing my collarbone and slipping lower to my chest. Her tongue drew lazy circles against my throat until I released her, her length now pressing against mine, my hands going to the small of her back to hold her there.

She raised her chin and I bent my head, capturing her lips, my hands journeying over her body, finding every curve and contour across the softness, reveling in the feelings she evoked inside me when she pushed her tongue into my mouth. We spent many long moments kissing and touching one another, the waves rocking us gently back and forth, pushing our bodies together before separating them ever so slightly.

The sun beat down but I was barely aware of its growing heat, Alexis' hands trailing over my skin sending hot flames from my stomach to the rest of my body. She tightened her grip at my neck and wrapped her legs around my waist, her tongue seeking mine with greater desperation. I gripped the outside of her thighs, bringing her even closer as I clamped my teeth on her bottom lip and pressed down.

She gasped, threading her hand into my hair. The temperature of my blood continued to rise, heightening to a dangerous level when she began to move against me. My hand remained at the small of her back, guiding her against my heated flesh, her breath shortening each time we met and it was not long before she found her end, immediately sliding her hand between us and ensuring I followed just as quickly.

"I must admit, I have enjoyed aspects of this trip far more than I expected to," I murmured, nuzzling my lips against her neck when our breathing returned to normal.

"I certainly did not expect to have so much time to … appreciate one another as we have," she replied with a laugh.

"Mmm. A fortunate set of circumstances indeed," I agreed. "Do you want to attempt the cliff jumping now?" Alexis nodded in reply. I released her and swam to the black rocks, hoisting myself out of the water and up the smooth face as Alexis followed.

We stood shoulder to shoulder on the top of the cliff, Alexis reaching for my hand with a slight tremor. "It is higher than I expected," she said.

I regarded her for a moment. "You are afraid?"

"A little," she admitted. "I have never been higher off the ground than Skotos or Calla's backs."

"It is thrilling to be so though, is it not?" I asked, squeezing her hand as I looked down into the clear water, my stomach fluttering with anticipation.

"I suppose."

"I promise it is safe. Shall I show you?"

Alexis hesitated, looking from me to the water below, swaying slightly before reaching back with both hands to grip the rocks behind her. "I can see you want to do it again."

I could not help the grin from breaking out, even though the fear and apprehension was clearly written across her face. "When you push off from the rock face, press your thighs together and wrap your arms across your chest. Hold your nose as well so the water does not go up when you hit it," I told her. "It is deep and I did not touch the bottom when I went in, so do not fear that." Alexis only nodded in reply. I rocked back and pushed off, grabbing my chest and taking a breath a moment before my feet touched the warmth of the water.

When I resurfaced, I swam back to the rocks and climbed up. "You are ready now?" I asked, wringing out my wet hair.

"Not yet. Perhaps you could show me again?" Alexis replied.

I nodded, turning so I was facing her. "Watch what I do with my body. I shall wait for you in the water this time." Alexis nodded once more.

I took a quick look behind me before positioning my feet and jumping out backwards. It was even more exciting watching the blur of rocks in front of me than it had been watching the water rise to meet me and I broke the surface again with a delighted cry.

Alexis gazed down nervously. "Just do as I showed you and I shall be right here," I encouraged.

"I … I cannot."

"Of course you can. Just do as I said and you shall be fine."

"It is too high. But I cannot climb back down the rocks; that does not feel safe either."

"You can do this. Just push back against the rocks and jump off." Alexis took a number of deep breaths, her hands still gripping the stones behind her. Her chest rose and fell and she closed her eyes for a long moment. When she opened them again, she looked down and gave me a tight smile.

Wrapping one arm across her chest and the other gripping her nose, she inhaled deeply and jumped off the rocks, hitting the water seconds later with barely a splash. She kicked up strongly, breaking the surface with a gasp of air and I swam the short distance to her with a grin.

"Well? Is it not wonderful?" I asked. I noticed Alexis' breathing was shallow and her face had paled. My smile faded. "Alexis?"

"It was … I do not want to do that again," she murmured, the skin on her shoulders puckered. I reached out and drew her against me, swimming back to the point where my feet touched the sandy bottom.

"I am sorry," I whispered into her hair, holding her tighter.

She shook in my arms, and I knew it was a mixture of the fear and excitement leaving her body. I had had the same response after the fight in Anticyra when I first picked up a weapon. It still happened now after battle. "Sorry," I murmured again. I released her and tilted her chin so our eyes met. Her color was returning to normal and her shaking eased.

"I should not have insisted you jump. I should have helped you down the rocks again."

She swallowed before replying. "I did not expect to have such a reaction. It is not as though the mountains we travelled through to get here were not high, nor the path over the Othrys Mountains to Epirus filled with the same." I noted the direction she spoke of to get to Epirus; it was not the same as the one Father and I had followed, but I did not question her on it. "It was just … I had no solid ground beneath me as the paths provide. I did not feel safe jumping out into the air. I did not know what to expect the water to feel like when I entered it. It was not hard exactly, but it was not as it is when we swim through it," she said in a rush.

"No," I agreed, with a shake of my head. "Apologies again for making you do so. Perhaps it is time we returned to the beach."

"Please," Alexis nodded. "I did not see the old woman this morning, but Thaddeus may now be awake."

"If he was awake, I am certain we would have heard him, I expect his leg shall be painful."

"If he had not been injured, perhaps he would have enjoyed the cliff jumping as you do."

"Perhaps, but I shall turn the activity from my mind and focus on what we came here for."

We dressed in silence before I took Alexis' hand, leading her across the sand and over to the temple buildings. She ran her fingers across the stone surface of the altar as we passed, her eyes lighting up when she caught sight of the yellow-centered flowers in the garden on the south wall of the temple.

"I believe this is the Heraion Aphrodite spoke of," I told her as she freed her hand from mine and reached out to stroke the white petals. The bush sat low to the ground, the flowers themselves rising up through narrow, pale-green leaves on brown stalks, the scent of apples wafting through the air when Alexis pressed the petals between her fingers.

"Hera is not one of the goddesses your people worship, is she?" I asked, picking one of the flowers and offering it to Alexis.

"No," she smiled, taking it from me. "But after you arrived in Trachis, your father and I had many discussions about Greek gods, what their names were, why they were worshipped."

"Did you?" I grinned, not surprised in the least.

She nodded. "It was how I knew I wanted a poet to speak of Aphrodite at the banquet."

"And now you have been fortunate enough to meet her in person," I said.

"Yes. I cannot wait to get back to Trachis so I can send Leandros a messenger to tell him of it."

"I hope you shall not give him too many details when you speak of our time in Corinth," I grinned, bumping my shoulder against hers.

"Definitely not," she replied, coloring slightly.

"Good," I laughed. "My father is aware of much of my past, but there are certain acts I would prefer to keep to myself."

"As would I," Alexis agreed with a nod. I took her hand again and, pointing out the other small temple, began back up the stony path.

"Do you want me to heal your arm?" Asclepius asked, appearing suddenly beside us. I jumped, automatically putting my body between him and Alexis and reaching for my sword.

"Apologies, I did not mean to startle you," he grinned.

"It is never wise to merely appear without announcement," I grinned, dropping my hand from my waist.

"You do not carry your weapons, so I considered myself safe," he replied, his smile widening.

"You are fortunate," I agreed. "And I appreciate your offer." I unwound the length of material above the gash Cleomenes' blade had made when he killed the boar. Dried blood stuck it to the skin in several places, making me suck in a breath as I separated them. I held my arm out and Asclepius closed his hand around the wound, bright light shining out between his fingers a moment later. The faint sting of the wound disappeared, replaced by a slight tingling throughout my body. I had experienced the sensation before and wondered, not for the first time, if I had been visited – and healed – by a god then also.

"Was it you who came to me in Trachis after I was hurt?" I asked.

"No," Asclepius replied, shaking his head. "Until we met in Epidaurus, we had never been face-to-face."

"Oh," I murmured, looking down at my arm as he released me; there was no sign of the wound, or even a scar where it had been. Had I indeed just dreamed the voices and presence of others as I lay in Trachis?

"That is amazing," Alexis breathed, smoothing her hand across my skin.

Asclepius smiled again. "There are those who wish to see you get what you seek sooner rather than later. You need not suffer from injuries when you receive their aid."

"Who?" I asked. "Aphrodite?"

"It would appear you are favored by her, yes. But now I must take my leave for I am required elsewhere."

"Wait," I called.

"Thank you," Alexis added at the same time. Asclepius disappeared as silently and quickly as he had appeared.

"I wish, just once, the gods would not speak in such riddles," I muttered. "First Aphrodite spoke of me being favored by an immortal, now Asclepius appears to be suggesting the same."

"You do not believe it to be only the two of them?"

I blew out a loud breath and shrugged. "I do not know. Come on." I took Alexis' hand and continued up the path. "When I was down by the water earlier, I thought about Hera and the tales I have heard of this place."

"It has been here for many winters?" Alexis asked.

"At least since the time of the Argonauts I referred to earlier," I replied. "You have never heard of the heroes and men who joined Jason in capturing the Golden Fleece in Colchis?"

"I know only part of the story; that Heracles was counted in their number. But he was not with them when they reached Colchis."

"That is true," I nodded. "Heracles remained in Mysia after his weapons bearer was lost when the Argonauts went ashore. He did eventually return to Greece, though I do not know if it was before Jason and his men did or not. Theseus too sailed to Colchis and back with them."

"I did not know that. Would you tell me how this place is linked to the Argonauts?"

I nodded. "When they arrived in Colchis, Jason met and fell in love with the king's daughter – Medea. Medea loved him in return and offered to help Jason steal the Golden Fleece if he promised to take her with him when he left. He agreed, succeeding in gaining the Fleece and returning to Iolkos. Not long after, Jason and Medea, along with their two sons, were driven from Iolkos after Medea had Jason's cousins cruelly kill their father. They settled in Corinth where, unfortunately for Medea, Jason's love for her waned and he fell in love with another king's daughter named Glauce, and asked her to be his wife.

"Medea was furious Jason had broken his vow to be with her forever and reminded him of all she had done to help him steal the Golden Fleece from her father. Jason told Medea he was merely thankful to Aphrodite for having her fall in love with him and giving him such aid. Medea took her revenge by presenting Glauce with a cursed chiton for a wedding gift which burnt her to death when she put it on."

"That is so similar to Heracles' fate, though his gift was given in error rather than malice," Alexis offered.

"Indeed. But Medea, fearing her sons would be killed or enslaved in retaliation for her actions, killed them and, it is said, she buried them here in a sanctuary to Hera."

"Medea killed her own children?" Alexis asked, horrified.

"That is how the tale is told," I replied.

"That is a terrible deed, especially for a mother."

"It is. When Jason learnt of it, he was devastated and searched for Medea to take vengeance. It was said that she went to Athens, but he never found her." I paused before adding in a quiet voice, "I would rather die myself than allow my child to pay for something I had done."

"Allow us to hope that is never the case," Alexis murmured, squeezing my hand. "We have spoken much of Heracles these past days; he is a hero both of us have admired for many winters, yet we are here to ask Hera for assistance or guidance in the two of us having a child. She despised Heracles so much, do you believe she shall aid us if she knows of our respect for him?"

I shrugged. "I cannot imagine Aphrodite would have suggested we journey here if Hera held that against us. Neither you, me or Thaddeus have found ourselves to be the child of an immortal parent so unless we give the gods reason to show ill-favor towards us by acting with contempt or disrespect towards them, I would hope we could ask them for help when we needed it. That is what they are there for, is it not?"

"Your words to Aphrodite could have made her turn from us, had she wished to."

I nodded. "I know. I am fortunate that she thought so highly of *you* to look past my actions towards her."

"Clearly I am your better half," she laughed.

"Oh, you think so, do you?" I asked, grinning as I raised an eyebrow in her direction.

"Sometimes," she replied.

"Well then I thank Aphrodite or whichever god or goddess would take credit for it, that I met you to keep me from incurring the wrath of the immortals," I smiled, leaning down and kissing her on the cheek.

Alexis laughed again. "As do I. Do you have other stories of this place?"

"I do," I replied as we reached the building we had slept in the night before. I gave Skotos a quick pat as I passed, entering ahead of Alexis, pausing suddenly in the outer area. Thaddeus stood upright in the doorway of the room we had left him in, a large bowl in his hand and his sword no longer attached to his leg.

"I hope you shall share them with me also," he said.

"Thaddeus?" I asked, surprised to find he appeared fully recovered.

# 32

"Good morning, or is it afternoon?" Thaddeus replied, grinning as Alexis pushed past me. She took his arms in her hands as she looked him over.

"Thaddeus. But ... you ... how?"

"Have you tasted this? It is the best I have ever eaten."

"We have," I replied, remaining in the doorway. "Your leg is completely healed?"

"Yes. How long did I sleep? Injuries as I suffered take a moon to heal at least. I gather we are at the Heraion?"

"We are," I acknowledged.

"We only arrived yesterday," Alexis added. "How is it possible you have made a full recovery? Your leg ... it was ... and your head," she reached up and pushed his hair aside; there was no sign of the cut.

"Yesterday? That cannot be true," he said with a frown.

"It is," I said, finally moving into the structure as Thaddeus set his food aside. I approached, checking his forehead for myself before dropping to one knee and examining his leg. There was no sign of injury.

"How?" Alexis asked again. "Could it have been the sap?"

"Sap?" Thaddeus repeated.

"No. It could not have done that," I murmured, returning to my feet. "It must have been Asclepius. What is the last thing you remember?"

"The snake. I lost my footing when Darko broke my hold on his reins and I fell backwards over the side. My leg smashed against a rock, I heard a snap, felt the pain of it, but then I hit my head, and next I knew, I woke up here and there was a delicious smell of cooked meat," he said, nodding in the direction of his bowl. "Should I ask about the resin?"

I grinned. "Used it on your head. It stopped the bleeding but there is no way it healed your leg, or made the gash disappear so quickly."

Thaddeus raised his hand to his head, smoothing his fingers over the unbroken surface. "How did I get here?"

"Skylar brought you back up the slope," Alexis replied before I could answer. "Your leg was … bent in the wrong direction. She put it back, attached your sword to it and tied you to Darko's back so we could ride faster."

"I owe you my thanks," Thaddeus said, holding his arm out.

I took it, gripping it briefly as I nodded. "You would have done the same for me had it been required," I replied.

"No question," he agreed. "So, we are at the Heraion. Do you know where we have to go to request Hera's assistance?"

"I have an idea," I nodded. "Come, I shall show both of you."

"Allow me to put on a clean tunic first," Thaddeus said. "If I am to meet a goddess, I want to look my best."

I smiled and shook my head. "I do not know if we shall actually meet the Queen of the Gods, though a new tunic would be advisable," I said, indicating the blood on the one he wore.

"You were fortunate enough in Epidaurus and Corinth to speak with Asclepius and Aphrodite, so I do not wish to take chance of offending the highest placed of them all if she should appear here," he said with a nod.

"I hope you brought more than two with you – one of them I used on your leg. I shall buy you a new one at the agora in Trachis when we return."

"I have another, do not allow it to concern you."

"We shall wait for you outside then," Alexis said, threading her fingers through mine. "Perhaps he shall join you at the cliffs here after all," she added quietly. I regarded her thoughtfully, but only nodded in reply.

When Thaddeus joined us a short time later, I pointed out the buildings around us he had missed the day before, adding the ones I had discovered earlier when we reached the harbor level. He did not enter any, heading to the water to clean his arms and face instead. "So, you were going to speak of what you knew of this place?" he prompted. "I should enjoy hearing of your Queen of the Gods."

"It was actually not Hera I thought of when Alexis asked it of me. I had just shared the tale of Jason and his wife Medea," I began.

"A story no father who loves his children as much as you do would wish to hear," Alexis cut across me.

"A different one then, perhaps?" Thaddeus asked.

I nodded in response. "I was thinking of Periander, for he too has ties to this place."

"I hope his time here was not for such cruel reasons as Medea," Alexis said.

"Er ..." I paused.

"Just tell it," Alexis groaned, rolling her eyes.

I nodded again. "Well, when he first came to rule Corinth, Periander was well respected and built Corinth into the major trading area it is today by utilizing both the Lechaeum and Kenchreai ports. Just as Cleomenes' brother, Dorieus, strives to establish colonies for Sparta, so did Periander; successfully achieving it at Potidaea in Chalcidice and Apollonia in Illyria. He was also held in high regard by the leaders of Miletus and Lydia in the east. But unfortunately for his people, it was through his association with Thrasybulus, the tyrant of Miletus, that he became less kind-hearted in his reign."

"How so?" Thaddeus asked.

"He wanted to know how to rule with both honor and fortune, so he sent a messenger to Miletus to seek counsel from Thrasybulus. When the boy returned, Periander asked what he had been told. He replied that Thrasybulus had told him nothing, they had spent weeks just walking through Thrasybulus' fields of corn. Each time the tyrant came across an ear that had outgrown the ones around it, he broke it off, throwing it to the ground before moving on.

"Periander's messenger mistakenly believed Thrasybulus gave him nothing to take back to his ruler, but Periander understood the tyrant's message clearly; to rule unopposed, he must negate those who stood above him, or who sought to rise above him."

"What did he do?" Alexis asked.

"He began to treat his people cruelly. Anyone who dared challenge him or speak out against his treatment was banished or put to death, depending on their supposed crime."

"When we were with Cleomenes, you said that Periander's cruel hand extended to his own family, did they speak out against him as well?" Thaddeus asked.

"Yes," I nodded. "Periander's sons escaped punishment, but for reasons known only to Periander himself, he killed his wife. He must have felt some remorse though for he ensured her body was sent to the Underworld in the proper manner with a coin on her lips for Charon."

"Did she meet her end here rather than at Corinth?" Alexis asked.

"No, but it is told that after she reached the other side, she returned to Periander, claiming she froze in the afterlife as he did not burn suitable clothing for her to wear. She appeared often to him, until he could no longer ignore her pleas. He ordered every wife in Corinth to come here to the Heraion wearing her finest garments. He convinced them it was a festival and when they were all inside Hera's temple, he had them stripped of their finery and jewelry, burning them as he called his wife's name, and on Hera, Goddess of Marriage, to ensure his wife received all she needed to be comfortable in the afterlife."

"It sounds as though he deserved to be haunted by his wife, what man murders his wife for her attempt to guide him towards kindness rather than cruelty?" Alexis asked quietly.

"A man who does not deserve to call her wife," Thaddeus said.

"She was not the first, and certainly shall not be the last," I added solemnly, lifting Alexis' chin so her eyes met mine. "But neither shall Periander be the last king or man to turn to harsher ways to rule his people."

"Not everyone who witnesses cruelty and tyranny, or hears how others rule, mirror those ways," Alexis said, holding my gaze.

"No. Not all who hold positions of power believe it to be the only way to bring about what they wish for," I agreed. "Some are removed enough to see that it is not always best. Sometimes. But sometimes it is how it must be." Alexis nodded and swallowed, her eyes sliding over to the water. I watched her for a long moment before speaking again. "Many sayings are attributed to Periander, two in particular have stuck with me."

"You would share them with us?" Thaddeus asked hopefully.

I nodded. "*Practice makes perfect* was the first I heard. As a soldier, I am certain you would agree with the sentiment, Thaddeus." He nodded when I caught his eye before I went on. "My father spoke the words as he taught me to use weapons and fight from atop Skotos in Amphissa when I was twelve winters. The second was *be farsighted with everything*. Again, I thought of it only in terms of battle plans which needed to be made before we engaged with an enemy, though it is one my princess and your wife are obviously familiar with," I grinned, giving Alexis' hand a squeeze so she returned her eyes to me, the question evident on her face. "The night you asked me to meet you after Melanthios and I fought at the baths; you and Hesper had the honey-sweetened bread in various stages of readiness, should your mother wish to check on the progress of my cooking lesson," I explained.

"I heard about that, and I would tend to agree. It is frightening what the two of them achieve when they set their minds to it," Thaddeus laughed.

"There was something very satisfying at outwitting my mother that particular evening," Alexis agreed with a grin.

"I was quite impressed, though perhaps that was the beginning of my bad influence on you, Princess," I smiled, leaning forward and pressing my lips against hers.

"Oh, it was far too late by then," she whispered, wrapping her hand around the nape of my neck and pulling me to her again.

Thaddeus shook the water from his hands and stood. "I believe it is time we found the temple for I am eager to return to my wife. Travelling with the two of you reminds me of what awaits me at home, and what I sorely miss. It is torture."

Alexis pulled away first. "Apologies, my friend," she said, offering me her hand. "Sometimes we forget others are present."

"Do not be, I recall what it was to be in love in the early days; the constant want to be together without interruption from anyone or anything."

"I remember losing Hesper for candlemarks on end. When she returned to me, she would not speak of what had transpired, though she always appeared happy ... and well satisfied," Alexis noted. Thaddeus cleared his throat, his neck darkening as he kicked at the dirt with his sandal.

"Come, you embarrass the man with your words, true as they may be," I laughed, planting another kiss on Alexis' mouth. Alexis pushed at Thaddeus' shoulder, still grinning, and the two of them followed when I started back towards the buildings.

"You know, I was always pleased you wanted to betroth Hesper, that you loved her as deeply as she loved you," Alexis said. "Though it took you long enough to speak of it with her."

"I wanted to be certain she felt the same. Unlike the choice made for you when you were made to marry Basileios, I was free to choose the wife I wanted. I did not need to choose a woman whose selection would firm up my position or power. I wanted my wife to choose to do it for the same reason."

"You were fortunate it could be so for you," I said with a nod.

"I thank the gods, and Agrias, every day," he agreed.

I led Alexis and Thaddeus between the Doric columns of the Heraion, pausing to allow our eyes to adjust to the dimness inside. As the other two made their way around the temple, taking in its unusual design and the low walls with their columns above, I headed for the statue of Hera I had seen earlier near the cross wall.

The goddess was crowned with a tall polos, one hand on the arm of the throne she sat upon, the other holding a pomegranate in her upturned palm. Her features were solemn, yet her beauty and power were captured perfectly within the bronze. The story of Heracles and Eurystheus' births fluttered to mind again and I wondered, if Hera was able to gift Alexis and me with what we wanted, she would be there when it came time for Alexis to bring our child into the world. I hoped she would and sent up a silent prayer to ask it of her; I still feared for Alexis' life when the day came.

Alexis joined me, sliding her hand into mine and leaning her cheek against my arm. "This is Hera?" she asked, her voice quiet, yet loud in the small space.

"Yes," I replied.

"She is very beautiful, majestic even, as a Queen should be," Thaddeus noted, joining us.

"Indeed," I agreed.

"What thoughts trouble you?" Alexis asked, her hand tightening against mine.

I exhaled a long breath before replying. "Hera is not just the Goddess of Marriage and Women, but of childbirth. She is the protector of the mother during that time, just as Artemis is protector of the birthing infant. If Hera favors you, she shall grant a successful labor, if not, death in childbirth or a prolonged birth can ensue." I paused, but neither Alexis nor Thaddeus spoke, allowing me to continue in my own time. I blew out another deep breath.

"When I was younger, I told my father that if I ever met the great goddess Hera, I would ask what my mother had done to incur her ill-favor and why she had seen fit to take her from the two of us."

"Skylar," Alexis whispered, taking her hand from mine and wrapping her arm around my waist.

"Ask your question, Child," a new voice said, the bright light which announced the presence of an immortal being illuminating the temple. I jumped, spinning around as I reached for my sword, momentarily forgetting I did not have my weapons.

Hera stood in the middle of the room, her face mirroring the one in her statue, the tall crown stiff and sharply pointed at the tip. Her eyes were a rich, warm brown, her hair almost the same shade, held back from her face in a tight knot at the nape of her neck. Her chiton was a brilliant green, lined with silver and reaching the floor, her feet hidden beneath the thick layers. Her eyes flicked briefly to my left arm and the mark it bore, though her face betrayed no hint of surprise or interest in it, and soon enough she met my gaze again. Ensuring my body was between the goddess and Alexis, I took a step forward. Hera remained where she was, waiting for me to speak again.

I swallowed before dropping my eyes from her, inclining my head and upper body in her direction. "Goddess Hera. I ... we ... are honored to find ourselves in your presence. Your temple is unique and befits your stature as above all other goddesses."

Hera stepped forward, reaching out with long fingers to lift my chin until our eyes met again. "You had a question you wished to ask me?" she said, her voice inviting me to speak words I had only ever dreamt of.

"Yes," I said, swallowing again as I straightened. "My mother ... she was ... you took her the night she birthed me. Why? Had she shown you disrespect or forgotten to call on you for aid at that time? What did she do that saw you deny me the chance to know her?"

Hera was silent for a long time as she regarded me, and I wondered if she intended to answer at all. Eventually her eyes found their way first to Alexis, then Thaddeus, before meeting mine again. "It is not always my involvement, or lack of, which sees mothers die during childbirth. The Moirai also hold power over the mortals – it is they who often determine the length of their stay within the realm."

"But you must ..." I began.

Hera held her hand up and I quieted. "I was not present the night you entered the world and it was not my influence which saw your mother leave you. I give you my word." I inhaled a long breath, blowing it all the way out again before nodding curtly. It was not a satisfactory answer by a long way, though the knowledge that my mother and father did not displease the great goddess was of some comfort; she may indeed aid Alexis and me in what we sought without holding me responsible for my parents' actions long ago.

Alexis stepped forward, bowing her head as I had to Hera. "Goddess Hera, we come to you on Aphrodite's insistence. She has spoken to you of our wish for a child?" she asked, her voice strong.

"She has, and I am willing to see it done, though I expect to hear you call my name when making your prayers and sacrifices from this time forward. Though your family follows the Macedonian ways, your father welcomes Greek customs, so I wish to be most honored amongst the other immortals you worship."

"Of course," Alexis immediately agreed. "We would see it done without hesitation, and you speak true of my father, he indeed wishes to embrace Greek ways. He has spoken of it even more often since Skylar and her father came to Trachis. Our child shall be brought up to speak your name first as he or she prays to the gods."

"You are willing also?" Hera asked, looking between Thaddeus and me.

"Yes," I agreed, Thaddeus echoing my words.

Hera nodded and indicated a wooden bench against the south wall. "Please, sit, there are matters to discuss before I grant you what you have come for."

"But you *shall* gift them with a child?" Thaddeus asked as he made his way to the seat. The goddess did not answer immediately, conjuring a large throne and settling herself opposite the three of us, her eyes falling upon Thaddeus when she spoke.

"The three of you have impressed me far more than other mortals I have met, enduring many tests to be here this day."

"Tests?" I repeated.

"Yes," Hera nodded. "When I was asked for aid, I said I would only appear if you all passed the tasks set before you. Thaddeus, it was I who placed you in Corinth. I, who ensured you remained in the company of beautiful young women for three days, any of whom would have willingly allowed themselves to be taken to your bed. You were far from home, alone, lonely without your wife. The women were available to you, and you had the means to afford many nights of pleasure with them, yet you did not. Remaining faithful in your wife's absence and spilling no seed."

"I wish for no other woman in my bed," Thaddeus said with a shrug. "Those women held no interest to me."

Hera smiled. "And that is where you differ from so many others." She turned her attention to Alexis and me. "And the two of you; in the midst of the hedonistic pleasures of Aphrodite's temple, Alexis chose *you*, Skylar, above all others. She chose to remain with the one she loves, rather than experience the touch of another. She was loyal to you where so many would have been unfaithful. You trusted one another enough to speak of fears and secrets not shared. You each trusted the other far more than had ever been asked before.

"Skylar, when you allowed Alexis to be with you in a way no-one ever had, you came to know just how deeply she cares for you; how she shall always care for you, just as you care for her. There is, nor shall there ever be, another lover in either of your hearts. In return, you allowed Alexis to know every part of you, of what you had experienced with other lovers before her, how you had lived, how you saw those women.

"You have all proven yourselves strong. Worthy of what you seek. The time for Thaddeus to spill seed has arrived and I shall see it so. The family you wish for shall be yours."

I looked to Alexis, who clasped one hand over her mouth muffling a cry of joy, as her other reached out for Hera's. The goddess took it, nodding in acknowledgement. "Deepest thanks to you," Alexis murmured, a tear escaping.

"We shall indeed favor you above others," Thaddeus added, rising and making his way to Hera, kneeling at her feet and placing a kiss on the back of her hand.

I swallowed loudly, unable to convince my limbs to move towards Hera as one question repeated itself inside my head. With my eyes on the goddess, I forced the question from my lips. "Do Alexis and Thaddeus have to lie together for it to be so?" Hera retrieved her hands from Alexis and Thaddeus. Alexis took mine instead and Thaddeus returned to his chair, both watching the Queen of the Gods as we waited for her answer.

Hera smiled kindly, shaking her head. "No. All shall remain faithful to the one they love."

"Then how?" I asked, frowning.

"All shall be revealed when it is time," Hera replied, smiling again. "Now we prepare."

# 33

"We shall need a pomegranate and a handful of chamomile flowers. Thaddeus, if you would be so kind as to collect the flowers, and Alexis, the fruit," Hera asked, waving her hand; the throne she had called forth vanishing. The other two stood, though Thaddeus appeared uncertain where he would find the named item. "They are the white flowers in the garden outside," I offered.

He threw me a grateful look and left the temple, Alexis following him, laughing quietly. "And what is it *I* can get for you?" I asked, uncomfortable at being the only one not given a task.

"Nothing. Yet. Though I wish you to answer me a question." I drew a deep breath but nodded as reply. "I understand you hold concern that you shall not love the child as deeply as Alexis if it shares no blood with you."

"Alexis has sought to assure me it shall not be so, but I do not know if that can be true," I acknowledged.

"Would it set your mind at rest if I was to tell you I could create a child who shared blood with you as well as Alexis and Thaddeus?"

"You could do that?" I asked, my heart beating faster at her words.

"There is much I can do," she smiled. "You need only say the words and it shall be done."

I hesitated only a moment before I replied. "Then consider them spoken. Thank you."

Hera inclined her head ever so slightly in acknowledgement. "Very well. Gather some lilies and flowers from the pomegranate's branches and bring them to me."

I gave a quick bow and made my way outside, a grin forming when I saw Alexis attempting to reach the fruit high above her head. I moved in close behind her, reaching up and plucking it from the branch before passing it to her. "Thank you," she said, taking it. She reached out again and ran her hand across the surface of the trunk in front of us.

"The bark is so rough, though not unpleasantly so, it reminds me how your palms felt when you first held my hand," she noted.

"Yours were, and still are, so soft in comparison," I smiled, placing one hand on her waist and trailing the fingers of my other over the back of one of hers. "As is much of your skin," I added, placing a kiss on her neck and resting my chin on her shoulder.

"There are several parts of your skin I have found to be soft also," she replied with a laugh, turning in the circle of my arms. "Hera did not ask you to collect items, did you feel uncomfortable in the goddesses' presence and wish to join us mere mortals outside?"

I tightened my grip, pulling her close as I shook my head. "She wished for quiet words before I collected further items."

"Oh? You do not appear concerned. What did she want?"

"Hera says she can ensure the child comes from us both, as well as Thaddeus," I said, my smile widening.

"How?" Alexis asked.

"I do not know," I shrugged. "But I told her it was what I wanted ... It is what you want also, is it not?" I asked, my smile suddenly faltering.

"Oh Skylar, of course. Nothing would make me happier," she assured me, pushing up onto her toes to kiss me.

"Good," I replied.

"We owe much to the Queen of the Gods."

"Indeed."

"Do you think this shall be enough?" Thaddeus asked, holding up a large bunch of flowers as he approached.

I laughed and nodded. "Yes. Come on." I plucked three pomegranate flowers from the tree, and a handful of lilies from the water as I passed, following the other two back inside where Hera stood, a tall table now in the middle of the open area of the temple. On its top lay several bowls and a marble mortar and pestle set similar to the one in the bathing area back in Trachis.

Hera took the items we had collected, dropping them into the separate bowls, and handing an amphora to Thaddeus. "Would you please fill this at the spring?" she asked.

"Of course," he replied, leaving the temple once again.

"Come, aid me in the preparations," Hera directed, holding one of the bowls out to me. Alexis and I moved to the table and I took it, noting it held the chamomile flowers. "Remove the petals from the stems, place the petals in this bowl and the stems in the one there," she directed, pointing to another at my elbow. "Alexis, I would ask you to do the same with the pomegranate flowers, though you may discard the stems. I shall take care of the lilies."

"You intend to make tea with these?" I asked, setting to work.

"Yes."

"Deacon, the priest at Epidaurus, gave me chamomile tea to aid in relaxing me, so I would find myself in Hypnos' realm faster," Alexis said.

"And I shall use it for the same purpose now, not for sleep, but to calm you," Hera nodded, putting aside the lilies. "To create a child, we must encourage a favorable atmosphere, and I have a number of ways to ensure it is so."

"You do not require dried leaves for the tea?" I asked.

"I do," the goddess replied with a grin. "And in a few moments they shall be just as I need them."

"How?" I asked, having finished separating the parts as she had asked me to. Hera did not reply, but held her hand over my bowl, removing it a moment later to reveal the now dry chamomile petals. "Impressive," I grinned.

"Thank you," she laughed as Thaddeus returned.

Hera took the amphora from him, holding her hand beneath it, flames suddenly appearing in her palm. I raised an eyebrow as Alexis gasped and Thaddeus jumped, his eyes growing wide. I chuckled at the satisfied look on Hera's face and nudged Alexis.

"You believe at times that I am a show-off, but I believe I have just been out-shone."

Alexis tore her eyes from the flickering heat and met mine. "If I ever saw you do that, I would be less impressed and more fearful."

"True, though you have to admit, just for a moment you would be impressed."

"Perhaps," she grinned, turning her face from me again.

"Add the chamomile please," Hera said.

I did as she asked, the first scent of the tea wafting from the top of the amphora barely a moment later. She poured out two steaming skyphoi, handing them to Alexis and me before setting the amphora down again.

"Drink the entirety of what I have given each of you whilst I prepare the incense. The lilies and flowers from the pomegranate tree are for the scent I most favor; flowers of the lily one of my favorites of all the blooms known. They signify optimism, fertility and creation. Do you know what significance the pomegranate has?" Both Alexis and I shook our heads, as did Thaddeus. "The pomegranate is, amongst other things, an emblem of fertility. I understand from Asclepius that your body is ready to receive a child, Alexis."

"Deacon performed a test, and says it is so," she nodded, reaching for my hand and threading her fingers between when they met. I gave her a smile before taking a mouthful of the tea, which had cooled faster than I would have believed possible, given that only a moment ago, steam had drifted from its top.

Hera took the lily and pomegranate flowers, placing them in the mortar and adding another ingredient we had not supplied her with as she pressed the pestle into the mixture.

"What is that?" Alexis asked, leaning forward ever so slightly.

"Styrax," Hera replied, not looking up from her task.

"Styrax?" Alexis repeated.

"It comes from particular trees," I replied before Hera had the chance. "It is akin to the sandalwood which was in the incense at Corinth. It is also often used as a middle note in a number of perfumes, just as cinnamon and sweet rush are."

"Indeed," Hera said with a nod. "Finished?" she added, nodding towards my skyphos.

"Yes."

"Good. Thaddeus, I would ask you to wait outside now. I shall join you momentarily and aid you in preparing for your part in this."

"Of course," he said with a nod in her direction.

"May we have a moment to speak before he leaves?" I asked, putting my skyphos on the tabletop again. Hera nodded.

"Skylar?" Alexis asked quietly. I gave her another grin, tugging gently on her hand and making my way to the entrance of the temple, Thaddeus following us closely.

"Is all well? You are not questioning your decision?" he asked.

"No. I just ... I wanted to say thank you. I know without you this would not be possible. When Alexis first spoke of her wish ... I believed, well, you both know what I thought of the suggestion. I did not want to imagine what would have to pass for it to be so. But now, here, with Hera's help, it appears it can be achieved in a manner we are all comfortable with. I have put behind me the fear and suspicion of why you agreed to help us Thaddeus. I know it was only your friendship that saw you make the offer. I hope you can forgive my words and treatment of you."

I held my arm out to him. He took it as he replied. "Of course. As I have said before, had I been in your sandals, I too would have hesitated in accepting such aid from someone I had known for less than a winter. I am glad the gods look down favorably on the two of you and see fit to grant you what you desire without Alexis and I having to lay together. You shall both make wonderful parents, and I am proud to assist and to call you both friend."

He released my arm as Alexis wrapped her arms around his waist.

"Thank you, Thaddeus," she said, hugging him tightly.

"You are welcome," he smiled. "I believe you know how fortunate you are that Skylar arrived when she did, and that she came to love you as deeply as she did. She saved you not only from an unpleasant future, but now travels far from home with determination and the co-operation of the gods to ensure you have the opportunity to have a family."

"I am well aware," Alexis replied, grinning widely, as she stepped back to my side and took my hand again.

"She is not the only fortunate one," I murmured with a nod to Thaddeus.

"No. You proved the depth of your love for my friend, my Princess, many times when you arrived in Trachis. You protected her before you loved her, before she became *your* princess too."

"How did you …?" Alexis began.

Thaddeus grinned, pressing on. "Because of you, Alexis remains in Trachis, which makes my wife happy, and that in turn makes me happy so I too thank the gods you came to us."

"Thank you," I said, a little embarrassed by his words.

"If you have said all you wish to, it is time Thaddeus joined me," Hera said, settling a hand on his shoulder.

"There is just one more thing," I said, delaying Thaddeus' departure once more. "*If* we are fortunate enough to have a child, I do not want anyone to tell him or her that you are their father. Alexis and I shall be the only parents it knows until we decide they are old enough to learn of your involvement."

"Of course, I would not wish to come between you," Thaddeus replied without hesitation.

I nodded, allowing him to move away as Hera addressed Alexis and me again. "Take the incense to my statue and make your offering and prayers. Skylar, given your knowledge of perfumes, I am certain you know what to do with lotus flowers and wine. There are klinai for your comfort also. If you are hungry, you may eat the pomegranates. When I return, we shall begin."

I only nodded in reply as Hera led Thaddeus from the temple. I returned to the table and collected the bowl Hera had mixed the lily and pomegranate flowers together in, noting two elaborately decorated klinai standing side by side in front of the statue of the goddess.

"So, are you going to tell me what the lotus flowers are for?" Alexis asked.

"After we make our offering," I replied, holding the bowl up and leading her to the statue.

"Why must we request aid when Hera has already said she is going to give us what we have come to her for?"

"Out of respect," I shrugged. "Mortals are not normally fortunate enough to actually meet the god or goddess they are praying to, indeed before we went to Epidaurus I had never met one, had you?" I paused, looking to Alexis who shook her head. "We have much to be thankful for. We must speak the required words." I knelt before the statue, Alexis joining me and placing her hand on the goddess' foot as I held the bowl up. "Do you trust me to offer words?"

"Of course."

I nodded, closing my eyes for a brief moment before beginning.

"O most blessed of goddesses, Hera
Many-named Queen of all and consort of Zeus
May you come to us this day
With kindness on your face and in your heart
Grant us what we seek in your presence
As only you can."

Alexis repeated it after me and I set the bowl on the bronze lap of the goddess. "Had Hera not appeared to us, I would have had us gather the same plants and spoken the same prayer. She said lily flowers were one of her most favored and as they grow abundantly here, we would have been expected to offer them to her," I told Alexis.

"You took notice of what grew, and what would most please the wife of Zeus."

I nodded. "The stories I was told of the gods as a child were not merely for entertainment; my father told them also to teach me. It was important I knew what god expected which specific flower or wine as well as or in place of sacrifice, libation or prayer. I am certain you were taught the same with the gods your parents favored."

"I was involved in so little of the celebrations and sacrifices as a child, and even less after I went to Epirus with Basileios. You appear to know so much about your gods, whilst the Macedonian ones remain a mystery, the specifics about them hazy to me."

"If you want to learn of the Greek gods, I shall teach you everything I know," I grinned.

"I would enjoy that," she replied, returning the smile. "The words you spoke, you had them in mind before we arrived?"

"Some, though the rest came to me as I floated in the waters of the harbor this morning." I got to my feet, offering my hand and pulling Alexis to hers to return to the table.

## 34

I hesitated a moment in front of the table before blowing out a deep breath and drawing the bowl with the lotus flowers in it towards me. I had never seen an actual lotus flower, though I had seen many drawings of its pointed-tip petals.

"When we were at Aphrodite's temple, were you offered anything to drink, other than wine?" I asked, pulling the blue petals from the stems and adding them to the bowl.

"No. Were you?" Alexis replied, watching me.

"Yes. I did not partake, but many of the hetairai consumed opium in its liquid form. It is made from the seeds of the poppies which were growing around the temple."

"The red flowers that were everywhere?"

"Yes."

"Why did you not join them?"

"I have never favored anything stronger than unmixed wine. It has never interested me to wake without recollection of my actions, or experience what I could not be certain was real."

"And that would have happened, had you taken it?"

"Perhaps. Opium is especially potent, causing the drinker to be far more aware of themselves than usual; not only emotionally but physically. Every touch, every caress is heightened, more seductive and addictive. The entire sexual experience is significantly enhanced."

"That does not sound so bad and it is no wonder it is so favored at the temple," Alexis said with a grin.

"True," I nodded, taking a warm, wine-filled amphora and pouring it over the flowers, adding a number of lotus stems and roots and stirring it so everything dissolved. "Though in large quantities it can make you see what is not truly there and for some, that experience is not a pleasant one."

"Oh," Alexis murmured.

"Perhaps if I had known you were on the other side of the door I would have tasted a small amount to experience its pleasant effects," I said nudging her with my shoulder. "But they passed around skyphoi of opium when we stood in the room before the choosing, and at that time I did not wish for anyone to place hands on me, or you. I did not want to be impaired when I attempted to stop you being with another." I blew out a long breath, recalling my unease as I stood waiting in the large room with Kalika and the other women. "Or perhaps I would have taken it to forget they were not your hands on me ... or to pretend they were."

"Skylar," Alexis murmured, covering my hand and halting my movements.

"Apologies, I did not intend to bring that up again," I said, turning my hand so our palms met.

She brought our entwined hands to her lips. "Idylla offered women to me, but there was never anyone other than you I wanted in that room with me. None of them held appeal or moved me to consider them. Always remember that." She turned me, moving closer and pressing her body against mine, thigh to thigh, chest to chest, settling my hands at her waist as she looped hers around my neck. "This body is the only one I want pressed against mine, the only one I want beneath me or above." She pushed into me, her chest rising and falling quickly when the heat between her thighs touched mine.

"I know," I grinned, kissing the tip of her finger when she ran it across my mouth.

"So, tell me what the lotus does, I gather it is similar to the opium or you would not have spoken of it," she said, her finger dipping lower to trace my collarbone through the material of my tunic.

"Somewhat, yes. Once the lotus flower is steeped in wine, you can drink it as you would wine, it is a stimulant; it brings out certain ... desires and wants."

"Indeed?"

"Oh yes – not that I have ever needed such encouragement to place hands on you," I replied, leaning down to kiss her firmly on the mouth.

"Mmm. I have noticed," she smiled. "Have I told you how much I enjoyed your arms around me that night in the kitchen? I almost kissed you then."

"Had your mother remained with Hesper much longer, perhaps you would have," I grinned.

"Would you have kissed me if I had not found the courage?"

"As I recall I was very close to doing just that when your father interrupted us after I saw you back to your room."

"He spoke words of apology after you left at having to interrupt what he saw developing between us. It was not my mother he was worried would catch us, but Melanthios."

"Perhaps he could have suggested we take it into the privacy of your room," I whispered, placing kisses against Alexis' neck and the curve of her shoulder.

"I wonder what would have happened if we had?"

"I have a few ideas …" I rumbled, pulling the fibula from Alexis' chiton and separating our bodies ever so slightly so it fell between us.

"I imagine you do, but I do not believe I was quite ready for what you would have offered at that time."

"But now you are?" I teased, drawing one finger up her thigh and over her ribs.

"Oh, yes." She closed her eyes as my mouth found the warm flesh of her chest. "Why do you believe Hera wanted you to make the lotus mixture for us?"

"I do not know, but if it pleases the Queen of the Gods, who are we to refuse?" I asked, my tongue finding the peaked flesh of her breast.

"You do not wish to pause to consider the request?" Alexis sighed.

"I did. When Hera mentioned it. I have never wanted, or needed it, to enjoy a lover's touch, but I shall set aside previous thoughts on the matter and surrender myself to new experience."

"As you have with so much since we met."

"Yes," I agreed with a grin. "Though I have not been alone there," I added, raising my face to Alexis' again.

"True and it was a wonderful awakening," she laughed.

"This is particularly wonderful also," I nodded, kissing her again. "The lotus-infused wine is ready, if you want to test it."

"I do, but I should re-dress."

"Oh no, I prefer you just as you are."

Alexis grinned and shook her head, but she did not reach for her chiton when I moved away. "How long shall it take to begin working?" she asked.

"The ingredients were fresh and I made the mixture fairly strong, so I would expect to begin feeling its effects almost immediately," I replied, pouring the rich, red liquid from the bowl and into two skyphoi. I handed one to Alexis, raising mine in her direction briefly before taking a sip; finding it quite sweet.

Alexis waited, a look of uncertainty crossing her features, until I nodded and she brought hers to her lips, swallowing a mouthful. "It is sweet," she noted.

I nodded and picked up one of the pomegranates, holding it up in silent question. She nodded in reply, taking another sip of her drink. Taking a dagger from the table, I sliced into the red fruit, picking up both halves and my skyphos and heading for the couches, Alexis following close behind.

"These are beautiful," she noted, running her hand across the top of the nearest klinai.

"As would be expected," I agreed, placing what I held on the table next to the couches. I turned, finding Alexis directly behind me. I slid my arms beneath her knees and around her waist, placing her atop the nearest one.

Settling myself beside her, I reached for my skyphos, taking another mouthful of the heady wine before setting it aside again. As expected, I could already feel the swirling effects of the lotus rushing through my head and warming my stomach. I rolled onto my side, facing Alexis, pleasantly surprised to find that even with my large frame, my feet did not reach the other end when I stretched my legs out. "It is potent," I noted.

"Indeed," Alexis said. "Though it is not an unpleasant sensation."

"No," I agreed. Alexis drained her cup and set it on the table on the far side, positioning herself along the klinai as I was. I leaned forward and was rewarded with a kiss. "I find it enhances my desire for you to a dangerous level," I murmured.

"That is indeed saying something, for your desire for me has always been easily stirred, has it not?" she grinned, sliding closer, her fingers tracing the outline of my hip beneath my tunic.

My eyes unfocused slightly as heat rushed through my blood, my stomach firing when Alexis ran her tongue over her lips. "A wild beast, begging to be released," I agreed, our bodies now only a hair's breadth away from one another.

"And what would it take to release such a beast?" Alexis asked, grinning wickedly as she drew the fibula from my shoulder and grazed her teeth over my collarbone.

"Little, if you keep touching me in such a manner," I replied, my breath hard to catch as my head spun and heat throbbed between my legs.

"Oh, I have no such intention," she grinned, her lips over mine. "I intend to have you beg, to feel as though you shall burst if you do not find release." She kissed me feverishly, her tongue pushing between my lips hungrily.

I slid my hand beneath her hair, pulling her against me, our naked bodies sliding where they met, a slight sheen of sweat coating us both. "As I recall, you are not skilled at such games. Perhaps you require further lessons?" I asked, separating only our lips. Alexis laughed, raising her body and reaching behind me, her breasts caressing my cheek. The lotus and wine had dulled my senses and I was not quick enough to take advantage of the tantalizing pink nipples before me. I slid my hands to her waist instead and pressed my lips against her stomach.

"Perhaps. Though perhaps *you* require further lessons in patience?" she asked, returning to the couch, one half of the pomegranate now in her hand.

"Oh?" I enquired, raising an eyebrow.

She scooped some of the seeds onto the tips of two of her fingers, opening my lips with her thumb as she brought her hand to my mouth. "Hungry?" she asked with a grin.

"For more than just fruit," I replied. Alexis slipped her fingers into my mouth, my tongue removing the seeds coating them. "Nice," I told her as I swallowed the soft, slippery pips.

She repeated the action, one finger lingering between my lips. "I believe you speak the truer of us both," she gasped as I trapped her finger in my mouth. I only raised an eyebrow in question. "I do not favor games in which I ask you to wait to touch me; I enjoy your hands on my body far too much," she admitted, grinning again as her cheeks colored.

I laughed, releasing her and rolling us so I lay above her. I covered the fruit in her hand with one of mine, my fingers pressing into the soft flesh and reminding me of how it felt to be inside her. I groaned and pressed myself against her. "Open your mouth," I directed, scooping out the seeds as she had.

She did as asked and I tipped my hand, allowing the fruit to drip from my fingers and find her tongue.

"Sweet," she murmured, smiling again. I allowed several more to fall into her waiting mouth, covering it with my own and tasting the sweetness on her lips. "It feels almost wrong to be acting in such a manner inside a temple, yet I do not wish to stop. I cannot," she breathed, her hand tightening against the small of my back.

"Agreed," I replied, the familiar stir of desire stoking as a flame when Alexis ground her lower body against me.

"Gods, I need you. Now."

"You have me," I assured her.

One of her legs slid between mine and her hands pressed hard into my skin. "Tell me you shall not stop, that you shall not hesitate in taking me to the heights only you can. Right … now," she whispered against my lips, her hips moving rhythmically below me.

"I shall not," I promised, my lips finding hers as I drove my body against hers, my heated flesh seeking its own relief.

# 35

"Mother," Ares called as Hera made her way from the dining building on the hill. "Is it done?"

"Not yet," she replied. She tilted her head ever so slightly to the right, a grin on her lips as she listened to the sounds emanating from up on the hill where she had just been, and on the lower level where she had left Skylar and Alexis. "But it shall not be long. I shall come find you when it is."

"Good."

"You offer no thanks?" she asked, raising her eyebrows at her son.

"When it is done," was his only reply as he disappeared again.

Hera shook her head, unfazed by Ares' lack of respect; she knew when he was intent on a specific outcome he wasted no words, nor time, on polite behavior. She continued down the slope towards the Heraion.

# 36

"It is time," Hera announced.

I lay atop Alexis, my breath shallow, the lotus and wine charging through my veins and quickening my heart, causing a certain restlessness. I did not know how long it had been since Hera and Thaddeus had left us, but I had called Alexis' name many times as we took each other over the edge of our desires and *still* it was not enough to sate my hunger or draw my hands from her.

I tore my eyes from my lover, turning them on the goddess and gasping as I took in the golden light that shone from the edges of her body. She stood out against the dimness of the temple around her, but my gaze did not linger long, Alexis' teasing tongue heating my flesh to a boil as her fingers twitched inside me.

Returning to the deep green of her eyes I pressed down hard, my impending release rushing down my spine as I arched my back. "Harder," I demanded.

Alexis entered me again, her teeth finding my nipple and gripping the already sensitized flesh. "Feel me," she said.

"I do. Gods, I do," I panted. My hips rocked against the heel of her palm, heightening the sensations she caused and my mouth hung open as I ground out her name. "Wait," I gasped in a moment of clarity. "She is luminous. She is here."

"What? Who?" Alexis asked, her eyes finding mine, though neither of us paused in our movements.

"Hera," I whispered.

"You are close. I can feel it."

"Yes," I agreed. "But ... the goddess ..."

"Can watch while we celebrate our love for each other here in her temple," Alexis said, quickening her pace beneath me. "After all, was it not she who suggested we take the lotus? She must have known what would happen. She wanted this."

"Yes," I said again as the wave hit me and my entire body stiffened.

I fed Alexis the remaining half of the pomegranate, her tongue and teeth teasing at my fingertips each time I offered them to her and sending dizzying desire scampering down my spine. Hera was bent over a small table which had replaced the larger one from earlier and three pyxides sat beside her as she prepared yet more concoctions. "I have what I require from Thaddeus, now it is your turn, Skylar," Hera said, joining us at the klinai with one of the pyxides.

Alexis attempted to focus on the goddess beside her as I reached out lazily to set the fruit aside. "Thaddeus is well? You did not harm him to get what you needed?" Alexis asked.

Hera laughed. "No, I did not harm him. He is well. Happy and quite satisfied when I left him." I opened my mouth to question the goddess further, but the points of Alexis' nipples pressed into my ribs and I forgot what I was going to ask. Her lips found the hollow above my collarbone. Her tongue tasting the gathered sweat. Her fingers danced across my stomach and I felt the caress deep beneath my skin. "Separate yourselves now so I can carry out the deed you have sought me for," Hera instructed.

Her words penetrated the haze the wine and lotus petals caused in my head, but Alexis continued to touch me, her fingers sliding lower with each stroke. "The sooner she has what she needs, the sooner we can return to the pleasures we have been enjoying," I murmured, lifting Alexis' chin so our eyes met.

"Hmph," she pouted, running a solitary finger from my throat to my stomach. "She is a goddess, can she not get what she wants while we continue to enjoy one another?"

"Alexis," I warned, covering her hand. Gods how I wanted her. I was perilously close to just allowing her to do what she wanted to me. I wanted to hear her call my name as she writhed beneath me. But I could not stroke her cheek or run my thumb over her lips. I could not tangle my hand in her hair as I pulled her body against mine. I could not kiss the jumping heartbeat at her throat. I could not touch her the way I longed to. Not yet anyway. It was torture. "We must do as she asks," I insisted.

"The two of you must lie on your backs so I can do what I must," Hera said firmly.

"That has often been my favorite position when with Skylar," Alexis grinned.

"Alexis," I admonished, clamping my hand over her mouth when she opened it to speak again.

The wine was bringing out a different side of my princess – an uninhibited, cheeky humor I had not witnessed previously. It did nothing to temper the desire coursing through my body for her and I fought not to pull her against me again. Long before I had fallen in love with her, indeed before I had even kissed her, I had found myself deeply stirred by just the sight of her. At times I had found myself speechless, unable to draw a full breath as I took in the true beauty she possessed both inside and out. And when she spoke simple, genuine words of comfort and question, she reached past all of my barriers. She drew me to share what I had with no other, whilst flaring my imagination and filling my dreams with thoughts and the sweet scent of her. She was intoxicating and I had wanted her then with almost the same intensity I did now.

My heart hammered in my chest, my resolve beginning to waver as pure lust coursed through me. When I first began to spend time with Alexis, I could not wait to hear the melodic sound of her voice when she spoke, to hear her laugh, or have her lay her hand on my arm in that comfortable way. I had wanted to know every part of her, not just her body but her thoughts, what her life had been, who was important to her or had hurt her. I yearned to know who she was and how it could be that she affected me so deeply when I barely knew her.

I swallowed, my gaze never leaving Alexis'. I wanted to caress every part of her with lingering touch, to recall how it had been that first time at the hot springs. Whilst at the same time I wanted to bring her to a quick end; hungrily, primal, as we had in the woods outside Epidaurus, at Aphrodite's temple or any number of times in Trachis. Had she still worn her chiton I would have gladly ripped it from her body, replacing it with hands and mouth.

My muscles tensed as Alexis wrapped her fingers around my wrist, as though she too sensed what I had been thinking. Heat lit in my stomach but my eyes flicked to Hera, who arched her eyebrows. I knew one of us was going to have to find restraint – and it became clear it was not going to be Alexis when she pressed the lower half of her body suggestively against mine. I drew a deep breath, taking my hand from Alexis' chin and getting to my knees. I slid one arm beneath hers and the other behind her back, lifting her across to the second klinai.

"That was a mistake," she smiled, gripping the back of my neck and pulling me down on top of her as her lips crashed against mine. For long moments I surrendered, feasting on her lips, the throbbing heat between my legs heightening to an unbearable level. With it, returned some clarity; what Hera was about to give us was what Alexis wanted; it was why we had travelled to Epidaurus and Corinth. It was why I had faced a past I had not wanted to, and asked questions of myself I had never dreamed I would. Alexis needed me to once again be strong for her and I would not allow it to be otherwise.

Reluctantly I separated her hands from my neck. "Stay," I ordered, softening my words by cupping her cheek and tracing the line of her jaw.

"Only you could ask it of me," she murmured, mirroring words I had used to her at Epidaurus.

I smiled and gave her a chaste kiss on the mouth, returning to my own klinai. Hera stirred her finger through whatever was in the pyxis, looking between the two of us when she spoke again. "I must ask you to drink this as well."

I pushed myself up onto my elbows. "What is it?"

"A combination of henbane, the root of white mandrake and wine," she replied, lowering the container and showing me the dark red inside.

"Henbane and mandrake are used for sleep when the body needs to heal itself, are they not?" I asked.

"Often times, yes. Healers have been known to favor their use, though one must be careful not to give too much, or the patient may never wake."

"You want us to sleep through what you are going to do?"

"No, the lotus you have already taken works to enhance the experiences, therefore, when both are ingested, you shall be neither sleepy, nor overly stimulated. However, you shall experience some pain whilst I extract what I must. This shall lessen the discomfort."

"Would it not have been easier to just have us take opium? In small doses it acts in the same manner as mandrake," I said, taking the pyxis Hera handed me and draining it before handing it back.

"I could have, but was it not more satisfying to enjoy one another for a time?"

I lowered myself back onto the bed, rolling my head to the side so I could look at Alexis again. "It was. Your thoughtfulness is appreciated."

"Perhaps that is how I have kept my title as Queen of the Gods for so long," Hera grinned. "And for you," she added, reaching across me to give Alexis a skyphos of the henbane. Alexis took it, finishing it as quickly as I had and handing it back to the goddess. "Ready?" Hera asked setting it back on the table and rubbing her hands together.

I nodded and took a deep breath, reaching out to take Alexis' hand as my other gripped the edge of the klinai. Warmth began to spread through my body and I became aware of my heart beating strongly in my chest, the room was suddenly cool against my heated skin. Alexis' fingers were hot between mine and I tightened my grip to anchor myself as the sound of my shallow breaths grew frighteningly loud in my ears.

I felt weightless, and at the same time my limbs were heavier than I had even known them to be; refusing to rise or obey when I attempted to bring my hand up to my face. The room darkened, casting long shadows up the walls and across the roof, broken only by what appeared to be flames flickering from an open fire such as Father and I had built many nights when travelling throughout the Peloponnese. Finally, I managed to turn my head, but there was no fire to my left. Hera no longer stood there either.

A flicker of movement caught my attention; the goddess was at the end of my couch, still rubbing her hands together as though she stood out in a winter chill and needed to warm them. She closed her hands into fists and released them twice more before reaching out and pushing her fingers through the skin at the bottom of my stomach. It was not painful exactly, but I could feel them as she moved inside me.

A laugh suddenly bubbled up, bursting from my throat without warning and I rolled my head to the side, meeting Alexis' wide eyes. "I have been fortunate enough to have a princess inside me, now there is a goddess. What a journey I am having!"

"Remain still," Hera ordered. I attempted to do as she asked, but another laugh escaped when Alexis began to snigger.

She turned onto her side, drawing my hand between her thighs. I gasped at the wetness. "I hope she does not satisfy you as I do when you find me there," she challenged, writhing against my trapped fingers.

"No. Ah … Gods," I stammered, swallowing loudly as the familiar insistent thrumming began between my legs. "She is … different … far less satisfying … I prefer …" I frowned, the movements the goddess made suddenly painful. "What are you doing?" I growled, my eyes returning to Hera.

"Getting what I require. You are not unaccustomed to pain. You have had your share of cuts and impalements when in battle. I imagine you simply gritted your teeth and continued with the fight, did you not?"

"No, I took revenge on the one who was able to get past my defenses to inflict such a wound."

"I would not advise you to pick up weapons against me at this moment," she said, removing her hands from my body, a number of small, silvery circles attached to the tips of her fingers.

"What is that?" I asked, taking my hand from Alexis' inviting flesh and attempting to prop myself up again, finding the movement painful where Hera had touched me.

The goddess turned her back and when she faced us again a moment later, the silver was gone. "Drink this," she directed, handing me another pyxis.

"What is it?" I asked, sniffing at the light red liquid suspiciously.

"A little opium mixed with wine, just as you suggested," Hera replied. "It shall help with the pain." I downed it promptly, the bitter taste of the opium not quite concealed by the wine. Hera took the container back, picking up another and moving to the end of Alexis' klinai.

"Do you intend to hurt her as well?" I asked sullenly, the pleasant desire Alexis had created now far from my mind.

"She may feel some discomfort but, if she remains still, it shall not last long. I give you my word."

"Skylar," Alexis said, drawing my eyes to hers with a hand beneath my chin. With only minor discomfort, I rolled onto my side, edging closer as she took my hand again.

"Do not fear. Hera is here to help us. Do you recall what I said in Corinth; that when I knew I wanted to be with you, I knew it would mean I had to endure some pain for it to be so? If that is what must transpire here too so we can have a child of our own, then I gladly welcome it."

"You remember what I said in response – that you should not have to experience pain to be with me," I began.

Alexis covered my lips with her fingers. "Perhaps that is how we know it is something we truly want – if we can endure the immediate pain then longer happiness shall find us."

I brought her hand to my lips. "You are far stronger than I ever believed you would be. I love you."

"I love you too. I want this so much, but before she ... does anything tell me it is what you want as well."

I leaned across the space between us, my hand on Alexis' cheek as I kissed her soundly. "I want this. I want you, and a child for us. I want us to be a family."

"And so we shall be," Alexis whispered, her eyes shining with unshed tears.

"Indeed," Hera agreed, dipping her hand into the pyxis she held. She brought out the shining lights again, though there were less and they appeared larger than before, brighter as well. Alexis gripped my hand and I squeezed back, never taking my eyes from the goddess as she reached inside Alexis' stomach as she had mine. Alexis tensed against the bed, her teeth grinding together as Hera worked. It took longer, Hera's hands moving deeper and more rapidly inside Alexis than they had within me.

Alexis moved her head from side to side, finally yelling out in pain, tears coursing down her cheeks. Wait," I shouted. "Stop, it is too much, she cannot bear it."

"Just a moment longer," Hera replied.

"No, stop. Now," I demanded, getting to my knees.

"Remain where you are," Hera ordered, looking up momentarily from her task.

"Skylar," Alexis cried. "Allow her to do what she must."

"No. That is enough," I replied, advancing on Hera.

The goddess barely nodded in my direction, but suddenly I could not move, it was just as it had been at Aphrodite's temple; my limbs refusing to budge, no matter how hard I attempted it. My jaw clenched as I struggled uselessly against invisible bindings.

"Done," Hera announced, taking her hands from Alexis. "We shall know in a few days if it is successful. Until I return at that time, you may remain here at the Heraion. I shall ensure you have all you need, including more opium for the pain."

Without another word she was gone and my arms and legs regained feeling, causing me to fall ungraciously back onto the bed. A skyphos appeared in Alexis' hand and she swallowed the entire contents of it, placing it beside her before reaching for me. I scrambled up to her, placing one hand on her cheek and the other against her stomach. "I am sorry, I should not have allowed her t–"

"Skylar, I am fine. You are fine."

"She hurt you."

"It is less than I have suffered before, indeed it is fading even as we speak."

"Sti–"

"No. Come, lie with me, I am exhausted. I need to feel your arms around me. I need only you." As I drew Alexis into my embrace, a light blanket materialized beside us. I draped it over our bodies and stretched out along the klinai, my eyes fluttering shut, my own body announcing its weariness.

"You have me. Forever and always," I murmured into Alexis' hair as I tightened my grip.

"Me too," she muttered sleepily.

## 37

Eos' dawn light had given way to Helios' bright sun when I woke the following morning. Long rays spilled in through the single high window, casting the inside of the temple with a warming glow. Alexis was still tucked into my body, though sometime during the night I had rolled onto my back and her head was on my shoulder, one arm draped across my stomach.

I kissed the top of her head and she murmured incoherently, wrapping herself tighter against me, her soft hair tickling my arm. I grinned, stretching the muscles of my stomach to determine the level of pain lingering from the day before, surprised to find no hint of discomfort at all.

"Must you do that? Some of us are still sleeping," Alexis mumbled, opening one eye as she tilted her head back and looked up at me.

"Apologies," I said, my grin widening. "How are you feeling?"

"I have woken up the way I most favor – with you beside me," she replied.

"Hmm ... I believed you favored another way far more."

"True, though clearly it is too late for that today so I shall have to settle for this."

"You could always go back to sleep and I could attempt to wake you again," I suggested, leaning forward to kiss her.

"Too late," she teased, scooting backwards and swinging her legs over the side of the couch. I growled, but allowed her to stand, content to watch the curve over her back as she stretched her arms over her head, pleased to see she too showed no signs of pain.

"When did we decide to sleep here and where did the blanket come from?" Alexis asked, turning back to me as she took note of our surroundings.

"Hera suggested it, and provided the blanket," I replied throwing it off and getting to my feet. "It was late, and we were both tired." I bent down, retrieving my tunic and Alexis' chiton, handing hers to her before pulling mine on.

"I remember drinking the lotus and wine mixture, but after that my memories become blurred," Alexis frowned, her fingers pausing over the fibula at her shoulder. "Did ... did Hera have her hands inside your stomach? Inside mine? Or was I already in Morpheus' realm when those images came to me?"

"It was not a dream," I replied, crossing to her and fastening the bone implement through the material.

"You recall what happened?"

"Yes. Though I am pleased to find I have no sore head this day as I have often woken with after celebrating with much wine."

She laughed and nodded. "As am I. I have never experienced it, but Hesper once attended a banquet with Thaddeus where there was a competition as to who could drink the most the fastest. She was not well when she woke the next morning, Thaddeus faring only slightly better."

"I have attended such festivities," I nodded.

"Tell me what you recall from last night."

"Later," I replied, cupping her cheek. "The water is warm this early, perhaps we could go for a swim? Then we should find Thaddeus and ensure he too is well." Alexis nodded, taking my hand when I held it out and I led her out into the warm morning air and down to the harbor. We stripped off our clothing again and stepped into the lapping waves.

"This is wonderful," Alexis grinned, making her way out into the deeper water.

"Yes it is," I agreed, stroking along behind her. "Hera said we are to remain here a few days and that she would provide us with whatever we needed."

"There are worse places we could find ourselves," Alexis smiled, placing her hands at my waist and pulling me close when I reached her.

"Indeed."

"Well, good morning," Thaddeus' voice greeted us. I looked back to the shore and he waved. I raised my hand in reply, squinting ever so slightly as a second figure appeared behind him.

"Is that Hesper?" I asked.

"It is," Alexis replied, waving enthusiastically at her friends. "I would ask how she got here, but I believe we already know the answer," she added, making her way back to the sand.

"Hera," I nodded, following her thoughts.

Thaddeus kept his gaze averted as we re-dressed but threw his arms around us excitedly as soon as we were done, Hesper hugging us tightly as well.

"When did you arrive?" Alexis asked as we sat down on the sand, the water soaking our toes each time a wave rolled in.

"Late yesterday," Hesper replied, taking Thaddeus' hand. "I had been beside myself with worry after Thaddeus' disappearance. I had dreams where a beautiful woman appeared and told me he was safe and that we would soon be reunited, but it did not dampen my fears."

"I am sorry," Thaddeus said. "I sent a messenger to speak words of the same, but he would not have reached you yet."

"Not to fear, we are together again now," she smiled before they shared a brief kiss. "Though truly, nothing can prepare you for the appearance of a goddess in your home; it was a surprise to say the least when Hera arrived."

"I can only imagine," I nodded. "Especially one you do not pray to."

"No, though it did not take me long to trust her when she said she could take me to Thaddeus. It was indeed a joyous reunion," she smiled shyly at her husband and I averted my eyes, a grin lighting my own face.

"Why did she bring you here?" Alexis asked after a moment.

"As reward," Thaddeus supplied before his wife had the chance.

"Reward?" I echoed, a frown touching my forehead.

"For remaining faithful to Hesper when I found myself in Corinth," he replied. "Hera wanted us to be together in an intimate sense, though she interrupted several times to take what she needed before allowing us to continue without further interference."

"Ah," I nodded. "Was it painful, when she gathered what she required from you?"

"Not in the least, frustrating, but not painful," he replied. I chuckled, imagining just how frustrating it would have been for Thaddeus – being so close to finding release only to be interrupted was an uncomfortable, and thoroughly dissatisfying, feeling. "Yes, well," Thaddeus stammered before clearing his throat.

Alexis shot me a look and nudged me with her shoulder. "Apologies," I whispered, swallowing my grin.

"Did she ask you to drink any sort of flower-infused wine?" Alexis asked. I concealed a further grin behind my hand; vividly recalling Alexis' lack of inhibitions when she had drunk the liquid she spoke of.

"No. She spoke of the two of you preparing some before I left though, why?"

Alexis raised her brows at me, challenging me to speak of what I had not with her. I shook my head, leaning close to whisper in her ear. "Believe me, you do *not* want me to give specifics of your lack of control in claiming my body for your own to your friends."

"Oh, I ... ah ..."

I leant back on my elbows as Alexis' cheeks darkened and turned my gaze back to Thaddeus and Hesper. "To ensure we were not in any discomfort," I told them. "I believe Hera gathered your essence and mine and placed them inside Alexis in order to create a child for us."

Alexis had regained her composure and placed a hand on her stomach, her eyes finding Hesper's as she spoke again. "How long until I am certain a child grows within me?"

"Not long, though your goddess may bring news of it earlier than most women would recognize the signs."

"I would agree, she told us to remain here for a few days so presumably she shall be able to confirm it by then," I said with a nod.

"You would not be offended if we did not remain with you until then? I am eager to return home and see our boys," Thaddeus said.

"Of course not, they must miss you terribly. Both of you."

"Hera has said she shall help the two of us and Darko to return to Trachis. She shall see us there in the same manner as Hesper was brought here, and I was taken to Corinth, so our journey shall be immediate."

"Oh, Skotos," I said suddenly, the mention of Darko reminding me my own steed was with us.

"He is well rested, and fed and watered, Hera has seen to that also," Thaddeus replied.

"Thank you," I nodded. "I shall visit him soon."

"Were you able to settle the boys with your parents before you came?" Alexis asked.

"Yes," Hesper replied. "Hera allowed me the chance."

"So, another late night for them?" I grinned.

"No doubt," Hesper laughed.

"Come, we should prepare to leave," Thaddeus said, standing and offering Hesper his hand, pulling her upright when she took it. I got to my feet as well, taking Hesper in an embrace when she held her arms out to me.

"I am glad to have found you all well, and that you and my dearest friend have been given the opportunity to become parents," she said, grasping me tightly.

"I believe it is I who owes thanks to you, without your allowance at having Thaddeus gift us a part of himself, it would not have been possible."

"I love him and Alexis almost in equal measure, and I have grown very fond of you since you arrived. If it was not so, then perhaps my decision would not have been as easy. I am glad you agreed to find out if it was possible for the two of you, that you could put your fear aside long enough to attempt it."

"Thank you," I said, releasing her. I held my arm out to Thaddeus but he shook his head and grabbed me in a tight hug.

"You make Alexis happier than ever before and I am thankful you have both chosen me to be a part of this," he whispered. "Though your child may not know who I truly am to them, I shall know, and I shall be proud to call them kin."

"Thank you, Thaddeus." I clapped him hard on the back, the truth in his words causing my breath to catch. Alexis and I waved Thaddeus and Hesper off, watching as they made their way back up the slope to the higher level of the area and into the dining building.

"Would you like to visit Skotos now, or can I interest you in a proper dip in the water?" Alexis asked, walking backwards and pulling the fibula from her chiton, allowing it to fall as she moved.

"Water. Definitely," I replied with a grin, discarding my own tunic as I followed her. Wrapping my arms around her waist, I pressed my length against hers, our lips meeting as we walked, the sun beating down onto us as I explored every rise and curve of Alexis' smooth skin.

*

When we had sated ourselves again, we stood looking out over the gulf, Alexis' back pressed against my chest as we remained in the warm water.

"It is beautiful here," she murmured.

"It is," I agreed, resting my chin on her shoulder and placing one hand against her stomach, my fingertips drawing patterns across the soft skin.

"How long shall it take us to get back to Trachis once Hera says we can leave?"

"A few days," I replied. "Though perhaps we could ask the goddess to escort us back in the same manner she intends to take Thaddeus and Hesper."

"You do not wish to make the journey with me as we have in getting this far?"

"I believe it would be safer to get straight back, I do not relish the idea of facing another wild boar or serpent along our path, especially if you are carrying our child," I said, laying my palm flat against her.

"A fair reason," she agreed, laying her hand on top of mine.

I was quiet for a few moments before I spoke again. "Had you been considering children for us for long before you spoke of it to me?"

Alexis drew a deep breath and then nodded. "Since before we were together."

"Before?" I asked, raising an eyebrow. "Before I told you how I felt about you?"

She turned, looping her arms around my neck as she smirked. "Do you truly believe I could not see how you felt about me before you spoke the words?"

"Perhaps not," I replied with a smile, sliding my hands around her waist to draw her close again. "But I do not understand why that would have made you think of children for us."

"I had been waiting for someone who would love me without wanting me as a possession. Someone who would not just see me as useful for giving them children to carry on a line with. I never wished – never believed – I would *want* to have a child with anyone. I would have of course, it was expected, but I did not truly wish for it. Perhaps that too hindered my ability to successfully carry a child for Basileios."

"Oh," I murmured, uncertain how to respond and dropping my eyes from Alexis'.

She put a finger beneath my chin, raising my face to hers again. "When I realized I had feelings for you – feelings which went far deeper than friendship, I knew if you spoke words of the same that I would do whatever I could to be with you, even if it meant leaving Trachis and never returning. Just as your father and mother did, so too I would have. You made me want things I never had before."

I smiled again. "As you did for me. No one had ever suggested I remain in one place with them. There was no one I would have wanted to do that for."

"So … in answer to your question; yes, I had thought of children for us because I wanted with you what I had not had before. I wanted everything a relationship promised, though I was afraid to speak of it to you before the last moon. I felt it would be too much, too soon. I was afraid you would not wish for it; that even though you changed what you had always done by remaining in Trachis with me, that this request would be too much. That is also why I spoke to Thaddeus first, to attempt to find solution to bring to you. To show you that it was possible if it was what you wanted as well."

I nodded slowly, exhaling a long breath before I spoke again. "Did you wonder if I would want to carry a child for us?"

Alexis hesitated, drawing in her own deep breath before she replied. "Wondered, but would never have asked it of you. I want to do this for us. You sacrificed everything you knew, your entire way of life, to be with me. I did not have to do the same. You freed me from Melanthios, allowed me to remain in Trachis with my family rather than joining you and your father on your travels. You adore me and show me the depth of your love without hesitation. I felt it was time I showed you how much I care for you. This was the way I wanted to prove it."

"Oh," I said again, her words touching me far deeper than she could ever know. I leaned forward and kissed her, hoping it could convey at least some of what I felt.

"Do you want to visit Skotos now?" she asked when we parted. I nodded and she took my hand, leading me back to the shore.

# 38

"You spoke of a test being carried out by the priest at Epidaurus indicating your body was ready to receive a child. What did he do?" Hera asked.

The three of us were once again back inside Hera's temple, Eos' dawn barely lighting the sky. Three days had passed since we said goodbye to Thaddeus and Hesper and Alexis and I had done little except swim in the Gulf, eat from platters left for us or revel in each other's bodies anywhere we found ourselves from the water, to the tree line at the edge of the Heraion Valley, to the buildings of the Heraion. Both of us carefully avoided speaking of children or speculating what Hera would tell us when she returned.

"Deacon lit a bowl of incense and I had to remain over it until he announced that he could smell it coming out through my mouth. When that happened, he told me my body was open and ready for a child to be placed inside me," Alexis replied.

Hera nodded, holding up a piece of linen. "I shall do the same now, though I have immersed this material in scents I favor and I shall not be setting it alight. If the child I placed inside you has begun to grow, you shall once again be closed and I should smell nothing, so let us begin and hope it is so." Alexis nodded and took the linen from Hera, placing it beneath her chiton and seating herself on one of the klinai.

The short nails of my fingers dug into my palms as I waited, barely breathing, beside her. "How long?" I asked a moment later, barely able to remain still as the silence descended around us.

Hera looked briefly at me before leaning close to Alexis' face. "Open," she directed. Alexis did as asked, her eyes finding mine over the goddess' head. Hera placed her hand on Alexis' stomach, speaking no words for a long moment. When she straightened up again, she was smiling. "You are with child," she said.

The breath I had been holding puffed out loudly.

"I am?" Alexis asked, tears forming as she looked between the Queen of the Gods and me. "I have ... we have a child?" she murmured.

"You do," Hera acknowledged with a nod.

I pulled Alexis from the couch, throwing my arms around her tightly as hot tears spilled down her cheeks and onto my arm.

"I am so happy," I whispered into her ear before pulling back far enough to kiss her. "I love you," I added.

"I love you," Alexis repeated, kissing me again before crossing to Hera and wrapping her arms around the goddess' waist. "Thank you."

Hera was momentarily taken back, but soon returned Alexis' embrace. "You are most welcome," she said as Alexis released her.

"Thank you, goddess Hera," I added, inclining my head towards her as well.

Hera acknowledged my nod with one of her own. "If you wish to know whether you carry a boy or girl, there is another test you can perform, though not for another moon," Hera said as Alexis joined me again.

"Do you?" Alexis asked, her eyes hopeful when she looked up at me. I smiled and nodded. "How?" Alexis asked, addressing the goddess again.

"Take some barley and wheat seeds and urinate on them. If the barley grows, you shall have a boy, if it is the wheat, then a girl."

"We shall, thank you again," Alexis grinned, sliding her fingers between mine.

"It is accurate?" I asked, raising an eyebrow.

"I have never known it to be incorrect," Hera replied.

I nodded and drew a breath before I spoke again. "When it is time for Alexis to bring our child into the world, shall you come and aid her?" I asked.

"If that is what you wish," Hera replied.

"I do. I have not had much experience with women birthing children and though I trust Gnosidicus and the midwife in Trachis, I would prefer to know you were there also. I want you to protect Alexis as she births our child and meet the one whose creation you made possible."

"Then I shall be there," she smiled.

"Thank you," I said again, turning to Alexis. "Whatever you need over the next moons, you need only ask it of me and I shall see it done. I wish for nothing but the most pleasant experience while our child grows within you."

Alexis smiled widely, taking my face in her hands and kissing me again. "Thank you for loving me as much as you do. I could not have asked for anyone better. I am so fortunate."

"As am I," I replied as our lips met again.

"You must excuse me for a short while, there is something I must tend to before I return you to your home as you asked."

"We shall ready ourselves and Skotos and wait for you by the spring," I replied, never taking my eyes from Alexis.

# 39

Hera appeared in the great hall of Olympos, finding Ares in a passionate embrace with his lover. Their moans echoed off the marble walls of the room, though the goddess did not wait for them to quiet before she spoke.

"It is done, my son. The mortal princess, Alexis, carries a child within her belly just as you asked."

Aphrodite stilled above Ares, embarrassed to find herself in such a position in front of his mother, but Ares continued to move inside her, his eyes locked on hers.

"Gratitude," he grunted, hoping she would simply leave again so they could finish.

"Why is it you show favor to these mortals specifically?" Hera continued.

"My reasons are my own, do not be concerned with them," Ares replied, Aphrodite again hesitating.

"Is it perhaps because Skylar bears the mark of your Keres? How is that even possible?"

"Again, Mother, I do not owe you explanation on this matter," Ares' voice was terse.

"Have I not always given you free rein in your affairs?"

"You have."

"Then, if you shall not favor me with answer about the mark, speak of why you did not simply go to Alexis in a guise you believed most suitable and carry out the deed of creating a child with her yourself?"

Ares blew out a deep breath; it was apparent his mother was determined to have words with him and he could not perform as Aphrodite deserved with his focus so divided. "Go, I shall tend to this and meet you at your palace. I shall not be long," he assured his lover, his hand finding her breast again.

She smiled and nodded, lifting herself off him, not daring to meet Hera's eyes before she disappeared.

Ares exhaled another deep breath, placing his hands on the armrests of his throne as he met his mother's gaze. "There is much that has been kept from Skylar already, I would never deceive her in such a manner. If I had gone to Alexis in the role of another – Skylar most probably as you suggest – she would have known no difference, but regardless of her insistence to it, Skylar would not believe her, for how else could it have come to be that a child grew inside her? They had to be together, to see for themselves that their bond was strong, and through it a new life for them could be created."

"You speak of deeds being kept from Skylar, she says her mother died in childbirth; that I was responsible for it, though I am certain I do not even know who her mother was. Would you care to share why she believes such a tale?"

"No," he replied. "I have somewhere to be mother, if that is all," he added, reaching for the leather pants which lay in a heap on the floor and pulling them on.

"We are not finished here," Hera said.

"We are," he insisted, silencing any further reply from her with his disappearance.

# 40

I tightened the rope holding our bag to Skotos' flank and patted his nose. The smile I had worn since Hera spoke of the child inside Alexis could not be wiped from my face, my lover finding the same true for her.

"I never believed I would be someone's mother one day; especially not after I realized I was attracted to women rather than men," I mused, checking the reins at his neck. "I told myself it could not be, did not see how it could be any other way. Told myself I did not wish for it, if I ever had."

"But now it appears you shall? You do?" Alexis asked and I heard the uncertainty behind her words.

I turned, the grin still plastered across my face as I reached over and pulled her to me. "Now I shall be," I said, leaning down and kissing her. "You recall Cleomenes saying he spoke of betrothing me to his brother, Leonidas, after Father and I aided him in expelling Hippias from Athens?" Alexis nodded. "I refused for obvious reasons, though he suggested that perhaps I would still lie with him and secure a royal child for myself, and for Leonidas."

"You did not consider it, even for just a moment?"

"No," I laughed. "Not even for a moment."

Alexis smiled, hooking her finger in the top of my bronze cuirass and pulling my lips to hers again, holding back just before they met to speak again. "You realize you shall have a child of royal blood after all, though it shall inherit the throne of Trachis, rather than Sparta?"

"Your father is going to name you as his heir?" I asked, the king having intimated as much before we left.

"Yes. Thaddeus agreed he would step aside if our current journey gifted us with a child," Alexis nodded.

"Our child would be the prince or princess," I murmured with a grin, realizing I had never considered otherwise when I thought of a child for us back in Epidaurus.

"It would and when my father passes from this world I shall become queen. My mother can choose to rule with me or step aside and allow me the task, my child in line after that."

"So ... I would be known as ... the queen's lover, her consort?" I asked curiously.

"No. You would rule beside me, and my mother if she chose to, as my queen."

"Would we not have to be betrothed for me to be allowed such an honorable title?" I asked, touched that Alexis would offer me such a position.

"I do not believe so. My father and I have spoken only briefly of it, though when we return I wish for all of us to speak of it in more detail, given the life that grows inside me now."

I retreated half a step so I could place my hand on her stomach, meeting her eyes rather shyly. "Would you want to be betrothed to me if we could?"

She smiled and placed her hand over mine. "In a heartbeat."

"Then perhaps I should ask it of the king when we return," I grinned. "When you first spoke of wanting a child with me, I told you I had never heard of two women being betrothed, but with the changes your father has made since leaving Aigai and settling in Trachis, perhaps this too would be something he would consider?"

"When we speak of how a god and two goddesses aided us and blessed us with the creation of this child, I do not see how he could refuse. I am certain he would not wish to incur the ill-favor of three such powerful immortals."

"It would not be wise," I agreed.

Alexis dropped her eyes from mine, finding an errant thread on my tunic to pull at as she spoke again. "So, are you asking it of me now, to be your betrothed?"

"No," I said, the inane grin remaining firmly in place. Hers faltered and she opened her mouth to question me. I leaned down and kissed her to keep her silent. "I must speak with your father first, Princess; that is the custom, is it not?"

"It is," she nodded. "But ... does this mean we cannot be together intimately until after our betrothal?"

"Not a chance," I assured her, pulling her against me as my lips found hers again.

"Thank the gods," she breathed when we parted some time later. Suddenly eager to return to Trachis and speak to Agrias, I called to Hera, telling her we were ready to leave when she appeared shortly after.

Though my father and I had shared many experiences, he had never had the opportunity to betroth the one he most loved. I hoped he would be as excited as I was that *I* would have that chance. I grinned, realizing I did not even consider Agrias would deny my request to wed Alexis. I was certain he would give us his blessing when I sought his approval and ensure that it would come to pass as soon or as late as I wished for it. And it would be soon – of that I had no doubt.

"What causes you to smile so?" Alexis asked.

"I just cannot wait to get home," I replied.

"Me either," she murmured, pushing up onto her toes to kiss me.

# ABOUT THE AUTHOR

Belinda Harrison was born and raised in a country town in North East Victoria, Australia. She spent some time experiencing 'big city life' in Melbourne and Sydney in her twenties where she held jobs in a packaging company, an online gaming firm, various temp positions and a hair loss treatment center before the lure of the country recalled her.

She joined her family's business in the world of retail plumbing and appliance sales – which is when she started writing the Thermopylae Bound Series before deciding to leave the familiar and join another well respected local firm in the Real Estate sector where she worked in Commercial Property Management.

Belinda then decided it was time for another change and moved across the road to the local newspaper where she looks after Circulation and the Kids' page, writing after hours, and sometimes during lunch.

Belinda holds a Certificate IV in Multimedia, which she has successfully used in her professional and personal life.

She currently lives in 'the best part of Victoria' with her fiancé Renee, daughter Ava, Charlie the dog, and cats Caesar and Max.

You can find Belinda on the following social media platforms: Instagram (belindagharrison), Twitter (beharrison78) or Facebook (Belinda Harrison Author). And don't forget to leave a review on Amazon or Goodreads to help spread the word.

www.ingramcontent.com/pod-product-compliance
Lightning Source LLC
Chambersburg PA
CBHW031727170626
46808CB00005B/1917